Harriet stood up, and her gaze wandered to the forest edge.

"It looks like something's wrong with our farmer," she said. "He's still lying there. Having a dramatic moment is one thing, but the rest of the people have left that side of the field and he's still in the same spot." She watched intently for a few moments. "He's not moving." She started to go down then glanced back at Mavis.

"You go ahead," Mavis said. "I'll catch up,"

Harriet hiked her skirt up and held it bunched in her fists as she hustled down the risers then continued toward the stage and the forest beyond.

"Where are you going in such a hurry?" Carlton asked as she brushed past him.

"One of the re-enactors looks like he's been injured at the edge of the forest," she said without stopping.

"I'll come with you," Carlton said and glanced at Bebe, who was standing in the shade of the stage, fanning herself with an ornate plastic-ribbed ladies fan.

"I'm not wearing this into the forest," she said and glanced down at her pink satin confection.

Carlton was obviously torn for a moment.

"You go ahead, baby," she said. "I'll keep your spot cool."

Harriet was already crouched over the man when Carlton arrived.

"He doesn't look too good," he said. "How is he?"

ALSO BY ARLENE SACHITANO

The Harriet Truman/Loose Thread Mysteries

Quilt As Desired
Quilter's Knot

The Harley Spring Mysteries

Chip and Die
The Widowmaker (2010)

QUILT AS YOU GO

A Harriet Truman/Loose Threads Mystery

BY

ARLENE SACHITANO

ZUMAYA ENIGMA

2009

AUSTIN TX

This book is a work of fiction. Names, characters, places and incidents are products of the author's imagination or are used fictitiously. Any resemblance to actual persons or events is purely coincidental.

QUILT AS YOU GO

ISBN 978-1-934841-58-7

"Zumaya Enigma" and the raven colophon are trademarks of Zumaya Publications LLC, Austin TX. Look for us online at http://www.zumayapublications.com/enigma.php

Library of Congress Cataloging-in-Publication Data

Sachitano, Arlene, 1951-
Quilt as you go : a Harriet Truman - loose threads mystery / Arlene Sachitano.
p. cm.
ISBN 978-1-934841-58-7 (trade paper : alk. paper) -- ISBN 978-1-934841-59-4 (electronic)
1. Quiltmakers--Fiction. 2. Widows--Fiction. 3. Washington (State)--Fiction. 4. Historical reenactments--Fiction. 5. Murder--Investigation--Fiction. I. Title.
PS3619.A277Q853 2010
813'.6--dc22

2009048445

ACKNOWLEDGMENTS

Many people support my writing efforts both directly and indirectly. My thanks go out to all of them. I particularly would like to thank my immediate family, Jack, Karen, Malakai, Annie, Alex, Amelia, David, Tanya, Ken, Nikki and Kellen. Thanks also to my sister Donna, who helped develop my creativity by drawing an endless herd of paper-doll horses on our many cross-country jaunts in the back of our parent's station wagon.

I would also like to thank my in-laws, Beth and Hank, not only for their support but also for their medical input as I try to figure out how to slay my characters. Nor can I forget Scott Ryon and Ed May, retired police people and active Ducks Unlimited members who are always willing to talk about the how-to of crime.

Supportive friends and relatives are also an indispensable part of writing my book. Brenda and Bob are unflagging supporters and promoters of my writing. Brett, Nathan, Jason and Chad provide support and let me use their names, so thanks, guys.

I'd also like to thank my knitting students for their patience and flexibility, especially when I leave them for promotional activities.

My critique group Katy and Luanne are always available to read pages and provide sympathy when rewrites are necessary—a thankless task, but thank you, ladies.

I'd like to express my appreciation to the many quilt store owners who allow me to do book signings at their stores and events. Their support is invaluable. Special thanks to Betty and Vern at Storyquilts.com—they started me on the path to quilt mystery novels with their Seams Like Murder Block of the Month series. They also generously share a corner of their booth at Quilt Market as well as a wealth of information about the quilt business.

Thanks, as always, to Liz and Tina at Zumaya for making all this work.

Last but not least, I'd like to thank my two Susans—friends, gym partners and willing listeners (no matter how many times I tell them slight variations of the same story).

Chapter 1

"Could everyone who will have a quilt for sale in our sutler's booth please put your name and a brief description of your quilt or quilts on this form?"

Harriet Truman held up the aforementioned piece of paper before handing it to her friend Jenny Logan. Harriet was a member of the Foggy Point Business Association, organizers of an upcoming Civil War re-enactment. In Civil War days, the sutlers were the mobile merchants. The Loose Threads quilt group had been meeting every day for the past week in order to finish their quilts before the opening skirmish in the re-enactment.

"Correct me if I'm wrong, but didn't the Civil War take place before Washington achieved statehood?" Lauren Sawyer asked. She gathered her straight blonde hair in both hands and raised it off her neck, letting the air from the open window cool her skin. "And why do we have to make quilts for people who relish violence so much they have to keep replaying it over and over again?" She loosened her grip and let her hair cascade onto her back again.

"Don't be so contrary," Marjory Swain scolded. She owned Pins and Needles, Foggy Point's only fabric store and the site of the Loose Threads' weekly meetings. Lauren couldn't afford to offend the older woman, so she held her tongue for once. "Here, tie your hair up and get back to your quilting." Marjory handed Lauren a lime-green fabric-covered elastic hair tie.

"I'm passing around another form," Harriet continued and held up a yellow piece of paper. "This one is to sign up for times to work in the booth. I do appreciate everyone's hard work. If we sell all the quilts we've collected so far, we'll have enough money to repair all of last year's storm damage in Fogg Park.

"I suppose you voted for that when I was in Angel Harbor last month," Lauren said.

"I'm sure even you can't have forgotten we were *all* in Angel Harbor, and no, we didn't vote then, it was after we got home, and yes, you weren't here for that meeting," Harriet challenged.

By the time she'd graduated from high school, she'd dealt with bullying schoolmates on three continents, thanks to her parent's international lifestyle and penchant for yo-yoing her in and out of boarding schools. At thirty-eight, she thought she'd learned to let go of the need to engage in schoolgirl trash talk, but when Lauren was involved, it all went out the window and she was back in the schoolyard.

"Ladies," Mavis Willis said in a no-nonsense voice, "this isn't getting us anywhere." Mavis was not only the oldest member of the Loose Threads but had also raised five sons whose antics were legend in Foggy Point Public School District lore. When she spoke, everyone listened. "What matters today is that we get as many quilts finished as possible before people start arriving on Thursday."

"If you have at least one quilt finished and ready to hang, raise your hand," Harriet said.

Everyone raised their hand.

"Robin and DeAnn have volunteered to gather what we have ready, put price tags on them and hang them in the booth. Anything we finish between now and Thursday can go on shelves at the back of the booth. The whole sutler's area will be covered with a canopy, so we don't have to worry about sun damage from hanging quilts early."

"I'll have seven quilts finished by Thursday," Sarah Ness announced.

"Here we go," Mavis said, covering her mouth and coughing to conceal her comment.

Sarah held up a simple quilt made from one of the pre-cut five-inch-square fabric packages known as charm packs. The colors were pastel pinks and blues and yellows. The prints were reproductions from an earlier age—the nineteen thirties.

"Okay, who's going to say it?" DeAnn Gault asked in a low voice, giving the rest of the assembled Loose Threads a sidelong glance.

Harriet shrugged, not up to that challenge. Mavis shook her head and smiled in anticipation of the coming argument. Lauren rolled her eyes toward the ceiling and went back to stitching the binding onto a quilt made with the Kansas Troubles block, done in shades of butternut and blue set alternately with unpieced blocks of the same size. She'd chosen small-print fabrics that were faithful reproductions of those used in the years leading up to the Civil War.

DeAnn gave the group one last pleading look before turning back to Sarah.

"While very lovely, your fabric is not a Civil War reproduction," she stated.

"It's a reproduction, that's all people care about," Sarah fired back. She folded the quilt and stuffed it in her large canvas carry bag, pulling another one out in the same motion.

Lauren groaned and looked away as Sarah unfolded her second quilt.

"I can't stand it," she moaned.

The quilt was made with the same Kansas Troubles block pattern Lauren had used, only Sarah had used yellow fabrics against a black background with pale blue and acid green accents. Technically, she'd selected fabrics from Civil War reproduction collections, but Harriet was pretty sure this particular combination had never been assembled before—not in Civil War times and not since.

DeAnn started to speak, stopping before recognizable words formed. Finally, she gave up, shaking her head and laughing.

"What?" Sarah asked, truly bewildered.

"Nothing," Harriet said, regaining her own composure, as long as she didn't make eye contact with DeAnn. "Thank you for your efforts. Give your quilts to DeAnn or Robin, and they'll record them and get them hung up at the booth."

She had been warned by the re-enactment consultant the Foggy Point Business Association had hired that some of their guests would be what were referred to as "thread counters"—people who obsessed over the authenticity of everything to the point of counting the threads per inch in all the fabrics used for uniforms, civilian clothing, bedding and supplies, checking to be sure they were true to the time period. The consultant recommended clearly labeling any items already known to be less-accurate copies from the period. He suggested phrases like "in the style of the Civil War period."

He had assured them that all types of history buffs showed up, and there would inevitably be family members of the hardcore re-enactors who would welcome the chance to shop for more contemporary items. As long as the majority of what was offered in the sutler's area were sincere reproductions, he was sure they would have a successful event.

"Does anyone have any questions?" Harriet asked before returning to her place at the big table the Loose Threads were clustered around. Normally, meetings were informal gatherings, with people drifting in and out as their schedule allowed or their project required. They met in the larger of two classrooms in Pins and Needles.

"Are we interrupting anything?" a stout, slightly balding man said from the doorway. He didn't wait to for an answer but came through the door and took the position Harriet had just vacated at the head of the table. A young, heavily made-up woman in a short pink skirt, silver tank top and pink alligator boots followed and stood by his side, a bored look on her face. Her long bleached hair was held up on her small head with a large silver plastic clam shell clip.

"We wanted to check and see how you gals were doing with the quilts for your booth. You know the quilt store is one of the most important booths in our whole vendor area." He made a grimace that was his version of smiling and directed his attention to Harriet, walking to her side of the table and sitting in the chair next to her. "Did you find vendors for the last three booths?"

He leaned eagerly toward her; the heavy gold chain he was wearing looped out through the open neck of his pink shirt. Harriet sat as far back in her chair as she could without being obvious.

As president of the Foggy Point Business Association, it was Carlton Brewster's job to organize the re-enactment. Since the association had agreed to hire a consultant, there weren't many jobs left for him to personally carry out, filling the sutler's area being his major one.

"Yes, they're filled. I got a candlemaker from Port Townsend who will do wax dipping demonstrations four times a day and will have candles for sale also. The knitting group that meets at the Lutheran church will sell handmade shawls as well as socks, hats and scarves. Luckily, they all had items they'd already made for a church sale that are historically acceptable, and they'll each turn out a few more items before the event. And for the last booth, the folk art school in Angel Harbor will set up a mini-bazaar like the women's aid societies ran to raise money for the war. They'll sell a variety of things—tobacco pouches, pin cushions, little sewing kits, children's toys, stuff like that."

"Well, good," he said. He clapped her on the back, causing the tea in the cup she'd just picked up to spill onto the table. "Seems like you have the sutler's area taken care of." He turned to his wife. "Bebe and I were just heading over to the country club. We figured people in Civil War times probably spent more time outdoors then we do. After spending all that money to make sure we have realistic costumes, we figured we better make sure our tans are up to snuff."

Harriet looked at Bebe, whose given name was actually Barbara. If she got any more tan her well-oiled skin was going to look like a piece of burnt toast.

"We wouldn't want that," she said.

His job for the day done, Carlton took Bebe by the arm and left.

Connie Escorcia got up and went to the bathroom, returning a moment later with a handful of paper towels. She glanced toward the door to make sure Carlton and Bebe were gone.

"Dios mio!" she exclaimed. "How dare he come in here with that…that…" She broke into rapid-fire Spanish even Harriet couldn't follow, but which apparently referred to Bebe, and not in a good way, either. Connie was a retired teacher and, at five foot even, made up for her diminutive size with her larger-than-life Latina personality. "He dumped all his jobs on you so he can go sit at the pool with her?"

Harriet picked up her quilt, a scrappy design made up of eight-pointed stars and rail-fence blocks, which were squares made from three equal-sized fabric strips of different colors or patterns. Like Lauren, she was hand-stitching the binding onto the edge.

"Somehow, when I agreed to take over Aunt Beth's quilting business, I didn't realize I was also agreeing to this whole business association hoo-ha."

"You're really good at it, though," Jenny offered. She was a slender, fiftyish woman whose sleek, shoulder-length hair was never out of place. Her taste in quilting normally ran to large pastel floral designs with a blended, low-contrast look. To her credit, for the re-enactment she was making a coverlet with roses and plumes cut from red, pink, yellow and green solids and appliquéd onto an off-white background. A ribbon of green stems with stylized rosebuds circled the rose blocks, forming a border. Jenny was still appliquéing the rosebuds and had arranged with Harriet to machine-quilt it as soon as it was done.

"You're definitely more competent than Carlton," DeAnn said. "If he was actually doing the job, he'd be making a mess of it, so we're better off with him sitting by the pool with the bimbo."

"DeAnn's right," Robin added. "The extra work he would have created would have been much worse to deal with." Robin taught yoga, and believed most problems could be solved with a few cleansing breaths and a stretch. If *she* condemned Carlton's management skill, Harriet had to believe it was bad.

One by one, the women around the table pulled their finished quilts from bags, or fetched them from their cars and stacked them in front of Robin and DeAnn for pricing and labeling. For their part, the two women had made three quilts together, sharing cut strips in shades of blue to make several variations of the Irish Chain Pattern.

Harriet was pleased to see the growing stack of quilts. Going into this event, she'd been concerned about asking the group for such a large commitment of time and resources. She was once again impressed by the willingness of the people in her new home town to pull together no matter what the cause. It didn't seem to matter that the current economy was tough—everyone in the group had donated at least one quilt, and most of them had contributed more than one.

"Honey, could you give me a ride home?" Mavis asked Harriet as she snapped her cell phone closed. "I dropped my car off for an oil change, but of course, Henry found a cracked hose and that worried him, so he wants to change all the hoses and he doesn't have time to finish it tonight."

"Sure, no problem," Harriet said. "I'll be done in a minute. I want to total up the asking prices DeAnn and Robin came up with for what we have here. We need to earn back five hundred dollars to pay for our share of the tent rentals for the sutler's area."

"That should be easy," Robin said. "All of the full-sized quilts are priced at least that high."

"You aren't serious, are you?" Lauren asked. "We'll have five hundred after the first hour."

"Of course, I'm not serious," Harriet said. She nervously tapped her pen on the page she was holding. "I just want to know what to expect profit-wise."

Robin put a garish purple-and-green quilt Sarah had made on the top of the stack.

"That's the last one for now," she said.

"Let me know if you two need anything," Harriet said. She finished adding up the figures on their list, wrote them in a small notebook and dropped the book into her bag. "You ready?" she asked Mavis, and when the older woman nodded, they left.

"Do you need to stop at the store or anything while we're in town?" Harriet asked.

Mavis declined, and Harriet pointed her car toward Mavis' cottage on the wooded shores of the Strait of Juan de Fuca.

Foggy Point is a peninsula on the northwest edge of Washington State. It resembles the head and small front claw of a tyrannosaurus, jutting into the inland waters that form the border between the United States and Canada. In earlier times, the jagged outline of the peninsula made a perfect hiding place for pirates and their sailing ships between forays. Eventually, one of the more successful among them, Cornelius Fogg, had settled down and founded the town of Foggy Point.

The downtown area of Foggy Point was situated on what would be the back of the T-rex's neck and spanned an area of six square blocks, with most of the activity centered within two blocks on either side of Main Street.

Harriet drove down the lane leading to the little house in the woods Mavis called home. Wild roses covered the fence that protected the yard of the fairytale-like cottage.

"Can you come in for a cup of tea?"

"Sure," Harriet replied. "Here, let me carry your bag." She got out of the car and grabbed Mavis' canvas quilting bag from the back seat.

Mavis led the way to the arbored gate and held it for her.

"Did you leave your door open?"

"No, I haven't left it unlocked since Bertie came calling." Mavis referred to an incident earlier that year when Avanell Jalbert had been murdered by her own brother Bertie, who had then come after Harriet, who was staying with Mavis at the time.

"I don't mean unlocked. It's standing *open*." Harriet started backing up, pulling her cell phone from her pocket as she went. "I don't have a signal."

"Let's not jump to conclusions. My boys all have keys to the house and some of their kids do, too."

"They *all* have keys? I don't even know where my parents live, much less have a key."

"You have weird parents," Mavis replied, being all too familiar with Harriet's history.

"Would your kids leave the door standing open?" Harriet asked.

"Not on purpose, but they might have forgotten you have to lift the knob when you shut the door or it doesn't catch."

Mavis brushed past her and went up to the porch. "We didn't see any cars along the road or in my driveway. I'm telling you, it was one of my boys." She pushed the door open. "Hello," she called as she went inside.

Harriet grabbed at her to slow her down but Mavis wasn't having it, so she followed her. The house was small; it only took a few moments to check the two bedrooms, bathroom, living room and kitchen. No one was there.

"There's no note, but that's not unusual." Mavis picked up her teakettle from the stove and added water before setting it back on its burner and turning on the power. "Sit down and put your feet up for a few minutes," she said and pointed to the living room. "Your aunt Beth told me you've been working late trying to finish the Civil War quilts as quickly as you can. You know that's why her shoulder went bad, don't you?"

"Yes, ma'am," Harriet said, even though she was pretty sure her aunt had damaged her shoulder long before she'd taken up long-arm quilting. Granted, running the quilting machine for hours on end hadn't helped.

"Have I shown you the new grandmother's flower garden quilt I'm working on?" Mavis was an old-school quilter who sewed the pieces of her quilt top together by hand. She quilted most of her projects by hand, too, although in the interest of time she'd let Harriet machine-quilt one of her Civil War offerings.

"No, but I'd love to see it."

"Katrina's pregnant again, and they just found out it's a girl." Mavis went into the spare bedroom that doubled as her sewing room. "I'm using…"

"Mavis?" Harriet called when her friend remained silent. Receiving no response, she jumped up and hurried down the short hallway that led to the bedroom.

Mavis stood clutching a worn quilt Harriet had never seen before. Tears streamed down her face.

Chapter 2

Mavis, what's wrong," Harriet asked as she eased her normally unshakable friend into a seat on the bed. She grabbed several tissues from a box on the fabric cutting table and handed them to her.

After a few moments, Mavis regained her composure. She stood up and, with a final swipe of her tissue, went into the kitchen, turned the kettle off and started making their tea. She gave one cup to Harriet then picked up the old quilt from the chair back she'd set it on and headed into the living room.

"Come, sit. I owe you an explanation." She spread the worn lap-sized quilt on the sofa between them. "I haven't seen this quilt in almost twenty years," she began. "I made this for my husband Gerald. The predominant plaid fabric is from one of his flannel shirts. He wore a brand-new shirt out in the garage to sharpen the blade on the lawn mower, and he caught the sleeve on a nail and tore it from elbow to cuff. Instead of trying to repair such a big tear, I cut the whole shirt up and used it in this quilt."

Harriet studied the plaid pattern, giving her friend time. Green, brown and blue shirtings had been used, giving the quilt its scrappy look.

"Gerald traveled some with his job, but after I made this, he never went on a trip without it. He said it made him feel like he had a little bit of home with him. He died on a trip to Malaysia, but when they returned his personal effects this wasn't with them. I thought it had been lost."

Harriet put her hand on Mavis's arm. "I'm so sorry."

Mavis just shook her head. She leaned back and stared into space as she silently sipped her tea.

Harriet wished Aunt Beth hadn't driven to Seattle for the day. She would know the right thing to say to her oldest friend.

"Do you want me to call the police?" she finally asked, knowing it probably wasn't the comfort Mavis needed, but she couldn't think of anything else.

"What for?" Mavis asked, a little more sharply than usual. "What am I supposed to say—'Oh, officer, a crime's been committed. Someone broke into my house to return a lost quilt to me?' I'm sure they'd rush right over to solve that one."

Harriet laughed softly, "I guess that's probably not a crime we need to dial nine-one-one over. But someone did come in here uninvited."

"We don't know that. Maybe Gerald left it with one of the boys, and they just now realized what they had. Things were pretty chaotic when Gerald died, him being overseas and all."

"It just seems like your sons would have left a note or called you or something."

"You'd think so, but the two unmarried ones are a little more scattered than the other three. Harry or Ben would have intended to leave a note, but I can easily imagine either one of them going out the door without doing it."

"Maybe we could call Darcy," Harriet suggested. Darcy Lewis was a quilter and sometimes Loose Thread, but she was also a criminalist based at the Jefferson County Sheriff's Office.

"You know better than anyone she can't do anything unless the sheriff's office or the Foggy Point Police Department sends her, and I'm not involving them."

Harriet heaved a weary sigh and finished her now cold tea in two large gulps.

"I better hit the road," she said. "I've got quilts waiting on me." She carried her cup to the kitchen sink, rinsing it before she set it on the counter. "Call me tomorrow if you want a ride back to the car dealer," she called before slipping out the front door.

Mavis didn't reply. Harriet could see through the front window that the older woman was sitting in her recliner, clutching Gerald's quilt to her chest.

She had almost reached her car when a strange-looking little dog with a too-round head and ears set at an odd angle ran up and started dancing around her feet. She bent down and patted her.

"Hi, Randy." She picked her up. "Where's your daddy?" she managed to ask as Randy licked her face.

"He's right behind you," a male voice said, in a falsetto, pretend-dog tone, from over her shoulder.

She turned to face Aiden Jalbert, Foggy Point's newest veterinarian, his arms already closing around her. She leaned into his solid chest—at six-foot-three, he was comfortably tall.

"I'll just stay here till after the re-enactment," she said.

She'd never thought of herself as one of those shallow women who judged men by their physical attributes, but Aiden's white-blue eyes, set at an angle like a cat's, and his blue-black hair, worn longer than was stylish unless you were a European model, made her heart flutter. The baggy running shorts that exposed his muscular legs only added to his physical appeal. Perhaps there were benefits to dating a man ten years her junior.

"Sounds good to me, as long as Mavis stays gone, that is."

"Mavis is inside in her chair. I brought her home—her car had to stay at the shop. It was good that I was here. Something weird happened." She told him about the open door, the quilt and Mavis's reaction to it.

Aiden thought for a moment. "I was pretty little when Gerald died." He looked up at the sky, thinking. "I don't remember anything other than Mom having to spend a lot of time with Mavis for a while."

"Maybe Mavis is right, and one of her sons dropped it off. It seems kind of insensitive to leave it in her house without a note or anything and then to leave the door open on top of that."

"Something's not right. I'll try to swing by here when I can."

"Speaking of that, what are you doing here, anyway? And dressed like that, too. You didn't get fired did you?"

Aiden lived on the other side of the large wooded area that ran along the shore of the strait. She had walked the trails through the woods with him and Randy on more than one occasion, but not during the workday.

"Your confidence in my abilities is underwhelming." He tried to make a sad face but ended up laughing instead. "Dr. Johnson decided to keep the clinic open late an additional night, and yours truly gets to be the first guy on the new shift. I came home to take Randy for a run, since I have a few hours off now in exchange."

"I guess that means dinner's off," Harriet said, trying for a smile but not making it.

"I could bring pizza by when I get off," he said and tilted her chin up with his finger and then kissed her gently on the lips.

"As good as that sounds, in reality I've got a lot of work to do. Maybe we should just postpone."

"I'll come by with a treat to reward you for all your hard work," he said with an impish smile.

She started to protest, but he pulled her into another kiss, silencing her. He brushed her short dark hair away from her face. "And I won't stay long and keep you from your work."

He let her go and called Randy, who ran up, her short tail wagging.

Harriet watched, her cheeks flushed and a smile on her face, until the pair had disappeared into the woods again.

Chapter 3

A long-arm quilting machine is really just a fancy sewing machine. It has a large frame that holds the quilt top, batting and backing under tension while the sewing head is guided over the taut surface, stitching as it goes. Completed sections are wound on a long roller as they are completed.

Harriet found the process relaxing—at least, she did when her thread didn't break and the requested pattern flowed easily. The one she was working on had a reasonable pattern, but the thread had been provided by the quilt maker; and although it was a lovely tea-dyed cotton, it broke every few feet, which translated to every few minutes for this pattern.

"You look like you could use a break," Aunt Beth said as she came into the studio through the outside door. Aunt Beth had given Harriet the long-arm quilt business as well as the Victorian house where she'd lived and worked back in April. Then, she'd retired to a cottage by the water.

Harriet still thought of both as Aunt Beth's even though her aunt didn't.

"I have a first-time customer who provided her own thread, and it's giving me fits. I don't have too much more to do, though."

"You keep stitching, and I'll make some tea," Beth didn't wait for an answer. She put her purse and coat on one of the wingback chairs in the reception area by the door and went through the door into the kitchen.

Aunt Beth backed through the connecting door again fifteen minutes later, a tray with a teapot, cups, sugar and spoons balanced in front of her.

"How's it going?" she asked.

"Perfect timing. I just finished. I'll take it off the frame when we're done with our tea."

"How are the preparations going?"

"I've got the sutler's area filled, no thanks to Carlton. And the Threads have our booth in good shape. As long as people actually buy our quilts we'll be good."

"Oh, honey, of course they'll buy our quilts."

"With this economy, I don't want to count on anything. I've tried to keep the expenses conservative just in case."

"That's a good plan no matter. If people don't spend much you'll be fine, but if they do, you'll have better profits." Aunt Beth poured the tea and handed her a cup.

Harriet inhaled the fragrance of bergamot. "Hmmm, Earl Grey?"

"Good nose," Aunt Beth replied. They both sipped for a few moments.

"I'm sorry you're stuck with Carlton," Aunt Beth finally said. "I'm so used to working around him I didn't even think to warn you."

"What I don't understand is how people like him get good jobs and positions of authority when they're completely incompetent."

"In his case, it was easy—his daddy built a company and brought him up through the ranks. When Daddy died, his only son got the keys to the kingdom. As one of the bigger employers in the area, he gets his pick of the positions in the Business Association. Actually, until he got married to Bebe, he wasn't that bad. I'm not sure he ever had an original thought, but at least he worked when you handed him a task. Now, all he can think of is her."

"On a different topic," Harriet said, changing the subject before she found herself ranting about Carlton for the hundredth time. "I took Mavis home from Loose Threads today and something really weird happened." She proceeded to tell Aunt Beth about the incident at the cottage.

Aunt Beth took her time before replying.

"Gerald worked for Foggy Point Fire Protection Company back then. That was when it was called Industrial Fiber Products. He was some kind of chemist. He traveled all over the world visiting customers. He died in a car accident in Malaysia. What was weird was that for some reason they never got his body back. A few weeks later, his ashes arrived in an urn. No one ever went to Malaysia; none of the family was present for the cremation. I'm sure there was some good reason. Maybe they automatically cremate people within a certain time frame, or something like that. I don't know." She rubbed her hands over her weatherworn face. "I guess everyone has their own way of doing things."

"Maybe that's why she got so upset at the sight of the quilt," Harriet said. "Did you ever ask her why she didn't go there?"

"Honey, there are some things you don't ask a person. Not when they've just lost the love of their life. I just trusted that she had a good reason. My job was to support her in whatever way she needed, not to challenge her decisions." She smiled. "I know what you're thinking, but you heed my words, some things are better left alone."

A tap on the studio door interrupted the silence that enveloped the room. Harriet got up and opened the door for Aiden, who carried a pizza box in one hand and a drink carrier in the other.

"I thought I might find you here," he said to Aunt Beth as she took the drinks from him. Harriet closed the door then held the connecting door to the kitchen open for them.

"How's Carla doing?" Aunt Beth asked when they were all settled on stools around the kitchen island, the pizza within easy reach. Aiden had chosen a nontraditional pie that included artichoke hearts, Kalamata olives and goat cheese. He'd also gotten a large Caesar salad for them to share.

"Getting better." He took a big bite of pizza.

Carla Salter was the youngest member of the Loose Threads. She'd joined after participating in a quilting group for unwed mothers that Marjory held at Pins and Needles. In addition to making a quilt for their own baby, each of the young women made a quilt to be donated to charity for other young mothers. Marjory gathered donated fabrics for the group to use, and when Harriet took over Quilt As Desired she'd also assumed Aunt Beth's donation of free machine quilting for all the quilts the group made.

Carla had caught the quilting bug and gotten a second job working at the quilt store to fund her new hobby. Unfortunately, she had lost her job at the vitamin factory Aiden's family owned and was living with her baby in a borrowed van until Harriet convinced Aiden to hire her to be his housekeeper.

"I stayed in my apartment over the clinic until a week ago," Aiden explained. "I thought it would be better for her to get settled at the house before I moved back in." He took another bite of pizza, and Aunt Beth waited patiently for him to finish chewing. "The first week I went to check up on her, and at seven o'clock at night she had the baby strapped to her back and was on the third floor scrubbing windows."

"Poor little thing," Aunt Beth said.

"So, I told her to restrict her activities to the first floor until we could figure things out. Then she didn't go upstairs at all, and one of the plants in the sitting room up there died and she was in tears over that." He sighed. "I had no idea how hard this was going to be when I agreed to hire her as a housekeeper."

"You must have had some idea—your mother had a housekeeper, didn't she?" Harriet asked.

"Of course, no one could take care of that huge house without help. I just didn't pay attention to who did what. And I was in school. I only know who took the garbage out—that would be me. And my sister was supposed to walk the dog, but she never did, so I did that, too."

"I've got a little time," Aunt Beth offered. "How about I go over and spend some time with Carla, and we can make a list of what she should do and a list of what things you should hire out. I know who your mama had do her windows and a few things like that."

"That would be great," he said with relief. "And could you ask her to stop calling me Mr. Jalbert? And also, when you make the list, you can give me some stuff to do, too. I never expected to have someone wait on me hand and foot. I know my mother still did some stuff around the house even though we had Rose. And like you said, she had other people who did stuff."

"We'll get things straightened out in no time."

"One more thing," Aiden said. "See if you can find out who her new friend is."

"Does she have a boyfriend?" Harriet smiled.

"Yeah, and he's not from around here."

"Did you check him out?" Harriet asked.

"No, I didn't check him out. She's a big girl. Besides, I just moved back, and she was already seeing him. If Beth can find something out, that's different."

Talk turned to Aiden's work and then the upcoming re-enactment. When they had eaten as much pizza and salad as they could, Aunt Beth got up and started clearing the remains.

"I'd better get out of here so you can get that quilt off the machine," she said.

"I better go, too," Aiden said. "Carla's friend was supposed to be dropping by tonight while I was at work."

"Okay," Harriet said. "I've got to go finish the quilt."

Aiden brushed his lips over her cheek in a quick kiss and left. She stood at the door looking down the driveway long after his car had rounded the turn and gone out of sight.

How pathetic am I? she wondered.

Aiden had spent months assuring her their ten-year age gap was meaningless, yet here she was wondering what it meant when he rushed off to check on Carla, of all people. In her heart, she knew he wasn't interested in Carla in that way, but an irrational part of her was hurt that he couldn't spare just one minute to kiss her goodbye properly.

Chapter 4

Harriet was in her sunny yellow kitchen the next morning when someone knocked on the studio door. It was barely eight o'clock, and she wasn't expecting any customers.

"Coming," she called out and set her empty cereal bowl in the sink and ran a splash of water in it before going through the connecting door and unlocking the exterior door.

"Hey, Chiquita," Connie said as she came in. She held a garment bag in her left hand. "I have your costume ready to try on."

Connie had volunteered to make Harriet's outfit since Harriet had no free time between making her own quilts and stitching everyone else's. After some discussion, they had agreed Harriet would quilt Connie's charity projects free of charge in exchange for the costume.

"Oh, Connie, I completely forgot you were coming this morning." Harriet put palm to forehead in a mock smack.

"Is this a bad time?"

"No, I was going to go check on Mavis, but that can wait."

"This won't take long," Connie said as she unzipped the bag and pulled out three hangers, each holding an element of the costume.

"The bodice and skirt aren't connected. Since it's hot out, I decided to make two different bodices to go with the skirt so you can have one to wash and one to wear." She had used simple cotton reproduction fabric in a pale brown that had a small light-blue flower in an all-over print. "Everything was in pieces in those days. Diós mio!" She pulled another hanger out of the garment bag. This one held a pale-blue apron. Clipped to the same hanger were three white cotton collars. "They didn't attach the collar to the shirt, so here are three of those. I was making one for each bodice, but they were so easy to do, I made you a spare."

"They wore all this stuff every day?"

"This is a simple outfit," Connie said. "The fancy outfits were much more complicated, with extra petticoats, under-sleeves and cuffs."

"I could make a lap-sized quilt with the fabric in this skirt," Harriet said as she pulled it on over her shorts.

"Take your shorts off," Connie ordered. "The waist has to fit well if it's going to hold all that fabric up."

"Yes, ma'am." Harriet wriggled her shorts off under the skirt.

"By the by, chiquita," Connie said around a mouth full of straight pins. "I went to coffee this morning with your aunt and Jenny and Mavis. It sounded like Mavis is leaving town for a couple of days. Her son in Portland called and said their babysitter had to go to an out-of-town funeral and asked if Mavis could come fill in until she gets back. I think she's going to do it. She told him she needed to be back for the re-enactment."

"Wow, that's kind of sudden," Harriet said, mentally scanning her remaining to-do list to see if she had any items with Mavis's name on them. She realized that what she'd needed from Mavis was moral support. Everything else was well on its way to being done.

Connie was just putting the last pins in the hem of the skirt when the door opened and Bebe Brewster came in without knocking, a cloud of designer perfume entering with her.

"Hi, Harriet," she said. "I need Mavis to remake Carlton's vest. She dropped it off this morning, way too early, I might add. Anyway, there must have been some mistake." She pulled a wool vest out of the paper bag she was carrying. "It's all dull and gray." She held it with two fingers as if it were contaminated then dropped it on a wingback chair. "This won't do. She needs to make another one out of a brighter fabric, something to match my dress."

"What color is your dress?" Harriet asked, afraid to hear the answer.

"Why, pink, of course. I had a dressmaker in Seattle make it."

"Men didn't wear pink in Civil War times," Connie said.

"We don't know that. No one knows what every single person wore back then. I'm sure there was a man somewhere who wore a pink vest, and Carlton is going to be like that man."

"Well, Mavis went to Portland, so I'm afraid you're out of luck," Connie said.

"Am I still out of luck if I'm willing to pay you three times what Mavis charged for this thing?" Bebe asked.

"Make it four times, and you have a deal," Connie said, knowing Mavis had charged a premium price for the first one and afraid of what Bebe might come up with if she *didn't* make it. She picked up the gray vest. "Did this one fit?"

"I'm sure it would have—Mavis is very thorough. But you already know that." Bebe pivoted on her pink patent leather heels and left as quickly as she'd come, her mission successfully accomplished.

"I can't believe you just agreed to make a new vest for Carlton when Mavis already made a perfectly good one."

"You need to learn to pick your battles, mija. Bebe is very young. Her world vision stops at the mirror in front of her. Some people are slow bloomers. Our Bebe is still a child. Besides, it won't take me any time at all, and I can always use more mad money."

"You're a nicer person than I am," Harriet said.

✂ ✂ ✂

"Meow," came a muffled complaint from the other side of the connecting door. The sound was repeated after a few moments, this time louder and more insistent.

"Okay, Fred," Harriet called out. "I'll be there in a sec."

DeAnn and Robin had dropped off two quilt tops they had made up at the last minute. They were to be lap-sized quilts, and the women had devised a scheme to sew the two tops together and use one big backing piece so they could be quilted as if they were a single big quilt. It was a clever plan and allowed Harriet to do one set-up instead of two. The pattern was the crosses and losses block, a design that used half-square triangle pieces along with solid squares of the same size as well as larger triangles.

Half-square triangles are made by stacking two layers of fabric, right sides together, and then cutting the resulting sandwich into a square, which is then stitched together on the diagonal with two lines of stitching placed a half-inch apart. When the unit between the two stitching lines is cut apart, the result is two squares each comprised of two different-colored triangles.

Several paper and fabric systems have been invented that allow a stitcher to lay two large pieces of fabric together then place a paper guide on top. The quilter stitches a continuous intertwined zigzag line following the printed guide then cuts along another guideline. The result is a lot of perfectly sized half-square triangles with much less effort. The latest twist on the guide system is to make it out of a very lightweight material that is permanently heat-fused onto the reverse side of one of the fabrics, eliminating the need to remove paper guide pieces.

Being reasonable women, they had chosen a simple feather pattern for the quilt stitching. The feathers would adequately anchor their quilt top to the backing without making Harriet go to undue trouble.

Fred meowed again, so Harriet opened the connecting door and let him come into the studio and weave between her legs while she shut down her machine. He had been banished to the kitchen several hours earlier when he had tired of their quilting project and started amusing himself by swatting her ankles.

"I suppose you're hungry again," she said, knowing the answer before she even asked. "You do know it was Aiden who put you on the hypo-allergenic cat food, not me. If you want to take it out on someone—"

"Hey, Fred," Aiden said as he came in from the studio.

"Don't you ever knock?"

"Don't you ever lock your door? Besides, if I had knocked I wouldn't have heard you bad-mouthing me to Fred here." He crossed the room and pulled Harriet into his arms, kissing her soundly on the mouth. "And no matter what the cat says, he has to stay on that food if you want his skin to clear up. Speaking of food, want to go find some? I have to go back to work for a meeting, but we're having a dinner break first."

"Would we have time to go by the battlefield before we eat? I'd like to take one last walk-through before the advance group starts arriving tomorrow morning."

Harriet had encouraged Carlton to pay a small group of experienced re-enactors from the Portland area to come several days before the main event to check out the battlefield, tent camps and sutler area to make sure they hadn't overlooked anything. Several of the women were quilters, and she had invited them to join the Loose Threads as they finished up their projects.

"I think that could be arranged," he said. "Let me call Jorge and see if he can start our dinners while we walk."

Jorge Perez owned a Mexican restaurant in downtown Foggy Point called Tico's Tacos. He had stepped in as a father figure after Aiden's own father had died when he was in grade school. Jorge's son Julio, an environmental lawyer in Seattle, was Aiden's best friend.

Aiden made the call from his cell phone as they drove down the hill, through downtown Foggy Point and on to Fogg Park, where the re-enactment would take place. Large areas of the park were barred to the public and had been sectioned off with yellow tape. Private security guards patrolled the perimeter to insure the fence segments, movable bushes and other props needed for the battles wouldn't be disturbed. As a result, the parking lot was nearly empty.

Aiden parked his vintage Ford Bronco at the curb, and they got out. The air was warm, and heavy with the scent of pine. Summer days in Foggy Point didn't often go higher than the upper seventies or low eighties. Harriet hoped their guests from warmer climates would be prepared for the cooler summer weather the locals enjoyed.

"What if no one comes?" she asked in a small voice when they had reached the middle of the battlefield.

"The City of Foggy Point would be stuck with a big tab and they would probably run you out of town on a rail," Aiden said in a somber voice.

Harriet looked stricken for a moment before she looked up and realized he was teasing her, at which point she hit his arm.

"You're not helping."

"You're being silly," he countered. "You have a zillion people signed up to attend the various events, you know all the hotel rooms in town have been reserved and the B-and-Bs are full. You also have two camps full of participants who have already paid to rent tents and tent spaces. It would take a full-scale disaster for this to be anything but a smashing success."

"I suppose. I've just never been in charge of an event of this size before."

"Well, you better get ready to do more. This is going to be a huge success, and then every fundraising committee in town is going to want your magic touch."

"Well, they're not getting it. This has been way too stressful. I'll need a vacation when this is over."

"No problem. I'll run away with you and we'll lie on some exotic beach till your stress goes away."

"Yeah," she said. "I'm sure you would. We both know you don't have any vacation days yet."

"I'll quit my job," he offered.

"Can we go look at the sutler's area, please?"

They started to walk back to the parking lot. The vendor area had been set up between the parking lot and the covered picnic shelter. Harriet stopped and put a hand on Aiden's arm, stopping him, too.

"Look. Is that a man between the woods and that section of fake hedge?"

"I don't see anyone," Aiden said, following the line of her arm as she pointed toward the woods.

"I'm sure I saw someone in a plaid shirt." She strained to see through the growing shadows. "He's gone now. I hope he didn't do anything to the hedge. You don't suppose the combatants would sabotage the battle site to gain an advantage, would they?"

"No, I think in most of these events the two sides take turns being the victors, so each one gets to win a couple of times throughout the weekend. It was probably a homeless person camping in the woods."

"Let's see if we can find one of the security guards and have him check it out."

The guard was a pudgy, sweaty fellow with bad skin and a skimpy mustache.

"I haven't seen anyone in the field or the woods, and I been here since three o'clock," he assured Harriet when she relayed what she'd seen. The fact they had found him sitting in his battered car did not inspire faith in his watchfulness.

"Maybe I should camp here overnight until people arrive," Harriet said when they were out of earshot of the guard.

"No, you shouldn't," Aiden said. "Everything's going to be fine. There's not enough here to worry about guarding. And besides, if you camp here, then I have to camp here to make sure you're safe, and I haven't been home from Africa long enough to think sleeping on the ground is fun yet."

"You're right—what could someone steal, a fake hedgerow? No one would do that."

"Can we eat now?"

Harriet looped her arm through Aiden's and turned him toward the parking lot.

Dinner was delicious, as usual. Harriet had her favorite chicken enchiladas with tomatillo sauce while Aiden had chiles relleños, and they shared a generous bowl of guacamole Jorge made fresh at their table while they gave him the latest updates on the reenactment.

"This has been wonderful as usual," Harriet said as they prepared to leave. "Thank you."

Jorge pulled her into a warm hug. "You come anytime, chica." He released her and grabbed Aiden's hand, pulling him in for a hug as well. "You don't be such a stranger either," he said. "An old man gets lonely, you know."

"Hey, I have to work," Aiden said as he stepped back.

"That's right, you go work and forget about poor Jorge," He frowned and tried to look sad; then he started laughing a deep hearty laugh that made him rock back on his heels. "Speaking of work…" He glanced toward the kitchen. "I got to get busy. See you kids next week."

"That was exactly what I needed," Harriet said. "I forgot all about the re-enactment when my enchiladas arrived. I should walk home to work it off. It's not going to be dark for hours."

Aiden pulled the door to the Bronco open. "If you do that everyone in town will be talking about how I took you to dinner and didn't drive you home. Half of them will think we broke up and the other half will think I lost my manners in Africa."

He had spent the three years prior to his return to Foggy Point doing research in Uganda. He didn't like to talk about the time he spent there, but the Loose Threads all assured Harriet he'd come home a changed man.

"Really?" she said.

"You think I'm joking, but when you've lived here longer, you'll realize nothing happens without everyone knowing about it."

Harriet got in the Bronco.

Chapter 5

The Loose Threads had agreed to meet at nine the next morning at Pins and Needles. The quilters from the advance re-enactors group were to join them after lunch.

"Can I help you carry quilts?" Carla asked. She'd seen Harriet pulling up to park and correctly guessed that her friend would have more than one armload of quilts for delivery to the other members of the group.

"Oh, thank you," Harriet said and handed her two cloth bags, each containing a quilt. "Is anyone else here yet?"

"No, just me and Miss Marjory."

Carla led the way into the shop. Harriet continued to be amazed by the changes in the young woman. They had met when Carla was helping a pregnant co-worker who was experiencing mental problems. She was barely keeping her own life together at that point, and things got worse before they got better. The loss of her factory job had not been her fault, nor was what followed Marjory's for being unable to offer her any more than part-time employment at Pins and Needles.

How quickly things change, Harriet thought. In a matter of weeks, Carla had gone from living in her van to what must seem like a mansion. Now that Aiden employed her as his live-in housekeeper, she didn't need the income from working at the quilt store, but she kept her part-time job in order to get out of the house, sending her daughter Wendy to a free toddler play program at the Methodist Church.

Carla had gained weight, and not in a bad way, Harriet noticed. However, the biggest change was to her confidence. It had been gradual, and someone who hadn't known her for a while would still think she was shy; but her voice was ever so slightly stronger, and she expressed her opinion on quilt patterns and colors without blushing when she spoke.

"Hey, Carla, Harriet," Jenny said as she came into the shop. "Has anyone started coffee yet?"

"Yes," Carla said. "I made the French roast. Can I get you a cup?"

"Sure. That would be nice." When Carla went into the kitchen area, at the back of the shop, near the two classrooms, Jenny continued. "Is our Carla growing up?"

"You didn't hear it from me, but Aiden says she's got a gentleman caller. He's not from around here, and Aiden wants us to see what we can find out. We need to be careful, though, I don't want to upset Carla when she's finally starting to have a normal life."

Carla came back, ending the conversation.

Harriet and Jenny went into the larger classroom, followed by Robin and DeAnn, who had just arrived, each carrying a tote bag with quilting supplies and fabric.

"We have twenty-five quilts priced and ready to go," Robin said as she set her bag down on the table in the center of the room.

"The prices range from a hundred dollars for the crib-sized ones to a thousand for Jenny's appliqué quilt," DeAnn added.

"Thanks for all your work on the pricing," Harriet said.

"Hey, it's nothing compared to your having to deal with Carlton," DeAnn said, and the rest of the group laughed.

"Does anyone else have quilts they're finishing that we'll need to price?" Robin asked the group.

"I'll have two more," Sarah announced as she came in, whacking Jenny in the back with her overfilled bag as she pushed past to reach her favorite spot at the table.

"Great," Robin said in a flat voice. She'd called Harriet the night before to discuss the ethics of redoing the binding on one of

Sarah's quilts. The binding had obviously been applied with great haste and had gaps where the machine stitching hadn't caught the edge, in spite of Sarah's use of a very wide zigzag stitch. Harriet had to agree with Robin that if the binding was so sloppy the quilt wouldn't sell it was better to repair it. It was, after all, an event to raise money for charity.

"Was that you I saw with the stud-muffin at the coffee shop the other night?" Sarah asked Carla. "What was he doing with you?" she pressed on. "He's obviously not from around here."

So much for subtlety, Harriet thought. Jenny looked at her across the table and made a small shrugging motion.

"Well," Sarah said. "Come on, spill."

For her part, Carla was beyond red-faced—she looked at her feet and stammered out, "Terry."

"What?" Sarah demanded.

"Let her be," Connie ordered. She'd come in during the inquisition and had used her best grade-school-teacher voice—something even Sarah wasn't immune to. "Carla will tell us about her new friend when she's good and ready, and if that's never then you just leave her be."

Everyone around the table suddenly became very involved with their hand work, digging in bags, threading needles and otherwise avoiding looking at Sarah, Carla or anyone else.

"How is everyone doing with their costumes?" Connie asked after a few minutes. In her years of putting on plays at the grade school, she had learned a number of useful costuming tricks, such as making bloomers from two pillowcases in under an hour, and she'd shared her know-how with the group.

The discussion went around the table, each person reporting on the status of their Civil War outfit. The Threads had planned their costumes in advanced to insure that, as merchants, they would be appropriately dressed. Everyone had chosen accordingly, with the exception of Sarah. Even Lauren would look similar to the rest of the group. She had added some fine embroidery to her collars, but Harriet couldn't find fault with that.

Sarah, on the other hand, had made her dress out of black silk-like synthetic, complete with black collar and black apron. With her pale skin, all she needed was black eye shadow and red lipstick and she would blend right in with the goth kids who congregated around the corner from the high school on week days.

Harriet chuckled to herself.

"Okay," Robin whispered to Harriet. "What was so funny?"

"Oh, just imagining Bebe and Sarah side-by-side."

Robin started laughing and had to go to the kitchen before anyone could ask her to say it out loud.

"Excuse me, chiquita," Connie said as she squeezed past Harriet's chair and headed toward the door. "I've got to find some thread to match Carlton's vest."

She was barely out the door when Sarah spoke in a quiet voice.

"So, Carla, who was the hunk?" she asked again, and glanced nervously toward the door.

"His name is Terry," Carla repeated without looking up.

"I got that the first time. I'm asking who *is* he?"

"Who he is, is none of your business," Harriet said. "I thought Connie made that clear. Since you obviously didn't understand, let me say it in simple terms—back off. Who Carla sees is her business. And she certainly is under no obligation to tell you anything about it."

"Well, excuse me," Sarah said. She broke eye contact and busied herself with her stitching. "I'm not sure who crowned you queen," she muttered.

Harriet knew enough to not press the issue.

✂ ✂ ✂

"Diós mio, that was delicious," Connie said and pushed her chair back from the table. Robin had picked up sandwiches from The Sandwich Board, a deli a few blocks from the quilt store. To keep things simple, the restaurant had prepared three options: a Reuben-style sandwich made with turkey pastrami, Swiss cheese and homemade sauerkraut, a vegetarian option on seven-grain bread with herb cream cheese, avocado, tomato and cucumbers and a smoked turkey on sourdough with thin sliced gouda and baby lettuce.

"Stop hogging the cookies," Lauren demanded. The Sandwich Board had sent along a tray of oatmeal raisin cookies that were still warm from the oven.

DeAnn pulled the plastic wrap from the tray and shoved it across the table. "Help yourself."

"Our visitors are due to arrive any minute," Jenny said. "Everyone here has worked very hard to make this re-enactment a success. I know we're all stressed by all the last-minute preparations. We're in the home stretch. In a few days, this will all be a happy memory. Until then, could we please just hold it together?"

"Hello?" said an unfamiliar voice. "The lady out front told us to come in here."

"Hi, I'm Harriet," Harriet got up and made her way to the door. She held her hand out to the woman who had spoken.

"Hi, I'm Sharon Davis," The woman shook Harriet's hand. "This is Ellen and behind her is Inez. I spoke to you on the phone."

The three women were dressed in identical gray T-shirts with a handmade logo identifying them as the Confederate Quilter's Club and denim capri pants. Harriet introduced them to the Loose Threads.

"Welcome to Foggy Point," Connie said. "Can we get you coffee, or tea?"

Inez held up a bottle of water. "No, thanks, we picked up waters on our way here."

Sharon and Inez, with their long gray hair wound into buns at the napes of their necks, appeared to be in their fifties. Harriet guessed Ellen was closer to her own age.

Jenny directed the women to the empty chairs she had pulled up to the table.

"I can't tell you how thankful we are to have you come early and check us out. None of us here has experience putting on a re-enactment of any kind. We've tried to follow all the rules the council forwarded to us, but we'll all feel better when someone who has actually been to one looks things over."

"We're happy to come help," Inez said. "The fact that you're putting us up in a nice B-and-B tonight definitely sweetened the deal, but we would have come even without that." She smiled warmly.

"I think you'll find re-enactors are like any other group of people you gather in one place," Sharon said. "Most are really friendly and just want to have a good time. They're interested in history and the Civil War, but mainly they like having fun with their friends. And no matter what you do there will be critics—nothing you do will please them, and they're unlikely to help in any way other than making suggestions about how you can do something differently, usually a way requiring more effort. Unfortunately, there is also a third group, the troublemakers. They aren't around all the time, but they do show up among us every now and then."

"We've had a little trouble at the last few re-enactments we've participated in," Ellen said. "Most recently it's been theft. Things have been stolen from tents during the major battles and quilts have been stolen—from tents, from the sutler's booth, even from unlocked cars."

"We mentioned that in one of our e-mails, so hopefully you've had time to address the security," Sharon added.

"We hired a private security company to patrol all the populated areas. We asked for two in the sutler's area and one each in the two tent areas. In addition, we'll have someone in the parking lot," Harriet said.

"That should help," Sharon said. "We all try to look out for each other, but a determined thief is hard to stop."

Harriet sighed.

"Don't worry," Inez said. "All you can do is take reasonable precautions and then whatever happens, happens."

"On a lighter note," Sharon said. "We brought our quilting along with us." Her lips curved in an impish smile. "I'll show you mine if you show me yours." She pulled a piece of quilting from her bag. It was about a foot square with a pieced top, batting and backing held together with pins." I'm doing a quilt-as-you-go project," she explained. "I hand-pieced the top in block-sized pieces, and now I'm hand quilting it block by block. When the blocks are finished, I'll hook them together with sashing pieces. This way my quilting is not only more portable, but I can change the outcome right up until the last block is finished." She held up the square she was working on. She had made four six-inch LeMoyne Star blocks from brown, red and beige Civil war reproduction fabrics, and had sewn them together to form the twelve-inch square.

Harriet pulled out her piecework. Mavis was trying to convince her of the joys of hand-piecing a quilt top; she was still playing with her stars-and-bars design. She didn't plan on hand-piecing the whole quilt, but she was going to at least make a few of the star blocks by hand just to try it out.

She'd chosen to start with Margo Krager's newest Dargate fabric line "Lavender and Mint" for her first block.

"I don't have much of a show-and-tell," she said. "I just finished a quilt for the store and now I'm trying to do some hand-piecing."

"It might grow on you," Sharon said. "We generally stick with hand-piecing or appliqué, since we can work on it during the re-enactment events."

"How critical are the other re-enactors about period authenticity?" Connie asked. "I've been making costumes, and I think the skirts and bodices I've made are accurate, but no one but the group gathered here have seen them."

"What Connie is trying to say, or would be if she wasn't beating around the bush," Lauren said, "is that we have a couple of people who are way off the charts. The husband is in charge of this whole wing-ding and his bimbo of a wife is going to be dressed like a tart." She looked expectantly at the newcomers. "Can we look forward to an ugly scene?"

"That's a terrible thing to say," Connie scolded.

"It would be if she wasn't right," Robin said and laughed.

Sharon looked at Inez, who nodded for her to go ahead.

"There will be a few thread counters who think nothing is right unless it's absolutely authentic," she said. "They are so picky they even want the reproduction fabrics to have the same thread count as the originals. Fortunately, they aren't in any official positions. They mainly want to criticize everyone but without doing anything to help with the changes."

"Reminds me of someone we know," Jenny whispered to Harriet, and they both concealed smiles behind their teacups.

"We were warned to expect thread counters in the sutler's area. Our consultant said as long as we posted a sign that said our goods were reproductions and not exact replications, we would be okay."

"That's good advice," Ellen said. "That won't stop all the comments, but really it's only one or two people. I wouldn't worry about it."

"Good," said Harriet. "That's one less thing. Did anyone see where Sarah went?" she asked the group as she stuck her needle into her fabric and put both items in her bag. "I need to get those quilts she mentioned."

"Or not," Robin said.

"She *has* been pretty scarce lately," Jenny said.

"We were supposed to go to dinner last week and she ditched me at the last minute," Lauren said. "She said she had to go to Angel Harbor. She probably has a secret lover."

"Our Sarah?" Jenny asked.

"You're right," Lauren said. "What was I thinking?"

Harriet thanked the re-enactors from Portland and arranged to meet with them the following day to inspect the event facilities, but not until they'd had a chance to thoroughly enjoy breakfast at their lodging.

✂ ✂ ✂

Beth waited in the circular driveway in front of Harriet's bow window as Harriet pulled in and parked. "I like the new planter," she said when Harriet was out of the car. She pointed to the cedar box that Harriet had added by the studio door. "I assume you still want to walk."

"I *need* to walk," Harriet said. "Between the long hours on the quilting machine and the stress of dealing with all these crisis, my poor back feels like it's being twisted into a pretzel."

Foggy Point was a great place to live it you liked to walk. There were plenty of wooded trails, but Harriet's favorites were the paths that went along the water. The peninsula had rocky shores with little or no sand, so there weren't beaches as such, but there were pathways through the rounded water-worn stone.

"Let's go down to the water," she suggested, and Beth agreed. "Do you mind if we drive over to the north side? I don't feel like walking from here."

"Whatever you want, honey."

Harriet drove back down her hill and through downtown Foggy Point. She was taking them to a beach along the strait side of the peninsula, just beyond the commercial docks.

"Well, what do you think?" Beth asked when they had parked and gotten out of the car. Harriet led the way toward the path. "Is everything ready?"

"With the exception of Sarah's last quilt or quilts, everything is done as far as the quilt booth goes. Connie gave me my costume, so I've got something to wear. Bebe came by and talked Connie into making Carlton a new vest. She didn't like the one Mavis made. She's insisting he wear pink to match her dress, so they will look like clowns. Other than that, things are great."

"At this point, the event is going to happen whether they have proper clothes or not, so I wouldn't worry about it," Beth said. "I just met with the ladies at the Lutheran Church and they're all ready to do admissions. They have their tickets and cash boxes, and their schedule looked good—they have two people plus a spare for each park entrance."

"It's unfortunate Mavis had to be gone," Harriet said. "There isn't really anything she needs to be doing, but I'd feel better if she were here."

"It seems strange the kids would insist on her helping out on such short notice when they know how involved she's been with this event."

"She said she'd be back in time for the re-enactment," Harriet said.

"How are things with you and Aiden?"

"We had dinner the other night, but he had to go back to work."

"He kind of left in a hurry on pizza night, I noticed."

"Yeah, well, he's worried about Carla. We both are."

"We all want to help Carla, but she's been on her own for a long time and she's done a pretty fair job taking care of herself and that baby so far."

"If he decides he wants to be with Carla, that's his business," Harriet said.

"I didn't mean to suggest he was interested in her in that way."

"You did, too, and if he's that easily distracted, we don't really have a relationship to begin with."

"Go ahead and take the high road, but I saw your face when he left the other night."

"I might not have wanted him to leave early, but I am a little curious about this guy Carla's seeing. Aiden hasn't met him yet, either. He said Carla was so embarrassed when he tried to ask her about him all he got was a bunch of mumbling."

"I'll see what I can find out," Beth promised. "I'm stopping by tomorrow to talk to her about housekeeping. And we're on the same shift in the sutler's booth."

"It just seems weird. I mean, Carla has made great strides, but her life lately has been all about working at the quilt store and getting acquainted with that big old house. So given that, I'm wondering where she met this new guy."

"Well, I read an article the other day that the grocery store is replacing the singles bar as a place to meet a potential mate," Beth offered.

"I don't want to see someone take advantage of her. Don't you find it the slightest bit weird that the rare stranger under the age of forty who comes to town manages to find the one girl who almost never goes out in public?"

"Maybe its fate," Beth said.

Chapter 6

Thursday dawned sunny and clear in Foggy Point. The weatherman was expecting the day to be hotter than usual, but that would still make it cooler than most of the visiting re-enactors were used to.

The first troops had arrived the night before. There were separate tent camps for the Union and Confederate soldiers in the main area of Fogg Park, but the people from both sides who had brought horses were camping near the river, away from the battlefields. Harriet had gotten the Lions Club to build a temporary corral, and there were already a few horses loafing around the water trough.

Harriet was just finishing her second pass through the park when she found Aunt Beth in the sutler's tent.

"How many times are you going to walk through the battlefield?" Beth asked.

She shrugged.

"You've been through twice since I've been here, and I don't imagine anything has changed either trip. People aren't supposed to start arriving until tonight."

"Some of them are already here."

"Is there anything I can help you with?"

"Thanks, but I'm waiting for Foggy Point Rent-all to deliver the portable bleachers that will be set up on the rise that overlooks the main battle field. After that, we just need the crowd to arrive." She looked around the parking area for the hundredth time.

"Tell me again why Carlton isn't doing this?"

"That's a rhetorical question, right?" Harriet glanced at her aunt.

"I know. He's too busy keeping Bebe happy." Aunt Beth smiled. "You know, Carlton didn't really date anyone until Bebe, and he was past forty when she blew into town. Old Marvin was so afraid his son would never marry he didn't even care if the bride was the assistant at his dentist's office. He'd given up on Carlton producing an heir. Fortunately, Carlton's sister Frances took care of that, although she had four girls. Still, he paid for that big house Carlton and Bebe live in—Carlton's reward for catching her, I guess."

"As long as he shows up for his welcoming speech before the main battle, I don't care what he does with Bebe. Like I said, it's easier to get most things done without him. I still can't believe someone so incompetent runs a company as big as Foggy Point Fire Protection."

"The only skill he needs to run the company is the ability to hire good people to do the work."

"Must be nice," Harriet mused.

Aunt Beth looked past Harriet's shoulder. "Here come your bleachers," she said.

"Want to meet for lunch when I'm done here?" Harriet waved to the driver of the delivery truck.

They agreed to meet at the Sandwich Board at noon. She reminded Beth to turn on her cell phone in case she needed to amend their plan.

✂ ✂ ✂

"Everything set up?" Aunt Beth asked as Harriet sat down at their table by the window three hours later.

"Surprisingly, everything went without a hitch. The seats are done, and the rental people will pick them up as soon as the final event finishes. I guess they have problems with drug users stealing pieces and selling them as scrap metal. They said we don't have to call them or anything."

"I tried to track Sarah down to get her last quilt for you, but I couldn't find her. I drove over to the Senior Living Center where she works, and they said she had taken a few days off."

"Look." Harriet pointed out the window. Carla was crossing the street with a stocky young man wearing a tight black T-shirt that showed every well-toned muscle. His hair was cut short, military style, and could have been blond or brown—she couldn't tell.

"That must be her new young man," Aunt Beth said and sipped her iced tea.

"He looks like he belongs on a recruiting poster for the police or military or something."

"She looks happy."

"I just hope he doesn't take advantage of her."

"Now, why would you think that? He looks clean and well dressed."

"In an army surplus kind of way. I'm just saying." Harriet smiled and held her hands up in mock surrender.

"You're just anti-men, with the rather glaring exception of a certain young vet who shall remain nameless."

"I am not. Don't forget Harold. We've been out to dinner several times."

"Forget is exactly what I'm trying to do when it comes to that guy. There's something shifty about him, I don't care what you say."

Harold Minter was the finance manager at the Vitamin Factory, which Aiden's family owned and had operated until his uncle was jailed for murdering his mother. The factory was temporarily closed while Harold and the other managers tried to sort out where the business stood once you eliminated revenue from the illegal activities Uncle Bertrand had been running. Carla had been one of the factory workers displaced by the shutdown.

"Just because he's a bean counter and bald doesn't mean he's shifty," Harriet protested.

"I don't trust him as far as I can throw him," Aunt Beth said. "That fella…" She pointed at the young man who was now helping Carla into a gray late model car. "…he looks trustworthy."

"A short haircut and muscles do not make someone trustworthy," Harriet countered.

Aunt Beth laughed and picked up her purse. "Come on, honey. We got work to do."

Chapter 7

The first full day of the re-enactment went by in a blur of activity. Skirmishes were fought, camps were made, Civil War life was imitated and quilts were sold. When the last major event was completed, the Foggy Point Business Association would be able to pat itself on the back for a job well done.

So far, everything had gone as planned. The planning group had used conservative attendance figures, and with one full day left to go they had already exceeded those numbers, both for participants and audience. The quilt sales had been brisk, and everyone agreed that anything they had left would be donated to the local women's shelter.

The main battle would be fought Saturday afternoon, after which participants would gather for a group barbecue. Harriet was working in the sutler's booth Saturday morning.

Mavis arrived mid-morning. She was wearing a gray dress with a subtle blue stripe that matched the blue of her apron.

"Connie did a nice job on your costume," she said.

"You're back!" Harriet exclaimed. "I was starting to get worried."

"I didn't think I was going to be gone this long," Mavis said. "Something was fishy about the babysitter's absence, though. I ran out of diaper cream, and since I had to go out anyway and baby seemed up for it, I went across town to southeast Portland so I could check out a new quilt store, Cool Cottons. We parked in front of a coffee shop, and while I was getting the stroller out, I looked in the window and there was MacKenzie, their sitter, big as life, drinking an iced coffee."

"Are you sure it was her?"

"She saw me and looked like she'd seen a ghost. She knocked a chair over on her way out the back door."

"What did your son say?"

"He said she told them she had a family funeral, and that everyone grieves in their own way." Mavis put her small cloth purse in a box under the table they were using as a sales counter. "I feel bad enough being gone, without having to wonder if their sitter was scamming them to get a few days off in the summer."

"Well, whether it was for a funeral or because your son got scammed by his babysitter, they still needed you and that's what's important."

"I guess." Mavis sighed. "It was just poor timing, is all I can say. You had enough to do without having to do my part, too."

"Oh, stop," Harriet said and gave her friend a quick hug.

The two women discussed what had gone on in Foggy Point while Mavis was gone as well as the new fabric she'd seen while she was in Portland.

"Robin and DeAnn should be here any minute," Harriet said, and looked at the antique brass table clock Aunt Beth had brought to the booth. Watches and cell phones were strictly forbidden. "I want to be in the stands when Carlton gives his speech and rings the bell for the grand battle. Want to come with?"

"I've missed so much work, I probably should stay here and try to sell some quilts," Mavis said.

"You did plenty of work before the event. Besides, there aren't that many quilts left to sell. I'm sure Robin and DeAnn can handle it."

"Someone talking about me?" Robin asked as she lifted a flap at the back of the sutler's booth and entered. "Actually, I heard you talking while I was behind the tent untangling my petticoats. I agree, Mavis, go watch the battle. DeAnn and I will be fine."

Robin adjusted her bonnet over her close-cropped blond hair. When she'd arrived at the booth Thursday, she'd had a costume wig with a bun under her hat, but it had proved to be too hot. Her usual mode of dress was the latest in yoga wear and was heavy on stretch. She was struggling with the voluminous skirts and associated undergarments worn by the Civil War-era women.

"I can't believe woman actually worked in this get-up," she said with a final yank at her apron.

"You just have to get through today," Harriet said. "Costumes are by choice tomorrow, while everyone is packing up to go."

"I saw your aunt on my way in, and she said to spread the word that anyone who wants to can meet at her place for pizza as soon as we close the gates today," DeAnn said as she came into the booth and added her cloth purse to the others under the table.

"You two should get going if you're going to sit in the bleachers," Robin said. "It looked like they were starting to fill up."

Harriet pulled her purse and an unbleached muslin bag that looked a lot like a pillowcase from under the table.

"I brought lunch," she said and held the bag up. "I've got enough to share."

"What did people eat for lunch in Civil War times?" Mavis asked as they left the booth and headed for the battlefield.

"Aunt Beth decided we would be Confederate army sympathizers—we get johnnycakes instead of hardtack."

They debated the merits of cornbread over crackers until they reached the bleachers. As Robin had reported, people were already filling the viewing stands, and she and Mavis were forced to climb up to the top level to find seats.

"What on earth is Carlton wearing?" Mavis asked once she was seated.

Carlton had taken his long-tailed frock coat off, revealing the bright-pink replacement vest Connie had made him. He was pacing in front of the raised stage that had been erected at the near end of the main battlefield. The bleachers ran along the ridge above the field, perpendicular to the stage.

The opposite side of the field from the ridge was obscured by a thick stand of trees. Several paths led out of the woods, and according to the plans provided by the re-enactment group, one of these would be used by the Confederate soldiers as an entrance point for this battle. The Union soldiers should be gathering on the adjacent soccer field preparing to join the battle from the end of the field opposite the small stage.

"That would be the vest Bebe had Connie make him. She rejected the original one because it didn't match her dress."

"She's wearing a neon-pink dress?" Mavis asked in disbelief.

"'Fraid so. I hate to sound mean, but she didn't seem to be able to grasp the concept of period authenticity. She had a costume made by a tailor in Seattle. Who knows if she even told the poor soul who made it that it was for a Civil War event?"

Mavis scanned the bleachers around them.

"Look—is that our Carla down there?" She pointed to a row near the front and at the opposite end from where she and Harriet were sitting. "Is she with that handsome young man sitting next to her?"

"She is," Harriet said. "That's her new boyfriend."

"I leave town for a couple of days, and Carla has a new boyfriend? How did that happen? And where did he come from? He's not from around here."

"I know—his posture is too good. I don't know who he is or where he came from, but he's so buff it seems to have turned the heads of the Loose Threads and made everyone but yours truly willing to throw caution to the wind on Carla's behalf."

"Well, he certainly seems to have put a bee in your bonnet," Mavis said.

"Aunt Beth thinks I'm turning into a bitter old lady, but I think it pays to be cautious where strangers are concerned."

"I can't believe Beth said that to you."

"Well, not in so many words, but it's what she meant."

"I still find that hard to believe."

A short bugle blast sounded, and the crowd hushed. Carlton welcomed the crowd then introduced the fifth grade class from Joseph Meeker Elementary School. Four girls and three boys each read a portion of the history leading up to the battle the audience was about to witness.

"Please join me in a round of applause for our young historians," he said. When the noise had died down, he continued.

"Thank you for attending our inaugural event. We hope this will start a summertime tradition for all of you as well as the merchants of the Foggy Point Business Association. The shops and restaurants downtown will be open late tonight for your post-battle enjoyment." He glanced at his notes. "Let the battle begin," he finished and raised his arm to ring the bell and signal the armies.

"Is it me, or was that rather clumsy?" Mavis asked.

"I'd have to say he's not a natural emcee. I guess we should be happy he didn't attempt a joke. I've had the misfortune of witnessing that pitiful activity," Harriet replied.

"Well, we need to consider getting a professional master of ceremonies next year—if there is a next year."

The Union soldiers took the field, complete with drum-and-bugle corp. Ranks of soldiers marched stiffly past in precise rows. While all attention was focused on them, a thin ribbon of Confederates began winding through the forest, just becoming visible as they reached the tree line.

When they had a line of soldiers that reached from one end of the field to the other, one of the "invaders" gave a rebel yell, and the rest jumped out of their concealed locations. Just as it seemed the Union soldiers were getting the upper hand, a troop of Confederate cavalry came thundering out from the middle trail and momentum shifted.

"Wow, that Confederate bunch is sneaky," Harriet said. "Look, they have men on the other trails waiting for an opportune moment to join the fray."

At the end of one path, about a dozen men were lining up, waiting their turn. On the trail closest to the broadcast booth, a lone man lay partially concealed by a tree stump.

"Where?" Mavis asked, and Harriet pointed to the two locations.

"I'm not sure that single guy is a Confederate. He doesn't look like he's wearing a uniform."

"Maybe he's supposed to be a farmer or something," Harriet suggested.

"Or maybe he's just an observer who wanted a better view."

They turned their attention back to the field, where the battle was heating up. The action shifted to the edges of the field, isolating a quartet of mounted soldiers who proceeded to put on a display of swordsmanship and riding, finally ending with the mock death of the Confederate riders, who made dramatic falls from their mounts.

When the "bodies" had been carried away, several cannons were wheeled onto the field by the Union Army. These were fired with a great deal of noise and an even greater amount of smoke. As the smoke cleared, the audience could see that the battleground was now filled with the prone bodies of gray-clad soldiers. The Union had carried the day.

After a few moments, the northern army organized back into their marching units and retreated to the soccer field, followed by the mounted soldiers. The audience clapped enthusiastically.

When the victors were gone, the defeated rose from the dead to take their bows. The crowd cheered even louder.

Mavis and Harriet stood and cheered along with the rest of the audience.

"Look," Harriet said, and pointed to the path where the lone farmer had been earlier. "It looks like the farmer got caught in the crossfire."

"That's kind of harsh," Mavis said. "I mean, we know farmers probably got killed, but this guy didn't look like the homegrown farmer-soldiers you see in history books, going to battle with their pitchfork as a weapon."

"You're right—he doesn't look like he even has a weapon. He's sure playing it for all it's worth, too. Look, he hasn't gotten up yet."

"Maybe he fell asleep while he was playing dead."

The two women sat back down and waited for the people below them to exit the bleachers. Mavis chewed on a piece of johnnycake.

"Do you have any honey, Honey," she said with a smile at her own pun.

Harriet pulled a small plastic honey dispenser in the shape of a bear from her lunch bag.

"Don't tell Aunt Beth," she said and handed it to her friend. "I couldn't figure out how they carried their honey around in those days, so I smuggled the bear this morning."

"Come on," Mavis said after a few bites. "I think the crowd has thinned enough that I can make it down the stairs without tripping on my skirt or someone else's. We need to find something to drink with these bricks."

Harriet stood up, and her gaze wandered to the forest edge.

"It looks like something's wrong with our farmer," she said. "He's still lying there. Having a dramatic moment is one thing, but the rest of the people have left that side of the field and he's still in the same spot." She watched intently for a few moments. "He's not moving." She started to go down then glanced back at Mavis.

"You go ahead," Mavis said. "I'll catch up,"

Harriet hiked her skirt up and held it bunched in her fists as she hustled down the risers then continued toward the stage and the forest beyond.

"Where are you going in such a hurry?" Carlton asked as she brushed past him.

"One of the re-enactors looks like he's been injured at the edge of the forest," she said without stopping.

"I'll come with you," Carlton said and glanced at Bebe, who was standing in the shade of the stage, fanning herself with an ornate plastic-ribbed ladies fan.

"I'm not wearing this into the forest," she said and glanced down at her pink satin confection.

Carlton was obviously torn for a moment.

"You go ahead, baby," she said. "I'll keep your spot cool."

Harriet was already crouched over the man when Carlton arrived.

"He doesn't look too good," he said. "How is he?"

The man hadn't moved. He was wearing jeans and a plaid flannel shirt and was lying on his side, his back toward her. She reached out to feel for a pulse in his neck, and when she touched him he flopped onto his back, startling her and making Carlton jump back a few steps.

The quantity of blood soaking the front of the man's shirt seemed to be more than a person should be able to lose and still be alive, but Harriet checked for a pulse anyway. He was dead.

Chapter 8

"Carlton," Harriet said.

Carlton didn't move. He was frozen in place, staring at the body, his face white.

"*Carlton*," she said again, more firmly this time.

"What?" he asked in a flat voice, still staring at the body.

"Listen to me. We need the police and the paramedics here immediately. I don't have a phone with me, and I assume you don't, either. I need for you to go back to the park office and ask them to call for the sheriff. The paramedics are in the parking lot, go get them."

He hesitated.

"Go!" she shouted and finally got through to him. He went back toward the stage.

Harriet turned to the body at her feet. A slight breeze gently ruffled his hair, overlaying the coppery scent of blood with the damp smell of pine trees and earth and briefly giving him the illusion of life. She didn't recognize him, but he looked vaguely familiar. Maybe he went to Aunt Beth's church, or drank coffee in the shop she frequented.

She was still looking at him when Mavis came up behind her.

Harriet turned toward her friend.

"Don't come any closer," she said. "There's been an accident."

It was too late. The blood drained from Mavis's face, and she crumpled to the ground, her full skirt billowing around her as she fell.

"Mavis!" Harriet grabbed at her, breaking but not stopping her fall. "Help!" she called.

A man dressed in the gray of the Confederate army was picking up debris left from the battle when he heard her call. He ran over and helped her ease Mavis onto her back.

"I'm a doctor," he said as he started loosening the bodice of her dress. He felt for the pulse in her left wrist. "Her pulse is strong." He continued loosening and checking. "Are *you* okay?" he asked Harriet as he straightened Mavis's legs and ran trained fingers along her shins to make sure she hadn't broken anything in her fall.

The doctor looked over at the man lying a few feet away.

"He's dead," Harriet said before he could ask, and the doctor refocused his attention on Mavis.

Harriet held Mavis's hand. The older woman's lips began to move; at first, no sound came out.

"It's him," she said finally in a garbled tone.

"What?" Harriet asked.

"It's Gerald," Mavis said, and tried to get up.

"Ma'am, you're going to need to lie down for a few minutes until the paramedics get here with their equipment and we can run a couple of quick tests." The doctor turned to Harriet. "I can't find any sign of injury, and I don't think its heat-related." He felt Mavis's forehead with the back of his hand again. "She's not hot enough for that. She just seems shocky." He looked back toward the body. "What's going on here?"

"I don't know. We were coming down the bleachers and noticed this guy hadn't gotten up when the rest of the re-enactors did. I came over to check it out and found him lying there with no pulse."

I know dead when I see it, Harriet thought. Her husband Steve had died five years before her return to Foggy Point—she'd crawled into bed after a late movie "night out with the girls" and rubbed her foot up his cold, dead shin. It took several years of therapy for her to just be able to sleep in a bed again—most of the time, anyway.

Yes, she knew dead.

"He has a chest injury, and there's blood everywhere."

"Will you stay with her and make sure she doesn't get up while I check him?"

"Of course," Harriet said and rubbed Mavis's hand again.

Mavis pulled her hand back and was trying to sit up when the paramedics arrived. A thorough evaluation proved she had suffered a substantial shock and fainted but was otherwise unharmed.

Dried grass clung to her skirt as Mavis rose to her feet. Harriet put her hand on her friend's arm, but Mavis pushed it away.

"I'm okay," she said, her voice sounding stronger. "This is just a bit of a shock."

"Who *is* that?" Harriet asked, lowering her voice as she looked over Mavis's shoulder at the crowd that was gathering on the battlefield a short distance away.

"That is, or was, my husband Gerald."

"*What?* Are you sure?"

"Of course, she's sure," Aunt Beth said as she joined them. "You can't be married to a man for thirty years and not recognize him, even if you haven't seen him in a while."

"A *while*?" Harriet said, quickly adding the numbers in her head. "A while like a twenty-year while? How can that be? Besides hasn't he been dead all that time?"

"Apparently not," Aunt Beth said. She patted Mavis on the back. "Do you think you can bear a second look? Harriet's right. It's probably best to be sure. I agree it looks like Gerald, but it has been twenty years."

"I don't need a second look. He's grayer and a little fatter, but look under his chin. See the scar on the left side, right at the beard line?"

Harriet and Aunt Beth leaned closer and looked.

"He did that when he stepped on one of Gerry Junior's little metal cars. He stumbled and hit his chin on the corner of the tile counter in the kitchen."

Beth put her hand on Mavis's arm and gently led her away from the body that had once been her husband. Mavis pulled a tissue from the pocket of her skirt and dabbed at her eyes.

"So, where's he been for twenty years?" Beth asked.

"That would be the question, now, wouldn't it?" Mavis answered.

A man in khaki shorts and a green polo shirt walked up to the paramedics, who were standing next to the body.

"I'm the deputy coroner; Neil Drake." He shook hands with all three. "What have we got here?"

Harriet drifted over to the group. A chubby paramedic with short blond hair and a sunburned nose answered.

"He was dead when we arrived. This here is Dr. Stahl. He was a participant in the re-enactment and heard this lady call for help. He can tell you the rest."

The paramedic stepped away and started gathering his tools and stuffing them into the large plastic box he'd carried to the scene.

"As the young man said, I heard this lady call for help." Dr. Stahl gestured toward Harriet. "Her friend, the woman in gray over there…" He pointed at Mavis. "…was in distress. The younger lady pointed out the man and told me she'd found him like that. The older woman was in mild shock, and the paramedics verified her vitals were acceptable when they got here. As for him—he was dead when I came over to help the ladies. He appears to have a large, blunt-force trauma wound in the middle of his chest. I have no idea how he received the blow."

The coroner bent down on one knee next to Gerald's body. The blond paramedic returned and stood a few paces away.

Washington State uses a medical examiner/coroner system for death investigation. In smaller counties like Clallam, where Foggy Point was located, the prosecuting attorney is also the coroner, with deputy prosecuting attorneys also being deputy coroners. The larger counties have medical examiners or forensic pathologists who are medical doctors with specialties in forensics and death investigation.

It would be the coroner's job to decide whether Gerald's death was explainable or suspicious.

"Can you cut open his shirt for me?" he asked without looking up.

The blond paramedic pulled disposable gloves from his shirt pocket and put them on. He then plucked a pair of bandage scissors from a loop on the right leg of his pants. He bent down on the opposite side of Gerald and gently cut through the blood-soaked fabric.

"I don't see a bullet hole," the coroner said, "do you?"

The blond tilted his head a little and looked from several angles, then gently probed Gerald's chest with his gloved fingers.

"There's no hole." He was quiet for a minute. "There were a lot of horses on the field at the end. Do you think someone riding out of the woods could have knocked him aside without realizing it? Maybe drove him onto one of the big tree stumps?"

"Anything's possible, I guess," the coroner said and stood up. "In the absence of a bullet wound or sword wound, it doesn't seem likely he was a victim of foul play. Did I hear correctly that you could see him from the bleachers?" he asked, looking at Harriet.

She nodded. "He was in our view, but with all the action, I can't say I was looking at him the whole time. I mainly noticed him because he didn't get up when the other dead soldiers did. I didn't see what happened to him."

"I'm going to talk to the local police as a precaution. They can investigate and see if they can find anyone who saw what happened. I'm declaring him dead and for now writing it up as unknown cause or causes. I'm afraid he's going to need a ride to the ME's office in King County when the forensic people are done taking their pictures."

The paramedic signaled his team members. One was in the back of their truck rustling supplies around, and the other leaned against the back of the vehicle, chewing on a piece of grass. He explained the situation and asked each one to stand guard on either side of Gerald's location until the police arrived.

✂ ✂ ✂

"What happened?" Carlton asked when Harriet passed the stage on her way to the quilt booth. He and Bebe had hovered there while the police arrived and then the paramedics left.

She quickly explained about finding Gerald's body.

"Oh, my gosh," Bebe said, covering her mouth with her hand. "How awful for Mavis."

"It's been quite a shock for her," Harriet agreed.

"I'm glad I wasn't there," Bebe said. "I've never seen a dead body before, and I'd like to keep it that way."

"Let's hope this is the closest you ever come," Harriet said.

"What shall we do?" Carlton asked.

"For Mavis?"

Carlton nervously shuffled his feet. "I was thinking about our guests," he said and nodded toward the tent encampments.

"I don't think we need to do anything with regard to them. As far as activities go, we only have the barbecue tonight and then the goodbye brunch tomorrow, and while it's a sad occasion for us locally, the death of Gerald Willis, even if it turns out it was the result of incidental contact with a participant's mount, really doesn't have anything to do with the re-enactment. We need to quietly help the police talk to the mounted re-enactors who were on the far edge of the field. Other than that, we kiss them goodbye and invite them back next year."

Carlton looked relieved. "Well, if you think that's best, we'll go with it. Since you have police experience, I think it would be best if you let the involved people know who needs to talk to them."

"Sure," Harriet said, her shoulders sagging slightly. He hadn't done anything useful yet. Why did she expect it to be different now?

"Carlton, baby," Bebe said. "My feet are just killing me. Can we go home now?"

He looked at Harriet.

"Sure, you kids run on home—you must be beat," she said.

"See you at the brunch tomorrow," Carlton said. Harriet's sarcasm was lost on him.

Chapter 9

Harriet waited until after the barbecue was well under way and the caterer had assured her they wouldn't run out of food before she joined the small group at Aunt Beth's house.

"Hey," Aunt Beth said as Harriet came in the front door. "We saved you some pizza."

She and Mavis were sitting on one side of the oak-topped kitchen table. Robin and DeAnn sat on the other side with Lauren at the end. Connie was in a wooden rocker by the window, her black-rimmed reading glasses on the end of her nose, her appliqué project lying idle in her lap.

"I don't know about you guys, but I'm sure glad that's over with," Harriet said and collapsed into the chair opposite Lauren, neatly avoiding the topic on everyone's mind.

"They made us wait until you got here," Lauren said, and she wasn't talking about food.

"We didn't want Mavis to have to tell her story more than once," Robin said.

"I've tried to tell you all—there's no story to tell. Gerald died almost twenty years ago in Malaysia. I received his ashes, and they're sitting on a shelf in my bedroom. How he came back to life only to die again during a Civil War re-enactment is beyond me."

"You don't need to talk about this right now," Connie said. "Take some time to catch up with everything that's happened."

"I don't need time, I need answers," Mavis said, some of her old fire showing at last. "I need to know what happened today, and I need to know what happened twenty years ago. And," she said and paused, "I need to know who or what is in that urn in my bedroom. I don't *want* to talk about it—I *have* to talk about it."

"Okay," Robin said. She pulled a yellow legal pad from the quilting bag hanging by the handles from the back of her chair. Aunt Beth got up and rustled the pens and pencils in the cup on her phone table by the back door. She selected two and tossed them onto the table in front of her.

Robin drew a vertical line down the middle of the page. *NOW* she wrote on one side and *THEN* she wrote on the other half.

"What do we know for sure?" she asked.

"Gerald's dead under now," Harriet started.

"And Gerald's not dead under then," Lauren added.

"Good point," Harriet conceded.

"His disappearance was planned," DeAnn offered. "We don't know if *he* planned it or someone else did, but the fact he 'died' the first time while he was in a foreign country can't be a coincidence."

Robin noted DeAnn's comments on the *Then* side of the page.

"Gerald didn't come forward when he returned to town," Aunt Beth said from the working area of the kitchen. She pulled a pitcher of iced tea from the refrigerator. "Anyone want tea?"

Several raised their hands, and she began filling glasses.

"What sort of work did he do?" DeAnn asked.

"Yeah, and who did he do it for?" Robin asked.

"Well, he worked for Industrial Fiber Products," Mavis said slowly. "Now it's called Foggy Point Fire Protection."

"Carlton Brewster's company?" Lauren asked.

"Yes, but Carlton's father was alive back then. He actually knew what he was doing," she said with a wry smile.

"What was Gerald's position?" DeAnn asked again.

"I don't remember what his official title was, but he was a chemist. He figured out formulas for synthetic fibers that could be used in various types of protective gear," Mavis said. "Just before he…died, he developed the formula used for the fireman's turn-outs."

"What did they make before that?" Robin asked.

"Oh, a little of this, a little of that. Carlton's daddy Marvin was a salesman at heart. He'd go out and sell a product before they'd even created it. Poor old Gerald would have to go to the lab and make it. Sometimes he could, sometimes he couldn't. More often than not, Gerald could make whatever Marvin thought up, but the company couldn't produce it for the price the customer wanted."

"What kind of things?" Lauren asked.

"Everything," Mavis said. "You know those suits people wear in fencing competitions? They sense when a blade touches the fencer and record it as well as protect the person from blade strikes? And they made fireproof cocoons for forest fire fighters, and oven gloves for both house and barbecuing needs." She paused and looked at the ceiling. "They made bulletproof vests, chainsaw chaps—you know, in case you drop the chainsaw, they keep you from cutting your leg off."

"I think they still make those," DeAnn said.

"Do we know who invents new products now?" Harriet asked.

"I don't know." Mavis said. "After Gerald died, I had nothing to do with the company."

"But you do get widow's benefits?" Robin asked. In addition to teaching yoga, she was a lawyer. She hadn't kept regular office hours since she'd given birth to her first child, but she kept her license current in case anything came up. It had come in handy recently when Lauren had run into trouble.

Mavis looked uncomfortable. "I do get a pension," she said. "Do you think they'll want the money back, now that Gerald wasn't dead all that time?"

Robin pulled a small leather-bound notebook from her bag and wrote a few words before shutting it.

"I'll check on that," she said.

"She didn't know he was alive!" Lauren said. "That's ridiculous."

Mavis glanced at her with a weak smile.

"Let's not get excited until Robin checks it out," Aunt Beth said. "We don't need to borrow trouble."

Robin turned back to the list on the tablet. "Let's get back to what we know about now and what we know about then. Mavis, can you remember anything unusual about how your husband was acting before he left for Malaysia?"

Mavis sighed. "Harry and Ben were in high school, Pete was in college, James was in graduate school, and Gerry was working with his dad at the factory. I was working as a cook at the senior center to help pay tuition, and when I wasn't there, I was volunteering at the high school so I could keep an eye on Harry. He felt like he had a reputation to uphold. Even when his older brothers tried to explain most of what he was hearing about them was myth, Harry felt like he had to prove he was the worst of the lot."

"So, about Gerald," Lauren prompted.

Aunt Beth put a quelling hand on her arm. "We don't have to do any more tonight," she said. "Mavis has had quite a shock today. She needs some time to digest it."

Robin laid her pen down. "Beth is right. We don't need to do this tonight."

"I'm fine," Mavis said. "That doesn't change the fact I can't remember what was going on with Gerald back then. I should have been more attentive. Don't think I haven't thought about that a thousand times in the last twenty years. I was just wrapped up with the boys and money and Gerald had to deal with his own stuff."

"Hey," Harriet said. "No one is suggesting you should have done anything different. Even if you'd been hanging on his every word, he still would have gone to Malaysia, right? You weren't driving the car that hit him or whatever happened to him…" She trailed off. Wow, she thought.

She couldn't keep on top of the fact that Gerald hadn't died twenty years ago and she'd found his body today. She could only imagine how hard this was for Mavis.

"Enough," Aunt Beth said in a firm voice. "I'm taking Mavis home now. You ladies can stay or go, but we're leaving."

She picked up Mavis's purse and held it while her friend stood up then handed it to her. Mavis was wearing a pair of gray sweatpants and a pink T-shirt Harriet recognized as belonging to her aunt. Mavis looked toward the bedroom where she had changed out of her costume. "We can deal with the costumes tomorrow," Aunt Beth said.

Harriet's own costume was wadded up in the back seat of her car. She'd changed out of it in the restroom at Fogg Park. She assumed the others had done the same, as they were dressed in an assortment of jeans, capris and, of course, Robin in her yoga pants.

"We don't have much to work with," Robin said as she studied the list.

"We need to do some digging," Harriet said. "When Mavis can handle it, we need to see Gerald's death certificate."

"Good point," Robin said. "Mavis would have been asked to produce it to change their bank accounts, insurance, mortgage and car registrations to her name only."

"And what about his life insurance?" DeAnn asked.

"Let's hope he didn't have any," Robin said. "If she collected very much, they'll come after her for repayment."

"What a mess," Harriet said.

"I'm going home," Lauren announced and stood up. "I'm guessing that if he was smart enough to stay hidden for twenty years he probably was smart enough to change his name, but I'll search it anyway just in case." She moved to the door.

"Let me know if you find anything," Robin said, and Lauren waved an acknowledgment as she went out into the night.

"I've got to go, too," DeAnn said. "I'm serving at the brunch tomorrow, and I need to get my beauty rest."

"Me, too," Robin said. "I'll call if I hear anything from Lauren. Will you call me if you turn up anything else?" She looked intently at Harriet.

"Sure," Harriet replied.

Connie got up when Robin was gone and started picking up the napkins and tea glasses and loading Aunt Beth's dishwasher.

"Dios mio," she said. "What are we going to do?"

"I hate to say it, but I think Lauren had the best idea. We need to see if we can find out where Gerald's been all this time. She's right, he probably changed his name, but maybe he kept his Social Security number. We need to find out from Mavis if they had friends who might have helped him—you know, in other countries or something."

"Friends who would lie to Mavis?" Connie asked. "What kind of friends are those?"

"Kind of like the friends who knew my husband had a terminal genetic disease and didn't think I needed to know."

"Now, mija," Connie said and put her arm around Harriet's shoulders. "Let's not go there."

"You're right, this isn't about me. But we do need to think about who Gerald would have turned to if he was in trouble. And I hate to even think about it, but someone needs to talk to Carlton."

"Good idea," Connie said, "at least in theory. We have to hope he paid more attention to his surroundings before Bebe came along, though."

They finished tidying the kitchen and left, locking the door behind them.

Chapter 10

Word of Gerald's death had spread among the re-enactors overnight. At the final brunch, Harriet paced behind the buffet tables while Connie dispensed warm cinnamon rolls from a large metal pan.

Harriet could see the Confederate Quilter's Club working their way through the line.

"Is it true the police think one of the horses pushed that man into a tree stump and killed him?" Inez asked Harriet when she'd reached the cinnamon rolls. Connie selected a large bun and put it on her plate.

"That was a suggestion made by one of the attending paramedics. Someone either overheard, or he repeated it," Harriet said. "I don't think they have any idea what happened."

"You have my contact information," Sharon said. "Could you let us know when they determine what happened? If a horse was involved, we'll need to look at what further safety procedures we can implement."

"We'll let you know, but I'll be surprised if it turns out a horse had anything to do with Mr. Willis's death."

They moved on, leaving Connie and Harriet to roll duty.

"Hey," Carlton said and held his plate out to Connie. "This looks delicious." His plate was filled with scrambled eggs, bacon and fruit salad. He'd left a large space for a cinnamon roll.

"Do you have any smaller rolls?" Bebe asked as she came up behind him. "My baby is watching his weight." Her plate held a teaspoonful of eggs and several pieces of fruit.

Carlton looked longingly at the pan of rolls before mumbling "never mind" and moving on to the end of the table to pick up plastic utensils and a napkin.

"She's a real piece of work," Connie said as she placed a roll on the next plate held out to her.

"Do you want me to hand out a few?" Harriet offered.

"I think I can handle it. Besides, you're making me nervous with all that pacing. Why don't you go find your young man and spend a little of that nervous energy on him?"

"If you're sure you don't need me."

Connie rolled her eyes skyward. "Go," she said.

The tables had been set up on a grassy verge that separated the battlefield from the sutlers' area. The two end booths in the sutler's area had been emptied and re-configured into a food service space. Harriet walked out onto the verge and looked for Aiden.

He spotted her first and waved, catching her attention. He was seated at a table on the far side of the eating area. She wended her way through the tables, greeting people as she went.

"Good job on all this," Aiden said and made a sweeping motion that encompassed the entire park. He rose and kissed her on the cheek then pulled out her chair before sitting back down, flicking a strand of his silky black hair from his white-blue eyes as he did so.

"I'm glad it's over. I just wish Gerald Willis hadn't been the grande finale."

"Yeah, that's pretty weird. I wonder if it's still considered murder if the victim has been dead for twenty years."

"That's one of the questions the Loose Threads identified last night. Not the murder question, but the declared dead part. We want to see his death certificate. We figure Mavis must have one."

"She probably does, but whether it's real is another story." Aiden leaned back in his chair. "I'll bet I could get on the internet and within five minutes have a copy of a Malaysian death certificate and with a little cut-and-paste I could make it be anyone's.

You copy it onto fancy paper, and who in Foggy Point is going to know it's a fake?"

"You're right. If she showed me a death certificate right now, I'd have no way of knowing if it was valid or not."

"How's Mavis holding up?"

"You know Mavis. She was shocked, but now she wants answers just like the rest of us. It has to hurt, though—they were married for a long time when he left."

"We don't know what his reason was, though. Maybe he had a good one."

"Yeah, well, I'd like to hear it. The re-enactors are all worried that one of their horses was involved. I think I'll walk across the field and check out the area where he died again. Want to come?"

"I'd love to, but..." He paused and pointed at the dark-haired toddler sitting and banging a pair of Styrofoam cups together in the grass just beyond the table. "I'm on nanny duty. Carla went for a walk with her friend."

Harriet got up. "Well, I'm going to look. I'll let you know if I find anything."

"Can you wait until Carla gets back?"

"How long is she going to be?" She could tell from his face he had no idea.

"I told her to take her time," he said.

Harriet reached out and turned his arm so she could see the face of his watch.

"I better go on and look—I have to be back in a half-hour to clean up after brunch."

"Stop here first and I'll help."

"If Carla's back, you mean."

"Come on, don't be like that. If you'd been there when Terry asked Carla to go for a walk, you would have offered to babysit, too."

"But she didn't ask *me*, did she?" With that, Harriet strode away toward the bleachers and the forest beyond the field.

The bleachers were all but gone. The rental people had been there for several hours disassembling the structure. She paused to look at the spot in the forest where she had first noticed Gerald.

From this distance, she couldn't see any large stumps or broken trees in the area where she'd found him. There were clumps of brambles and vines separating two pathways that went deeper into the forest; she'd have to take a closer look to see if the berry vines were hiding a secret.

The dry grass crunched as she circled the end of the battlefield and moved along the edge of the woods. Since the re-enactors were still in the park, the police had removed their yellow crime scene tape as soon as they were finished documenting the location. Carlton and the mayor both had spent the morning circulating through the brunch, glad-handing the out-of-town visitors and encouraging them to come back next year while downplaying Gerald's death at the same time.

Harriet wasn't sure what she was looking for. The grass was still flat where Gerald had collapsed. She squatted on her haunches to take a closer look. There were a few dark streaks of what must be blood. Not really that much, considering a man had died, she thought. She scanned the area to the left and then to the right.

A fine white powder dusted the area to the right of where Gerald's shoulders had been. She ran her fingers through the grass, picking up powder in the process. She expected it to feel slightly sticky, as pollen might have, but it was very smooth. She made a mental note to ask Darcy, a sometimes Loose Thread member and crime scene technician, if the criminalists used powder in their processing of an outdoor scene.

Harriet heard a branch rustle. She stood, and could see the leaves of the tree above her head moving in the slight breeze. She looked back across the field and spied Aiden's dark head as he sat at the table, Wendy in his lap. She turned and went farther into the woods in the direction Gerald must have come from.

A loop of root caught the toe of her shoe. She bent down to free her foot, and a small blue cylinder caught her eye. She reached to pick it up, and a burst of pain shot through her shoulder as she was smashed to the ground.

She heard a scream and realized it had come from her. A wave of nausea swept through her as she sank deeper into the prickly vines she'd landed on.

Strong hands lifted her.

"Are you okay?" a male voice asked.

"Aiden?" she mumbled and opened her eyes.

Instead of the ice-blue eyes she expected to see, a stranger's dark-brown ones looked intently at her. His hair was close-cropped, unlike Aiden's dark silky locks that hung below his ears.

"I can't feel my right arm," she replied.

"Here, let me help you to that log." Without waiting for an answer, he guided her to the end of a downed tree that lay parallel to the path. He didn't let go until she was seated.

"Harriet, what happened?" Carla asked. She'd apparently come from deeper in the woods while Harriet was moving to her current seat. "We heard someone scream, so Terry ran ahead to see what the problem was."

"I don't know what hit me. My foot caught on a root, and I bent down to free it and something hit me from behind. Do you see a tree branch where I was?" She leaned in the direction she'd come from. "I think a big branch fell on me."

"Harriet, that doesn't make sense," Carla said. "It's not windy or anything, why would a branch that big suddenly fall?"

Terry stepped back to where Harriet had been sprawled on the ground. He reached into the berry vines beside the path and pulled out a club-like branch about the size of a baseball bat. He held it up.

"This isn't big enough to knock you down unless someone was swinging it."

"There must be another, bigger one," Harriet insisted.

"If there is, I don't see it."

The feeling was starting to return to Harriet's arm, and it wasn't a good thing.

"I don't want to seem ungrateful, but who are you, anyway?" she asked the man. She realized an instant later it was obvious who he was. This had to be Carla's new friend.

"I'm Terry," he said and held his hand out. "Terry Jansen. I'm a friend of Carla's."

Carla's cheeks turned pink. Harriet tried to extend her hand to shake his but winced in pain when her shoulder moved.

"We've been gone a long time," Carla stammered, her previous confidence fleeing. "I need to check on Wendy. I'll tell Aiden what happened." She didn't wait for a reply, just turned and hurried toward the battlefield.

Terry looked exasperated as he said, "Wait," to her retreating back. He turned back to Harriet. "Let me check your shoulder."

"So, who are you and why are you in Foggy Point?" she asked. "And why should I let you check my shoulder?"

"My name is Terry Jansen," he repeated. "I'm in town doing a little genealogy research, and I was a combat medic for two tours in Iraq."

She gingerly pulled her shoulder out of the sleeve of her hoodie—she was wearing an off-white linen tank top underneath. She tried to turn her head to see the top of her shoulder, but it hurt too much.

"Don't move," Terry said. He gently probed her shoulder. "You're going to have a nasty bruise when the redness subsides." He probed some more. "I can't feel any obvious breaks, but you should probably go by the emergency room and get it x-rayed."

"Get what x-rayed?" Aiden asked as he arrived, breathless from running. "What happened to her?" he asked Terry.

"It looks like someone clubbed her on the shoulder."

"Hello," Harriet said. "I'm here. You can ask *me* what happened. And by the way, what are you doing here and where's Wendy?"

"Wendy and I were on our way over here when we ran into Carla. She said you'd been hurt, so here I am."

Harriet recounted her story again.

"My arm hurts, but I'm sure it will be fine," she finished.

"Did you hear anyone or anything?" Aiden asked.

"No," she said and then paused, wondering if the blue cylindar was worth mentioning.

"What did you see?" Terry asked.

"I didn't see anything. I thought I heard the bushes rustling, but I think the wind was blowing so I can't be sure."

"Let's get you out of here," Aiden said. "And I don't want any arguments. We're going to the emergency room, and you need to talk to the police."

"There's nothing to tell. I don't know if anyone actually hit me, and if they did, I didn't see anything useful."

"Thanks for helping her, Terry," Aiden said. "I can get it from here."

✂ ✂ ✂

Harriet protested all the way to the emergency room. "This is so embarrassing," she said as they settled in their cubicle to wait for a doctor.

"Yeah, you have been kind of a regular here since you've been back in town," Aiden said. "But shoulders are nothing to mess around with."

Aunt Beth arrived as the nurse was leaving—she'd brought Harriet a fresh ice pack and offered to call the police. Harriet had declined. She looked at Beth and shook her head, but said nothing. The nurse was the same one who had tended to Harriet's head wound a few months earlier when Aiden's uncle had tried to discourage her from digging into his business.

"Honey, are you okay?"

"I'm fine, my shoulder hurts, and my collar bone has a crack, but otherwise nothing's wrong that won't heal."

"She's lucky the blow wasn't a few inches either way from where it was. It could have crushed her jugular vein on one side or torn up her rotator cuff on the other."

"Thanks for that bit of cheer," Harriet said and glared at Aiden. "He exaggerates," she told Aunt Beth.

"Well, never you mind, I'm staying with you until you're better."

"You don't need to do that," Harriet protested.

"You're not going to be able to run Mable for a week or two, so since I'm going to be over there anyway, I can cook and take care of Fred. And don't try to tell me you don't have jobs lined up. I saw your receiving shelf."

Harriet rolled her eyes heavenward. She knew there was no hope. "Fine," she mumbled.

"I can take it from here," Beth said to Aiden.

"Okay, I need to go check a couple of my patients if you're sure you can contain our patient here." He leaned toward Harriet and kissed her gently, being careful not to jostle her shoulder in the process.

"You run along," she said. "Come on, honey, let's get you dressed. The doctor said he's got someone bringing you an arm wrap of some sort to immobilize your shoulder."

"What happened to doctor-patient confidentiality?"

"I've known Burt Pattee since he was in high school and used to come to the door selling coupons to raise money for the Foggy Point High School football team. Besides, having your arm in a sling isn't exactly a sensitive communication. In a few minutes, everyone's going to know about it anyway."

"You're impossible."

Chapter 11

Mavis pulled into Harriet's driveway just as Aunt Beth was helping Harriet out of her car to go into the house.

"Thanks for getting here so quickly," Aunt Beth said.

"You called her?" Harriet asked her aunt, the disbelief clear in her tone.

"Of course she called me," Mavis answered. "Did you imagine I'd be sitting home crying into my tea cup?"

Harriet cringed. That was exactly what she'd been thinking.

"Look, Harriet, Gerald died almost twenty years ago."

Harriet started to say something, but Mavis raised a hand to silence her.

"To me," she finished. "That man you found in the woods—he looked like my Gerald but he wasn't my husband. My husband has been dead for a long time. I don't know who you found, but he wasn't my husband."

Harriet stopped and looked at her friend for a long moment before her aunt broke the tension by taking Harriet's good elbow in her hand and moving her up the stairs. Harriet pulled her arm free.

"I'm not crippled," she said and opened the studio door and went inside.

No one said anything as Harriet dropped her purse in the wing-backed chair and then went through the interior door into the kitchen.

"Can you sit with her while I go pack a bag?" Aunt Beth asked Mavis.

"Sure," Mavis said. "Let me put the kettle on, we've some detecting to do."

Beth raised an eyebrow.

"I'll fill you in later," Mavis said in response to the unspoken inquiry.

A few minutes later, Mavis had Harriet settled on the velvet chaise lounge in the sitting room. She had propped Harriet's arm on down pillows from the upstairs guestroom and had pulled a dark cherry side table closer so Harriet could reach it with her good arm.

"Are you comfortable?" she asked, and when Harriet nodded she disappeared briefly, returning with a canvas bag containing the plaid flannel quilt.

"I brought Gerald's quilt," she said and unfurled it. "This has to be a clue."

"I suppose it *would* be too much of a coincidence for it to have been returned by one of your kids only a few days before your. . ." Harriet caught herself before she said *husband.* "Gerald died," she finished. "But what on earth does it mean?"

"That's why I brought it." She laid the quilt in Harriet's lap. "I've tried to look at it, but all I see is memories." She sighed.

"Let me give it a try." Harriet ran her left hand over the surface of the quilt. It was amazing how different things could feel when you were forced to use your off hand, she mused. She felt with her left hand all the time when she was holding the quilting machine control in place— which hand she used depended on which edge of the quilt the machine head was close to. Somehow, though, it was different when you didn't have a choice.

Gerald's quilt had narrow sashing—the strips of fabric that framed the sections of the quilt. Sashing could form a grid or lattice, depending on the size and placement of the strips and was often a solid color, enabling a quilter to correct for any variations in the size of the blocks that occurred. A sashing strip that was an eighth or even a quarter-inch wider or narrower than its fellow strips was not noticeable in most cases.

When the sashing was narrow, it was often an indication the quilt had been produced using the quilt-as-you-go method. Individual blocks were completed through the quilting step then connected using the narrow strips.

Harriet fingered the sashing in several places. Knowledgeable fingers could detect the break in the batting that occurred between the quilt-as-you-go blocks.

"So, this was a quilt-as-you-go project?" she asked to be sure, and Mavis nodded. "And I'm guessing you hand-pieced and hand-quilted the blocks."

Mavis again agreed. "That didn't exactly stress your detection skills," she said and smiled. Mavis rarely did anything but hand assembly. She knew how to machine-piece and quilt—she just didn't prefer the method.

Harriet continued feeling the individual blocks. "Have you thought about what you're going to do about a funeral?"

Mavis was silent.

"I hadn't thought about it, to tell you the truth," she admitted finally. "I've wondered where he's been, and I've wondered why the elaborate disappearance charade, but I guess in my mind I've already had his funeral. The one we did twenty years ago."

"I just thought that, since you're his next of kin, his body would be released to you."

"I suppose you're right. I'll have to talk to the boys about it. Ben and Harry are pretty angry, as you might expect, them being the youngest. Pete and James were more indifferent than mad, and Gerry was upset—but then, he and his daddy worked together, so they had a more adult relationship. None of them said anything about doing a memorial, but of course they were in shock when they found out, as we all were."

"If you need any help, I'd be happy to do whatever you want."

"Oh, honey," Mavis said, then stopped as she noticed Harriet pressing one of the quilt blocks between the palms of her hands. "Did you find something?"

"I'm not sure." Harriet continued to manipulate the section of quilt. "Did you use fusible material in any of the quilt blocks?" Heat-activated adhesives were used in a variety of ways by quilters.

The most common use was to attach cut-out pieces of fabric to background material with fusible fiber using an iron. The completed image could then have a line of machine stitching placed around its perimeter, creating the appearance of appliqué without all the fine hand-stitching.

"No, why would I? The whole quilt is nothing but various plaid flannel blocks."

"That's what I thought. This one block feels a little stiff, though, like it has fusible on the back of the flannel. Here, feel it." She held the quilt out.

Mavis folded the quilt section back and forth in several directions.

"You're right," she said, and set the quilt on the sofa beside her. "It feels like something's in there."

"Let me look again," Harriet said. She held the quilt closer to her face, looking carefully around the seams that joined that block to the rest. "The stitching looks different on this one edge. Look."

"There's one way to find out," Mavis said. "I'll be right back." She got up and went to the kitchen. Harriet heard the door to the studio open and close again. When Mavis returned, she had a pair of sewing scissors in her hand. She took the quilt and sat down on the sofa again.

"Are you cutting into the quilt?" Harriet asked, her voice rising slightly.

"Well, Gerald isn't going to have any use for it, and we need to know what's going on."

She carefully cut the stitches holding the sashing to the square of flannel that was the top layer of the suspect block. She worked carefully, and in a few minutes had an opening about four inches long. Harriet moved closer to watch.

"Oh, honey, you shouldn't be up." Mavis said as she clipped stitches.

"Let's look," Harriet said.

Mavis bent the top edge of the fabric back, exposing dense, dark-gray fiber where they should have seen soft off-white quilt batting.

"Whoa," she said. "What's that?" She grabbed the strange material by its corner and tugged gently. When it didn't move, she pulled harder. A dark square slid free of the quilt.

"What on earth is that?" Harriet asked, and tilted her head to examine it from all angles.

"If I had to guess, I'd say it's a sample of Gerald's work. When he was alive—" She stopped then started again. "When he still lived at home, he was forever bringing pieces of test fabric home from the factory. I've still got some of the oven gloves we field-tested. And one time I had to sew pieces onto the knees and rear ends of the boy's jeans. He glued some onto the bottom of Pete's tennis shoes another time, and Pete had to wear those shoes every day until the stuff wore through. He got real tired of those shoes, and ended up growing out of them before they wore out."

"That must have kept life interesting," Harriet said.

"I suppose. I never gave it much thought. With a houseful of boys, I was too busy to think about much besides filling the refrigerator, doing laundry and running the home taxi service."

"I wonder what he was testing," Harriet mused aloud, and felt the other squares that made up the quilt. "I don't feel any other squares like that one."

"I didn't feel any, either," Mavis said as she folded the quilt and stuffed it back into the carrier bag. "As sample pieces go, it seems kind of small. He usually brought much bigger pieces home, but who knows what he was doing."

Harriet worried the fabric between her fingers. It had a woven appearance but didn't ravel at the edges, as if it had been woven and then pressure- or heat-treated.

"Not to change the subject, but I met Carla's friend earlier," Harriet said. "It wasn't under ideal circumstances, since I was on the ground writhing in pain when he found me, but he seemed okay in a military sort of way."

"So, you approve?"

"I wouldn't go that far, but compared to whoever hit me, he was a real gem." Harriet paused. "Actually, now that I think about it, maybe *he* was the one who clubbed me."

"Beth told me he was walking with Carla in the woods when he found you."

"It isn't a perfect theory. I suppose she'll claim he was with her until they heard me scream."

"I suppose she will," Mavis said with a smile. "Well, I'm glad she's met someone nice."

"The jury's still out as far as I'm concerned. He's passed the forest rescue test, but he's still not proven his worth as a boyfriend for Carla. I'll need to see more to make that call."

"Carla's lucky to have such a caring friend, as long as you don't run him off in the protection process. I don't think she'd appreciate that."

✂ ✂ ✂

"Are you still downstairs?" Aunt Beth said a few minutes later when she came into the living room with her overnight bag over her shoulder and carrying a small white bag. "I picked up your prescriptions," she said as she rattled the bag. "Let me put my stuff down, and we can get you started on the anti-inflammatory medication. It wouldn't hurt if you took a pain pill either."

"I'll help you upstairs," Mavis said. "You should lie down and try to rest."

Harriet thought briefly of protesting, but her shoulder did hurt and a few hours of sleep would be a blissful relief.

✂ ✂ ✂

Mavis and Connie sat on stools at one side of the kitchen island as Aunt Beth spooned scrambled eggs onto their plates from the opposite side; she was also making toast and frying potatoes when Harriet came downstairs several hours later.

"Oh, honey, are you sure you should be up?" Mavis asked.

"Dios mio," Connie said and rose. She hurried to Harriet's side. "You must be in terrible pain. Here sit down, and we'll fix you a plate."

"Connie, you're smothering the girl," Mavis scolded. "Give her some room. Here, honey." She pulled out a stool and patted the seat. "Sit down."

"I'm fine," Harriet said.

"Honey, you have a broken collar bone—that's not 'fine,'" Aunt Beth said.

"It's not that bad." She looked at each of the worried faces in turn. "Really, it isn't. As long as I don't move it, it doesn't even hurt." She sat down between Connie and Mavis. "So, what are you guys up to? And don't try to tell me you're all here because of my shoulder."

"Of course we're here because of your injury," Mavis said. "Not the injury itself, mind you. Ben and Harry each broke his collar bone, and they heal quite nicely. No, we're talking about why someone would attack you just for looking at the place where Gerald was found."

"We all agree Gerald wasn't accidentally bumped into a stump or log or whatever nonsense the police are saying," Aunt Beth said, and set a plate of eggs, potatoes and toast in front of Harriet. "Do you want the catsup?"

Harriet nodded, and Connie passed it to her.

"So, we agree it wasn't an accident, but we don't know where that leaves us," Mavis said.

"It leaves us with murder, that's where it leaves us," Connie said.

"Why would someone kill a man everyone already believed to be dead?" Aunt Beth asked.

"Because they benefited from his absence?" Harriet suggested, and then realized what she'd said.

"I guess that puts me at the top of the list," Mavis said before Harriet could take it back.

"Not necessarily," Harriet said. "Weren't you better off financially when Gerald was alive?"

No one spoke for a moment.

"What?"

"Gerald had a large life insurance policy through his work. The company paid for part of it, but then he added the maximum amount they allowed the employee to contribute. The result, along with our own personal savings, provided me and the boys with more income than Gerald made when he was alive. Remember, the company hadn't invented the firemen's turnouts back then, so Gerald got paid with a lot of promises of future riches. Deferred compensation, I think they call it."

"That alone doesn't make you a suspect," Harriet protested, but they all knew, as she said it, that it was exactly what it made their friend.

"Robin called while you were napping," Aunt Beth said, ending the discussion of Gerald. Mavis visibly relaxed. "She totaled up the quilt sales, and we did very well. Even after you pay the expenses, she thinks we'll clear at least five thousand dollars."

"We'll only have to donate four quilts that didn't sell," Connie said. "And before you ask, no, they weren't all Sarah's."

"Aiden came by, and we told him you were resting, and he said to tell you he'd call you later," Aunt Beth reported.

Harriet yawned. "I don't see how I can be tired after that long nap."

"Your body has had a shock," Connie said.

"And you're taking pain medication." Mavis added.

"I think I'll go lie down again," Harriet said, and headed for the stairs.

Chapter 12

Fred was sitting on Harriet's pillow, inches from her face, when she awoke the next morning. She started to reach for him with her right hand and moaned with pain. In her early morning stupor, she'd forgotten her arm was strapped to her side.

He pawed her nose, making her sneeze.

"Fred, you're killing me here," she said and sat up, dislodging him in the process.

She looked toward the alarm clock on the nightstand beside her bed. It began buzzing, and she twisted to reach it with her left hand. Aunt Beth came in and hit the switch for her.

"I can't seem to make Fred understand how annoying it is when he wakes me up moments before my alarm goes off."

"Don't blame him," Beth said. "I changed your alarm after you fell asleep last night. He actually let you sleep in."

Harriet moaned and leaned back on her pillow.

"How are you feeling?"

"Actually, I'm feeling better. All this sleeping has done me good."

"I think it has as much to do with the re-enactment being over as it does with your shoulder healing."

"You're probably right."

"Do you feel up to going out?"

"Sure," Harriet said. "Where are we going?" She pushed her tangled covers aside and got out of bed.

"I told Mavis I would go by the Methodist church and see the pastor about funeral arrangements for Gerald. Connie is going to talk to the women's auxiliary and see if they can put together some food, and Robin is tracking down Sarah to sing. DeAnn says she and Jenny can get enough flowers from their yards and that Jenny knows how to arrange them."

"Does Mavis—or better yet, her sons—have anything to say about the funeral?" Harriet asked.

"Let's just say Mavis isn't in the mood to give Gerald anything, much less a funeral. None of the boys stepped up and volunteered, so she didn't want to push it. We all thought it would look better for her if he had a nice funeral, though."

"So, has anyone questioned Mavis yet?" Harriet asked.

"You mean besides the Threads?"

"Yeah, besides them. Have the police questioned her, or her sons?"

"Not yet. I saw Darcy at the coffee shop this morning and asked if she's heard anything, and after giving her usual criminalist disclaimers she said Gerald's cause of death is still listed as unknown. She says they won't come after Mavis until there's an official declaration of homicide, but she said everyone's working on the assumption that the status will be changed at any moment."

"It's unfortunate Mavis had to go babysit. Otherwise, she would have been in the booth before the final battle and there wouldn't be any question."

"It's more than unfortunate. After Mavis left last night, Connie pointed out that her sudden absence just makes her look even guiltier."

"The killer couldn't have planned it better," Harriet said.

"Do you need help getting ready?"

"No, I'm allowed to take this contraption off to shower." They agreed to meet in the kitchen in thirty minutes.

"Come on, Fred," Beth said. "She's not going to do you much good when it comes to opening your food can."

Aunt Beth had made Harriet a breakfast burrito using some leftover eggs from the previous night by the time she came downstairs and into the kitchen. "Here, you can eat this on the way," she said and handed it to her.

Beth picked up both of their purses and led the way to her car, holding Harriet's and then putting it by her niece's feet, once she was seated, before taking the driver's seat herself.

"We're hoping to keep this event low-key," she said.

"Have the police said when they're releasing Gerald's body?"

"They were expecting to release him today, and I've got Lyon's Funeral Home on standby to pick him up."

"Sounds like you've got things under control," Harriet said and busied herself adjusting the straps on her sling.

Aunt Beth drove down the hill and through the downtown area, and then turned toward the strait. The majority of Foggy Point churches were within a one-mile stretch along the top arch of the Foggy Point peninsula. When pirate Cornelius Fogg founded the town, he had decided that, in order to attract respectable people, he needed churches. He gave free land and the money to build a church on it to the first five people who agreed to establish a congregation in Foggy Point. In later years, as the peninsula became more settled, it had become tradition for new churches to build along the arch.

Aunt Beth drove past the Unitarian church and pulled into the Methodist parking lot. The building had a single spire that rose two stories above the roof and terminated in a large cross. A black Volvo station wagon was in the spot closest to the church office, located in a wing that had been added in recent years as Foggy Point's Methodist population had grown.

Aunt Beth parked one space over and helped Harriet out. The door into the reception area was propped open to let the cool breeze in.

Harriet entered and heard the muffled sound of voices coming from an inner office. She cleared her throat and shuffled her feet, making just enough noise to let the speakers know someone was within earshot of their conversation.

A door squeaked open, and Pastor Mike Hafer came out, closing his office door behind him.

"Beth," he said, and clasped Aunt Beth's hand. "And Harriet." With a nod in her direction. "We're glad you've come back to us." He gestured toward a small conference room that opened off the reception area. "We have a bit of a situation. Here, come sit down so we can figure this out."

Harriet and Aunt Beth looked at each other then went into the room he indicated.

"Can I get you some water? Or lemonade?"

"What's going on, Mike?" Aunt Beth asked.

Mike Hafer stroked his dark, neatly trimmed beard. "As you know, this is a rather strange situation, what with Mr. Willis having apparently died nearly twenty years ago, only to return and die again two days ago."

So what? Is there a double jeopardy rule regarding funerals? Harriet wondered. Didn't presidents have multiple events?

Pastor Hafer picked up a pitcher of water from a credenza at the back of the room and poured water into three glasses. He set a glass in front of Harriet and Aunt Beth then took a long drink from his. It was pretty clear he was preparing them for something.

"There is a woman sitting in my office right now who says she is Gerald's wife. She came to me to make arrangements for a memorial service."

"How do you know she's his wife?" Harriet asked.

"I didn't ask to see her marriage certificate, if that's what you're asking," Mike said. "But why would a stranger walk in off the street and want to put on a funeral for someone they weren't related to in some way? Think about it."

"I hadn't even thought about this possibility," Aunt Beth said. "When I saw him lying there on the ground, I just assumed that since Mavis hadn't remarried Gerald hadn't either, but twenty years *is* a long time."

"We need to talk to her," Harriet said.

"Do you want to think about it first?" Mike looked from her to Aunt Beth and back. "I think she's going to be surprised to learn Gerald had a family in Foggy Point."

"Not that her," Harriet said. "Mavis. She needs to be here for this."

"Oh, honey, do you think?" Aunt Beth said.

"She's right," Mike said. "She needs to hear this first hand, and it might help both parties to meet here." He went into his office to sell the plan to Gerald's alleged wife while Beth went back to her car to get her cell phone and call Mavis.

"She'll be here in a few minutes," she said when she rang off. "I didn't want her stressed out while she was driving, so I didn't tell her what was going on, just that a complication had developed and we needed her here."

"Should we call Connie?" Harriet asked.

"Not yet. Let's wait and see if we need her."

Aunt Beth took the opportunity to use the restroom, and Harriet went outside and paced in the parking lot. Mavis arrived in less than ten minutes.

"What's going on, honey?" she asked as she got out of her car, dropping her keys into her purse and hoisting the strap onto her shoulder in one fluid move.

"We've had a curious development, but Pastor Mike needs to tell you about it," Harriet said, feeling guilty for not telling her friend the news before she walked in on the other woman.

"Mavis," Mike said as he came out to meet her. "How are you doing?"

"I'd be better if you-all would tell me what's going on."

"Come in, I'd like to talk to you." He opened the door and ushered her into the reception area. Harriet followed.

"Hi, Beth," Mavis said. "I don't suppose you can tell me anything either."

Beth gave her friend a weak smile. She started to follow when Mike let Mavis into his assistant's office.

"If you don't mind, I'd like to talk to Mavis alone," Mike said.

Harriet and Beth went back into their conference room but left the door open.

Aunt Beth only lasted five minutes before she got up again and went outside. Harriet looked out the open door and could see her aunt was talking on her cell phone. Probably updating the other Threads, she mused.

She was tearing small pieces off a napkin with her left hand and rolling them into tubes then attempting to make them into knots one-handed. She hadn't been successful yet when a slender blond woman who looked to be only slightly older than she was walked into the reception area.

"Excuse me," the blonde said, and leaned into Harriet's room. "Do you know where the restrooms are?"

"Sure," Harriet said. "I'll show you." She led the woman down the short hallway that divided the office area. "I'm sorry for your loss," she said.

"Thank you," the woman said as tears welled in her eyes. She was older than Harriet had thought at first glance. She adjusted her guess upward to mid-fifties. "This is just such a shock."

Harriet kept silent and tried to give what she hoped was an encouraging look.

"I felt terrible following Gerard," the woman continued. "I mean, I trust him. I really do."

Harriet listened intently. The woman had a slight accent she couldn't quite place. Scandinavian, maybe?

"It's just that this trip came up so suddenly. Right after he got a series of late-night phone calls. He had told me years ago about his estranged son, and I heard him call the person he was talking to 'son,' so I thought they were reconciling." She looked at Harriet, who was working hard to keep her face neutral. "I'm sorry to dump this on you. I'm not usually like this." She gestured toward her puffy, tearstained face.

"Oh, no problem," Harriet said. "Sometimes it helps to talk about things."

"I shouldn't have followed him. I knew it was wrong when I booked my tickets. But if he was coming to meet his son, why didn't he say so?"

"Where did he say he was going?" Harriet prompted.

"He said he was meeting an old college friend to go fly fishing. But I knew that wasn't the truth. He didn't take his flies or his travel rod—he had a special rod he took on trips. It fit in a custom tube he could carry on the airplane. And he left his vest home. I mean, what kind of a fishing trip was this?"

Tears well up again, and Harriet handed her what was left of the napkin. She hadn't realized until then she still had it in her hand.

"I should have never come here," the woman said again, and dabbed at her eyes.

They had arrived at the restroom, so Harriet had no choice but to leave her and return to the conference room.

"Where'd you go?" Aunt Beth asked when she returned.

Harriet explained her mission of mercy and the information she'd gathered.

"So, it sounds like maybe she didn't know anything about Foggy Point and Gerald's life here."

"That would be my guess," Harriet said. "She seems way too shaken up, and she's feeling guilty about coming here to boot."

They heard a door open, followed by Mavis and Mike entering the reception area.

"I think we'll all be more comfortable in the conference room," Mike said and ushered Mavis in. "I'll go get Mrs. VanAuken."

The blonde returned from the restroom, and Mike brought her into the room.

"Mrs. Willis would like to have her friends here with her for support," he said, turned to Mrs. VanAuken. "Is that okay with you?"

"That's fine," she said.

"A man has died, and each of you..." He looked first at Mavis then at Mrs. Van Auken. "...has expressed a desire to provide a celebration of his life and to give him a proper burial. I'd like you each to hold on to that fact as we try to understand how you both came to be in this unusual situation."

He proceeded with introductions, and they learned the blonde's name was Ilsa Van Auken, and she had been married to Gerard Van Auken, an American ex-patriot living in the Netherlands, for fifteen years.

Ilsa learned that her husband had not lost his wife of ten years and that their only son, being raised by his wife's sister, was largely fiction.

For the most part, Harriet and Beth kept their own council and let the two shocked women exchange information—tentatively at first and then like two survivors of a natural disaster. When they finally stopped talking, exhaustion clear on both faces, Pastor Mike stood up.

"You two will have a lot to talk about in the coming days, and when you're ready we can move forward with the funeral. Would you each take the hand of the person on either side of you," he said in his gentle voice. "Let us say a prayer for our brother who is no longer with us."

They bowed their heads and let his soothing words flow over them.

"Where are you staying?" Mavis asked Ilsa when the prayer was over and everyone had gone outside.

"I've been staying in Port Angeles. That's where Gerard's reservation was." She blushed and looked away for a moment. "I checked the history on his computer when he left and found his maps and reservations and then I followed him. Of course, I didn't stay at the same hotel, but I was nearby. I followed his rental car to Foggy Point the day I arrived, but I lost him. I came every day after that, but I didn't see him again until after he died."

"Can we help you find a place to stay in town?" Aunt Beth asked. "Our friend DeAnn has a couple of guest cottages she rents out. They're empty now that the re-enactment is over."

"That would be nice," Ilsa said with a sniff.

The women exchanged information and agreed to meet for lunch the following day at the Sandwich Board.

"I called Jenny and told her to hold off on picking the flowers," Aunt Beth said when they were underway again. "I also called Carla and told her we would stop by and see how she's doing with her new housekeeping plan. I hope that's not going to be too much for you."

"I'm not a shut-in, for crying out loud," Harriet said as she fumbled with her seatbelt latch.

"Here, let me do that," Aunt Beth said, and rammed it into its fitting with a satisfying click.

Carla had hot water ready when they arrived and showed them into the downstairs parlor. Randy ran into the room when she heard Harriet's voice and wove between her legs, making little yipping noises until Harriet bent down and scratched her odd little ears.

"How's your arm doing?" Carla asked. "Have they figured out what happened to you?"

"There is no 'they.' I didn't report it to the police."

Carla's eyes widened in surprise, but she didn't say anything.

"I told her she should call them, but no one listens to me," Aunt Beth said.

"I've been through this a few times, you know," Harriet said. "And frankly, telling the police when someone banged me on the head didn't do anything for me—twice."

"Gommy," yelled a little voice as Wendy came running into the room, launching herself at Aunt Beth when she was close enough.

"How's my girl," Aunt Beth asked in a high-pitched voice and scooped the child up in her arms, tickling the girl's belly as she did so.

Wendy shrieked in delight.

"Okay if we go find a treat in the kitchen?" Beth asked Carla.

When Carla nodded agreement, Aunt Beth carried her squirming armload out of the room.

"Can I pour you some tea?" Carla asked.

"Sure," Harriet replied. "I'm having a little trouble with activities like that right now."

"It's no trouble." Carla picked up a cup, placed a tea bag inside and poured steaming water over it. "Who do you think hit you?" she asked as she handed Harriet the cup.

"I truly have no idea. This whole business with Mavis's husband showing up dead is a real mystery. And I can't figure out what I was doing at the scene of his death that could be interpreted as a threat to anyone."

"So, what did you see while you were out there?" Carla asked and looked intently at her.

"The only thing I remember is the grass had something white and powdery on it. It felt smooth. I'd planned to talk to Darcy and see if that was something the criminalist's had used. I went a little farther and my toe got stuck in a tangled root. I bent down to pull it free, and I saw a blue plastic cylinder. I was about to pick it up for a closer look when something hit my shoulder."

"Do you know what it was?" Carla asked. "Was it a shotgun shell casing? Sometimes those are colored plastic."

"It was about that size, but more solid. It reminded me of some of the plastic creations people made in machine shop when I was in junior high school."

"I thought you went to fancy schools," Carla said, momentarily distracted.

"I came back here a couple of times for a few months at a whack."

"At least you got to go sometimes," Carla said.

Harriet was trying to think of the right way to explain how much she cherished her time in Foggy Point and resented all the others, without coming across like a drama queen. She was spared by the appearance of Carla's new friend.

"I hope it's okay that I'm here," Terry said. "The lady in the kitchen let me in."

"Of course it's okay," Carla said, her cheeks a little pinker and her eyes a little brighter in response to the new arrival.

"I couldn't help but hear your description of the piece of plastic you found," Terry said. He was wearing baggy khaki cargo shorts and a form-fitting red T-shirt. "Do you have it with you?"

"No," Harriet replied. "I was just about to pick it up when I got hit. Why?"

"What you're describing sounds like a sabot. It's a piece of plastic that can be shot out of a shotgun. It can do a lot of damage without leaving a recognizable gunshot wound. Without seeing it, I can't be sure."

"If you don't mind my asking, how do you know that?" Harriet asked.

"I've used something similar," he said.

"Terry's in the navy," Carla explained.

"And in the navy you shoot guns filled with plastic?"

"I'm a SEAL—we do a lot of stuff."

It was obvious to Harriet that Terry was well-trained in how to avoid answering questions.

Chapter 13

Can I get you a something to drink?" Carla asked Terry, and when he requested water, she left Harriet alone with her visitor while she went to the kitchen.

Harriet sipped her tea, and Terry sat on an uncomfortable looking velvet sofa, saying nothing.

"Are you from around here," she finally asked when she couldn't stand the silence.

"No."

"Visiting?" Harriet guessed.

"I guess you could say that."

"Will you be staying long?" Harriet persisted.

"Are you an undercover policewoman or something?" he asked with a smile.

"No, but Carla's my friend. And I'm not buying your family genealogy story. You could do that on the internet, you wouldn't need to come here in person if that's all you were doing. Carla doesn't need someone laying on the charm and trying to take advantage of her."

"Why would you assume I'm trying to take advantage of her?" he asked, the smile leaving his face.

"I'm not assuming anything. It's just that she's my friend, and she's vulnerable, and I want to be sure."

"Fair enough," Terry said. "I *am* here doing some family research. When I was young, we lived in Foggy Point. My father died, and my mother moved us to Seattle. I had some leave, and I wanted to try to understand who my father was. My mom won't talk about him. This seemed to be a logical place to start. I met Carla at the grocery store my first day in town, and she was friendly. I like her—simple as that."

"So, have you learned anything?" Harriet asked.

"Not as much as I'd hoped. I think he worked at a place called Industrial Fiber Products, but that doesn't exist anymore."

"That's what they used to call Foggy Point Fire Protection," Harriet offered.

"So I've been told," he said and stood up to pace. "I went out there to see if anyone who knew my dad still worked there." He fell into silence again.

"And?" she prompted.

"And…nothing. They said they couldn't give out any information on who did or didn't work there. I didn't get any further at the library."

"What was your dad's name? My aunt has lived here forever. Maybe she knows something."

"His name is the same as mine—Terry Jansen."

"I suppose you've tried the newspaper?"

"Not yet, but it's on my to-do list."

"You might give it a try. They have a pretty good archive."

Carla returned with Terry's water, followed by Aunt Beth and Wendy, effectively ending the conversation.

Chapter 14

Harriet and Beth returned to the car and headed home. "Could we swing by and see Mavis?" Harriet asked.

"Sure, I wouldn't mind checking on her, but what are you thinking?"

"I've been thinking about that quilt that showed up at her house the other day. Now that we know Gerald was likely in the area at the time, it seems probable he was the one who put it in her house."

"Just don't upset her. She's been through enough. You better call Lauren, too. She needs to know the name Gerald was using and about his wife."

Lauren was the last person Harriet wanted to talk to, but she knew her aunt was right, and Lauren *was* the computer maven of the group. She pulled her cell phone from her purse and balanced it on her leg while she dialed with her good hand.

"Talk to me," Lauren answered without preamble. Harriet silently counted to ten.

"We have a name." she said. "Gerald was going by Gerard Van Auken. He married a lady named Ilsa in the Netherlands."

"The Netherlands is a big place," Lauren sniped. "Could you be a bit more specific?"

"No, I can't," Harriet shot back. "I think she's going to be staying in one of DeAnn's guest houses, so maybe you can call her for more info."

"Fine," Lauren said and hung up.

"She's such a ray of sunshine."

"It'll be worth it if she can come up with something," Aunt Beth said.

✂ ✂ ✂

"Come in," Mavis said when she opened the door to her cottage and found Harriet and Aunt Beth on the small porch. "Let me put the teakettle on."

The two visitors sat on the sofa and waited for their hostess to reappear.

"Here, let me get this out of the way," Mavis said, and moved a stack of fat quarters in shades of brown from her coffee table. "I like that stars and rails pattern you used for your re-enactment quilt, so I thought I'd try it out," she said to Harriet. "I'm cutting enough out to make a table runner, and if I like I how it looks I may make it bigger."

"Do you have enough fabric?" Aunt Beth asked.

"It's going to be scrappy, but within three or four color families. I think using lots of different prints is more in keeping with how quilts actually looked during the Civil War." Mavis went into her sewing room and brought out a few more pieces of brown fabric for Beth's approval. The women rearranged the material into several piles until the sound of the teakettle whistle interrupted.

"How are you feeling about things," Harriet asked when Mavis came back to the living room carrying a tray with three mugs of tea on it. "Are you up to looking at Gerald's quilt again?"

"Of course," Mavis said. "And I'm not sure how I'm feeling about things, but the options are running towards angry and frustrated."

"We don't need to do this now if you don't want," Beth said.

"Don't be silly. I want to get to the bottom of this, and the sooner the better. The quilt's in my sewing room. I'll get it." She went back into her sewing room and returned with the plaid quilt draped over her arm and the piece of strange material in her hand. "I figured this is what you really want to look at," she said and handed Harriet the black square.

"There must be something special about this material," Harriet said. "Why else would he hide it, yet keep it with him. And what about this would make him come back?"

"It *is* strange-looking," Mavis said.

Harriet raised an eyebrow. "How so?"

"It's the only black one I've seen. The samples he usually brought home were white or off-white or dingy gray or yellow. Nothing I ever saw was black."

"Huh," said Aunt Beth. "So, this isn't a memento from his final success, the fire cloth?"

"No, that stuff is yellowish-white, but it could be an earlier version. Let me get a match." She went to the kitchen and came back with a box of wooden matches. "Here," she said as she positioned the black square in Harriet's hand. "Now, hold it out while I try to burn it."

Harriet did as she was instructed. The fabric resisted burning, but it got so hot she dropped it, and when she grabbed at the falling square, she jostled her sore collar bone, causing her to yelp and jerk back onto the sofa. In the process, she slopped her tea onto the square and knocked Mavis's appliqué scissors off the table. The scissors ended up stabbing point-down into the floor, impaling the wet black square in the process.

"Well, that eliminates a few experiments we might have done," Mavis said. "It's neither waterproof nor scissor-proof, and from your reaction I'm guessing it wasn't protecting you from the match."

"What are we missing?" Aunt Beth wondered. She picked up the flannel quilt and felt the intact squares as Harriet had done before. "I don't feel anything out of the ordinary," she said when she'd finished.

Mavis took it from her and took a good look at both sides. When she didn't find anything, she folded it, placed the black square on top of it and returned both to her sewing room. "With him dead, we may never know what was going on," she said when she came back. "It may simply have been a wear test." She went into the kitchen and made Harriet a fresh cup of tea.

"What are you thinking regarding the funeral?" Aunt Beth asked when Mavis was settled in her chair in the living room again.

"I go back and forth," Mavis said honestly. "For the boys' sake, I need to do *something*, and if that Ilsa person really was married to him for fifteen years, she needs to be involved. I'm just so angry at Gerald." She stared out the window for a moment, gathering her composure. "But I guess that can't be helped. And anyway, on a cheerier note, it seems like I'm no longer alone at the top of the suspect list."

"There is that," Harriet said. "By the way, we have Lauren on the case, computer-wise. She'll see what she can find out about Ilsa and also see what she can find out about Gerald's activities over the past twenty years."

"Why does she need to be involved?" Mavis asked. "Let's get Ilsa over here and grill her."

"I think we should do that, but I also think Lauren can help us know if Ilsa is telling us the truth," Harriet said. "I mean, we have no reason to believe she isn't being truthful, but on the other hand, she could be anyone."

"Why don't we invite her to our Loose Threads meeting tomorrow?" Aunt Beth suggested. "Then it won't seem so much like an inquisition."

"Does she quilt?" Mavis asked.

"I don't know," Harriet said. "But I think Aunt Beth's right. I'll call DeAnn later and see if Ilsa's arrived."

"Well, we better get going," Aunt Beth said and drained her cup. "I've got some quilting to do while someone..." She glanced at Harriet. "...gets some rest."

"Hey, you were the one who insisted on taking over."

"Okay, missy, how are you going to stitch the orders you have with one arm tied to your side?"

Harriet smiled. "I don't know, maybe I can train Fred to help."

"That's what I thought. Come on, we've got work to do."

"Bye, Mavis," Harriet said. "See you tomorrow."

Aunt Beth hugged her friend and then ushered Harriet out to the car.

✂ ✂ ✂

"Wake up, sleepyhead," Aunt Beth called from the top of the stairs. Harriet looked at the clock beside her bed and was shocked to see she'd been asleep for almost two hours. "Carlton's here," Beth continued.

Carlton was the last person Harriet wanted to see, but she was pretty sure he wouldn't leave if she refused to come downstairs, so she got up and went to the bathroom to splash cold water on her face.

"Carlton," she said as she came into the long arm studio a few minutes later. "How can I help you?"

He was wearing a pink Hawaiian shirt over khaki shorts. His basketball-shaped stomach held the shirt away from his waist, and his thin legs looked stick-like coming out of the stylishly baggy shorts. He watched the stitch head on the long arm machine as Aunt Beth guided it around a large quilt that was made up of circles in squares. The woman who'd made the quilt had chosen sunflower colors—gold, forest green and brown with touches of orange and lime. She'd incorporated sunflower prints in several scales in the circle parts. It would make someone a nice late-summer bedcover.

Carlton turned toward Harriet.

"How's the arm?" he asked in his slightly too loud for indoors voice.

"Its fine, Carlton, but I'm pretty sure you didn't drive over here to ask about my health." She was still annoyed about the workload he'd dumped on her during the re-enactment and was pretty sure he was here to ask for something more.

His face turned a pink color that matched his shirt. "Of course I'm concerned about your arm." He was obviously stalling as he shuffled his feet and then studied their new positions.

"But you'd like to ask me to do something?" Harriet prompted.

"Well, now that you mention it, the city council is having a meeting tomorrow and wondered it we could provide some information about our event. I was hoping you could put a few figures together for me."

"Are you sure you don't want me to just come to the meeting?"

"Oh, I couldn't possibly ask such a thing while you're wounded."

Of course not, Harriet thought. People might realize who'd really done the work, and that would never do.

"I'll see what I can come up with," she said. "I'm not promising anything—after all, it's hard to work with my arm like this." She already had the information, but she wanted to watch him squirm. "Now," she continued, "I have a couple of questions for you."

"Sure, ask away. I have no secrets."

"This isn't that sort of question." Harriet led him to the sitting area near the front door and gestured for him to sit down, then took the wing back chair opposite him. "Think back about twenty years, to the time just before your dad's company became Foggy Point Fire Protection."

"You mean when Gerald disappeared?" he asked.

Maybe he was sharper than she was giving him credit for.

"Yeah, around that time. Do you remember what products were under development?"

He was silent for a few minutes. "Nothing stands out. Back then they made a lot of low-volume products. They were trying to make a fabric shielding sleeve that could be used to fireproof cable bundles, but I don't think they got very far with it. I could try to look in the company archives, but I'm not sure we kept the data on products that didn't go anywhere."

"That would be useful," Harriet said. "I'd like to see a list of everything Gerald was working on, successful or not."

"Sure, I'll get my secretary right on it." He pulled a smart phone from his pocket and keyed in a reminder note.

"Oh, and one more thing," she said. "Do you remember an employee during that same period named Terry Jansen? I don't know what sort of position he held."

Carlton appeared to be thinking. Finally, he shook his head. "No, it doesn't ring a bell. That's not to say there couldn't have been, but one of my jobs was to sign Christmas and birthday cards from my dad for each employee. There weren't a lot of employees back then, you see. Dad wanted people to feel like the company was their extended family. When we got bigger, we had to do away with the personalized stuff."

It must have really made the people feel great to get a card from the company owner that hadn't even been signed by him, Harriet thought, but then focused on the task at hand.

"If you could check the employee rosters I'd appreciate it."

Carlton looked skeptical about adding another task to his list.

"Perhaps you could give me that information when I bring you the information for your meeting?"

His shoulders sagged, and he tapped on his phone again, adding the additional request.

"What time is your meeting?" she asked.

"After lunch," he said.

"I'm coming downtown for a Loose Threads meeting," she said. "I'll swing by on my way."

"See you tomorrow, then." He stood and turned toward the long-arm machine. "Good to see you as always, Beth," he said, and let himself out.

"Is there anything I can do to help you?" Harriet asked her aunt when Carlton was gone.

"I can't think of anything you could do left-handed that would help." Beth said. "Your job is to rest up and heal."

"How about I walk downtown and get us some dinner?"

"Are you sure you're up to it?" Aunt Beth asked. She looked at her closely.

"I'm fine, really. I've had lots of rest."

"Okay, but take your cell phone with you, and if you're not back in an hour, I'm coming looking."

"I'll be back, don't worry. If I get too tired, I'll call and you can come get me, but I won't need to."

She went into the kitchen and picked up a thin brown flowered nylon shopping bag that folded up in a small pouch she could carry in her pocket until she needed it. She took money from her purse, wrestling left-handed with her wallet until she finally was able to extract enough bills to cover the anticipated cost of dinner.

"Do you have any preference?" she asked Aunt Beth when she'd returned to the studio.

"Honey, if I don't have to fix it, anything sounds great."

Harriet headed out of the studio and down the driveway. She still was undecided about what dinner would be.

"Hey, doll," came a male voice from behind her. A familiar vintage Ford Bronco cruised into view, inching forward, keeping pace. "Want a ride?"

"Sure," she said.

Aiden stopped and jumped out to open the door. She was still on a neighborhood street, so no traffic was in sight.

"I'm on my way to California," she told him.

"I'll go anywhere with you," he said. "Let's go."

"Don't you need to pick up Randy?"

"Nah, Carla will feed her eventually."

"You're impossible," she said with a smile. "Actually, I'm on my way to pick up dinner for my aunt and I. Would you like to join us?"

Aiden was silent. Harriet looked at him. It was unusual for him to not have a ready quip. "What?" she finally said when he continued to stare out the windshield. "Do you have a date?" She was joking…until he didn't answer. "If you have a date, just say so. It's okay."

"I don't have a date," he said. "Not like you think, anyway. It's just…" He broke off, obviously choosing his words carefully.

"Just what?"

"It's just that I promised I'd be a guinea pig for Carla tonight."

"That's okay," Harriet said. A deep stab of pain knifed through her stomach; or maybe it was her heart—she wasn't sure. "Carla needs you."

"She wants to have Terry over for dinner, but she's afraid her cooking isn't up to snuff. I've tried to tell her what a great cook she is, but she wants to try the dinner menu first, just in case."

A great cook, Harriet thought. She supposed she shouldn't be surprised. Carla was his housekeeper, after all. But now she was his cook. His "great cook," she amended.

"That's fine. I realize I was inviting you at the last minute."

"You don't have to give me notice," he said. "You know that. I'd rather eat with you, but Carla was so worked up over having

Terry over, I agreed. If I'd known you were going to ask me, I'd have said no."

"It's no big deal," she said. "It's my pain meds talking. Of course Carla needs your support. Are you going to be there when Terry comes to dinner?"

"I told her I'd take Wendy to Tico's Tacos and introduce her to Mexican food."

Harriet looked out her window. Aiden reached over and turned her face toward him.

"I can get one of the vet techs to babysit. I'm sure Carla wouldn't mind."

"It's not that," Harriet said. "I'm actually worried about Carla being alone with that guy so much. There's something off about his genealogy story. He claims he's trying to get to know his father by retracing his past. He says his dad used to work for Carlton's dad, but Carlton doesn't remember him."

"And that surprises you?" Aiden asked.

"Actually, it does. Carlton's dad made him write out the birthday and Christmas cards for all the employees back then. He wrote every name at least twice every year for some number of years. I realize he could forget someone after twenty years or more, but when I told him the name, it didn't trigger anything."

"Carlton's a weasel—I wouldn't put faith in anything he remembered or didn't remember. I can guarantee you the only thing he thinks about these days is Bebe."

"Still, I don't trust Terry."

"They're just having dinner. They're not even leaving the house."

"Unless they go for a walk by the strait. Then he could kill her and dump her in the water and we might never find her."

"You have been watching way too much television," Aiden said. "Terry is not out to kill Carla."

"Maybe not, but he's lying about *something*—I can feel it."

She sank back in her seat, and Aiden drove in silence.

"Have you decided where you want to get food?" he finally asked as they approached town.

"Tico's sounds good and easy to carry, too."

"I'm going to drive you home when you get your food," he said. "I don't have to be home for a while." He looked down when he said the last part.

"It's okay, really," she said and put her hand on his arm.

Aiden guided the Bronco into the small parking lot at the side of Tico's. He got out and came around to Harriet's door, opened it and pulled her carefully into his arms, making sure he didn't jostle her collarbone.

"I'm sorry I can't come to dinner. I really want to."

"Look," Harriet said as she leaned back and gazed into his ice-blue eyes. "I just overreacted there for a minute. Like I said, it was the pain meds talking. I really do want you to help Carla, and more important, I want you to protect her."

"Are you sure?"

"I'm positive," she said, and almost meant it.

She leaned toward him. Aiden steadied her face with his hand and gently brushed his lips over hers. She smiled against his mouth, and he kissed her more deeply, being careful still of her wounded shoulder.

"Please, amigos, get a room," came a booming voice from the back door. "You're going to drive my business away."

Jorge laughed and waved the dish towel he was holding at them. Harriet laughed, too.

"Busted."

"I guess we better go in," she said.

"Yeah, he's probably on the phone with your aunt already."

"*What?*"

"You heard me. Jorge is as big a gossip as any of the Loose Threads."

Harriet finished getting out of the car, pushing him out of the way.

"I don't need them talking about me any more than they do already."

"Do you two want food today, or are you just here to make out?" Jorge asked when they came into the restaurant.

Harriet's face burned, and she took a deep steadying breath before she spoke.

"I actually came to order take-out for my aunt and I."

"What? No food for the señor?"

Jorge couldn't have missed the look that passed between Harriet and Aiden. He clapped his large hands together.

"Well, then, mija, what did you have in mind for dinner? You want to try something different? How about some nice barbacoa burritos?"

"Sounds good," Harriet said.

✂ ✂ ✂

There were more than burritos in the bag when she unpacked it. Aunt Beth came through the studio door into the kitchen as Harriet was pouring a glass of lemonade for each of them. She glanced at the two place settings on the island bar, and her eyebrows rose.

"No Aiden?" she asked.

"He had to be home for dinner," Harriet said, and busied herself dividing the generous carton of guacamole into two smaller bowls. She pulled out a small bag of tortilla chips from the main package and poured them into a basket she placed within reach of both places.

"Are you regretting sending Carla to be his housekeeper?"

"No," she said, too quickly. "No. I couldn't in good conscience let her continue living in a car with a baby." She set a container of salsa by each plate—mild for Aunt Beth, medium for herself.

"You didn't have to suggest Aiden. She could have stayed here." Aunt Beth settled at the bar, and Harriet handed her a plate with a foil-wrapped burrito.

"Aiden does need a housekeeper. It works for both of them. He would have had to pay someone anyway. It might as well be Carla. It's a win-win." She knew her response lacked the enthusiasm usually associated with such words. She set her own plate and burrito on the counter.

"But…"

"No but," Harriet said and sat down beside her aunt. She unwrapped her burrito and carefully folded the used foil with one hand. "It's just that I'm starting to feel like the other woman. They have all kinds of plans, and I have to fit in around the edges."

"It's only natural for people who live together to have to coordinate their schedules."

"How many times did Avanell have to miss dinner out with the Threads to be home to eat with Rose?" Harriet asked, referring to Aiden's mother and their family housekeeper.

"That was different. Rose came to Avanell and George when they had their first child. She helped with the baby and took care of the house. They were both working, and she had to contend with their schedule initially. Then, as the kids got bigger, she had to work around their classes and activities, too."

"A big part of me totally gets it. I want Carla living there where she and Wendy are safe and Aiden can keep an eye on her new boyfriend. I just liked it better when she was living at his house and he still had the apartment over the vet hospital. I was getting used to having him around all the time."

"Are you sure it isn't that you liked having everything your way?"

"Thanks for your caring support," Harriet said and dipped a tortilla chip into her bowl of guacamole.

"What good would I be if I only said what you wanted to hear?"

"You're right. It's one more reason why Aiden and I don't belong together. I got used to having things my way. I'm not used to accommodating anyone else's needs anymore."

"That's not true," Aunt Beth said around a bite of burrito. "You can be a very flexible person. Look how you helped Lauren through her tough spot. And you don't even like her."

"You're right. I can be. It's just hard. Aiden and I are still figuring out our relationship. Adding another person or persons makes it harder."

"I'm going to be going over there tomorrow after Threads to see how the changes she and I talked about are working out, housekeeping wise. She feels so grateful—she thinks she has to work constantly to earn her keep. She may be using the time we freed up from cleaning to cook. I'll see what I can do."

"Don't tell her I said anything."

"Don't be insulting," Aunt Beth said and then smiled. "I'll feel Marjory out, too. She cut back Carla's hours at the quilt shop when the girl moved to Aiden's so she could get settled. I'll put a bug in her ear about restoring the old schedule. If Carla doesn't have so much time on her hands, it'll be easier for her to stick to a reasonable housekeeping schedule."

"You're the best," Harriet said and hugged her aunt with her good arm.

Chapter 15

Harriet and Fred were in the kitchen the next morning when Aunt Beth came downstairs.

"Are you trying to put me out of a job?" Beth said when she saw Harriet's cereal bowl.

"You're helping enough, taking on all my quilt jobs; especially the one for the woman in Angel Harbor."

A woman they had met at quilt camp had pieced a quilt she hoped to enter in the upcoming Jefferson County Quilt Guild show. It was a blended floral quilt, and the woman had asked for stitching that suggested a small iris image combined with some equally small cross-hatching. It would take at least twice if not three times the amount of time to finish as for an average quilt of the same size.

"Honey, I could do that job in my sleep," Aunt Beth said.

Beth's familiarity with the long arm machine aside, Harriet knew her aunt was more tired than she let on. In the few short months since retiring, she'd become accustomed to a life of leisure, or at least a life of not being on her feet all day.

"My collar bone and shoulder are feeling a lot better already. I'm supposed to start exercises today."

"For your shoulder?" Aunt Beth asked in disbelief.

"No, no, not my shoulder—my wrist and elbow. It says so on that paper they gave us when I left the emergency room. I'm supposed to squeeze a rubber ball. I thought I'd squeeze a needle through fabric at Loose Threads today instead. I was going to go rummage through projects in the studio when I finished my cereal and see if I could find something I'd already cut out that would be easy to hand piece."

"You have so many UFOs that shouldn't be too hard," Aunt Beth said, making reference to the euphemism that quilters used for unfinished projects or "objects."

Harriet laughed as she got up and put her empty cereal bowl in the sink.

"Come on, Fred, we have work to do."

It was a good thing I started early, Harriet thought later. It had taken almost thirty minutes to wade through her partially started projects one-handed. She'd finally picked up a Lemoyne star project she'd started in a class years ago on one of her visits to Aunt Beth. The stars were made up of eight diamond-shaped pieces with setting triangles and squares in a background color. Harriet had cut her diamonds from brown-and-red print Civil War reproduction fabrics. Fred batted at the pieces as she tried to gather them up and put them into her quilting bag.

"You're not helping, you know," she scolded. "This is hard enough one-handed without having to pick pieces up off the floor where you keep knocking them."

"Are you ready?" Aunt Beth asked as she came into the studio, her purse in one hand and her quilt bag in the other.

"I am in spite of excessive feline help."

✂ ✂ ✂

"I got decaf or fully leaded here," Connie said and held up a coffee carafe in each hand. "Anyone?"

Jenny held up her cup and pointed to the decaf. Sarah held her mug out for the caffeinated coffee when her turn came. Connie filled her own cup with a blend and returned the pots to the shop kitchen. The rest of the Loose Threads seated around the table in the large classroom at Pins and Needles were drinking tea of one sort or another.

"No Carla today?" Harriet asked, a brief vision of Carla and Aiden dead on the floor of his house, killed by Terry, flashing past her consciousness. She pushed it from her mind. It had to be the pain medication talking, if you considered the two ibuprofens she'd taken that morning pain medication.

"She's in the back room pricing fabric," Robin said. "She said Marjory got in a big shipment from Kona Bay she had to check in."

"So, Ilsa agreed to meet us here?" Jenny asked.

"Yeah," DeAnn said. "I asked her if she quilted, and it turns out she does, so it was easy. She had to go by the police station this morning, and then she should be joining us."

"Harriet?" a little-girl voice called from the shop. "Are you here?" Bebe Brewster leaned into the room. "Oh, there you are," she said when she spotted Harriet sitting between her Aunt Beth and Mavis. "Carlton asked me to come by and have you fix this report."

She tottered to Harriet's side on the impossibly high heels of her gladiator sandals, a process made more difficult by the tight strip of pink fabric that surrounded her hips. The girl was wearing fishnet tights, and Harriet wasn't sure if the pink piece above them was supposed to be a skirt or an artfully placed shawl. Bebe flipped the papers in her hand back and forth, not quite fanning herself.

Harriet turned toward her. Bebe continued flipping the papers without handing them over. Aunt Beth finally reached out and grabbed the girl's left hand.

"Wow," she said. "That's, ah…" She paused a moment, trying to find the right word to describe the obscenely large bauble adorning the younger woman's finger. "That's some ring you have there. What's the occasion?"

Bebe grinned and batted her eyelashes. "This ole thing?" She held her hand out, tilting it from side to side, catching the light with the stone and sprinkling the resulting twinkles around the room. "It's me and Carlton's one-year anniversary. I know it's supposed to be paper or clocks, but I didn't want a watch, so Carlton decided to super-size my wedding ring." Her smile widened as the Loose Threads ooh-ed and ahh-ed over the ring with a lack of sincerity that went right over her head.

Harriet cleared her throat and waited. When Bebe ignored her and kept talking, she grabbed her arm.

"The papers," she said. "There's a problem?"

"Oh, yeah," Bebe said, and laid the papers on the table. "Carlton said there was a mistake in the security costs." She pointed to a line that had been highlighted in yellow. "He said the cost went up the second and third day for the same amount of hours."

"See the little star beside the figure here?" Harriet pointed to a number on the page. "That star refers to a note at the bottom of the page." She moved her finger to the bottom of the page. "See, it says here the on-duty Foggy Point policemen had to be paid at their overtime rate per hour. They get paid time and a half for overtime, so that's what we paid. Most of the security force was made up of private security people, but your husband made a deal with the mayor to use policemen, too. This is the price we paid for that deal."

"That wasn't very clever, was it?" Bebe asked.

"I'm sure he had his reasons," Harriet said, hoping that would end the conversation. She wanted to talk to the other Threads before Ilsa arrived.

"Would you like some coffee or tea?" Connie asked Bebe.

"Oh, that would be real nice—coffee please."

Connie pulled out a chair on the other side of Aunt Beth, and Bebe carefully sat on the edge, folding her long legs to the side. When she was settled, Connie retrieved the coffee pot and filled a cup, which she set on the table in front of her.

"Are you doing anything special for your anniversary?" Jenny asked politely. Harriet thought the ten-carat rock should be special enough for ten anniversaries, but she didn't say anything.

"I wanted to go to Cabo, but Carlton can't get away from work." Bebe made an exaggerated pout with her pink-painted lips. "He's going to charter a plane and take me to San Francisco for dinner and the opera, you know, like in that movie."

Only you're no Julia Roberts and Carlton is definitely not Richard Gere, Harriet thought, and wondered if Bebe even realized she'd cast herself in the role of a hooker.

Bebe took several nervous sips of her coffee then set the mug on the table.

"Thanks for the coffee, but I better get these back to Carlton."

She stood up but then didn't leave. Harriet followed her gaze toward the door to the classroom. She could see Ilsa coming down the short hallway.

"Who's that?" Bebe asked, the curiosity clear in her voice.

Ilsa's sharply creased linen pants and her violet silk tank top were a notch above the usual garb worn by locals in Foggy Point. The single strand of pearls around her slender neck perfectly coordinated with her neat shoulder-length bob and was pure classic. Bebe could only aspire to the easy grace the woman exuded.

Ilsa held a cream-colored soft leather tote bag over her left arm. She looked at DeAnn.

"Am I too late?" she asked when no one said anything.

"Of course not, come on in," DeAnn said.

"Where are my manners?" Connie exclaimed. "Here, you can sit by Beth." She gave Bebe a pointed glare. "Bebe was just leaving."

Bebe held her hand with the diamond out to Ilsa in an awkward, reverse handshake.

"I'm Bebe Brewster," she said in her little-girl voice. "My husband Carlton is president of the business association. I was here on business, but I have to go." She said it in a way that implied she had more important things to do.

Ilsa took Bebe's hand in both of hers. "How very nice to meet you. I'm sure I'll see you again around town."

Ilsa was smooth—Harriet had to give her that. She sat in Bebe's chair and accepted the coffee offered by Connie.

"Thank you for inviting me to quilt with you," she said when she was settled, breaking the silence that had once again descended on the group. "No matter how stressful life gets, I always find peace in my quilting."

She pulled a partially completed block out of her bag, followed by a handful of fabric pieces that looked to be similar in size to the fat quarters the Loose Threads were familiar with.

"Your fabric is beautiful," Aunt Beth said. "What are you making?"

"These are eighteenth-century Dutch reproduction fabrics," Ilsa said. "I'm doing a simple geometric pattern with squares and triangles. I don't know the English name for it."

"What's the fabric made of?" Robin asked. Ilsa's fabrics were dark-colored prints with a shiny surface.

"These fabrics are all Dutch chintz," Ilsa explained. "Cotton, basically. The Dutch East India Company brought fabric to the Netherlands in the sixteen hundreds, and then they brought instructions on how to construct fabric mills and create the fabric. By the seventeen hundreds, the Netherlands produced their own fabric, but as you can see, it was still heavily influenced by the patterns produced in India."

She pointed to a modified tree-of-life pattern on a red background. She picked up her stack of fabric and handed it around the table.

"This is beautiful," DeAnn said, starting a round of marveling over the fabric that led into a discussion of chintz and then quilt block patterns, and before the group knew it, it was lunch time.

"I'm glad we can make our own quilts again," Sarah Ness said when the conversation lagged. "I mean, charity is all fine, but I want to work on my own designs."

Mavis rolled her eyes when Sarah looked away. "Anyone want to go get a salad at the Sandwich Board?"

"I've got to get back to work," Aunt Beth said. "Someone's business is awaiting my return." She smiled at Harriet.

"Hey, you volunteered," Harriet said.

"We'll make sure Harriet gets home to keep you company after lunch," Connie said.

Sarah and DeAnn both had to return to work, but Jenny, Lauren and Robin were able to join Mavis, Harriet, Connie and Ilsa for lunch.

"Do you do a lot of quilting at home?" Harriet asked Ilsa when everyone was settled around three tables the group had pushed together at the Sandwich Board.

"I do more in the off season," she said. "I have a flower shop, and we stay pretty busy in the spring and summer. In the winter, the shop closes earlier and I am not so tired when I go home. That is how I met Gerard," she said tentatively. "He came into the flower shop."

She paused, and Connie smiled in encouragement. The Threads were all listening intently—finally, they were getting to the good stuff.

"He wasn't a customer. He works for a tulip farm," She looked down, realizing her mistake. "He worked for a tulip farm. It was a family business. He delivered flowers, sorted bulbs—he even helped Joris set up a computer program to track the bulb plantings."

"And you had no idea he had another wife and family?" Lauren asked. Connie coughed to cover the small gasp that escaped her lips.

"It's okay," Ilsa said, looking at Connie as she said it. "We need to get this out. It's like I said at the church, Gerard told me he'd been married for ten years and had a son he'd been estranged from ever since." She looked at Mavis. "He had a cousin in Amsterdam. We went to dinner at their house on Sundays."

She said the last part in a rush, as if the cousin made the wife and son more real.

"He does have a cousin in Amsterdam," Mavis said slowly. "Theobald."

"That's right." Ilsa became more animated. "Theobald and Uda. They have two daughters, Elsbeth and Karyssa."

"Well," Mavis said after a moment, "at least he told the truth about that."

"Okay," Lauren said. "So, why has he been hiding all these years?"

"Lauren," Connie scolded.

"Well, it's what everyone wants to know," she said.

"I wish I knew," Ilsa said.

"You and me both," Mavis muttered.

"What about Ger—" Harriet paused. "I'm going to call him Gerald, no offense." She directed her attention to Ilsa. "His quilt."

"I understand," Ilsa said. "What quilt are you referring to?"

"Gerald returned a quilt to Mavis when he came back." Mavis started to interrupt, but Harriet held her hand up. "Mavis found a quilt she'd made for Gerald before he left. It's been missing, and it suddenly showed up in her cottage. It's made from plaid shirting flannel. It has narrow sashing and was made with the quilt-as-you-go technique."

"I know that quilt. He said his sister in the States had made it for him before he left for the Netherlands. He told me it reminded him of home."

A tear spilled down Mavis's cheek. She dabbed at it with her crumpled napkin.

"I'm sorry," Ilsa said as she reached out and patted Mavis's age-spotted hand.

"No," Mavis said. "You have nothing to be sorry for. I need to hear this. *We* need to hear it. It's the only way we're going to figure out what happened. We need to know why a reasonably happy, successful family man would abandon his family and start a new life half a world away."

"And having done that," Ilsa said, "why would he come back after all this time?"

"Okay," Harriet said. "Let's be a little more methodical about this, construct a time line, maybe."

Robin pulled a tablet from her purse. "I'll take notes," she said.

"Start at the beginning. Mavis, what can you tell us about the time right before Gerald left."

Mavis recounted what the rest of the group already knew about Gerald's last weeks before he disappeared. He'd been working a lot. He'd just perfected the fire protection fabric. He was working a lot of hours but seemed upbeat about the new product. Gerry had started working at the factory, and he and his dad were spending more time one-on-one talking about the job.

"He worked in a factory?" Ilsa said in disbelief.

"He was a fiber chemist," Mavis said. "He invented the fire protective fabric that is still made in Carlton Brewster's factory."

Ilsa sat back in her chair. "I can't believe it," she said. "I mean, I believe you. I just can't believe he worked anywhere that was inside. He told me he loved living things and had always worked out-of-doors."

"He did have a green thumb," Mavis offered. "He had quite the garden at home."

"A garden," Ilsa said. "Not a small farm in a green valley in northern California?"

"'Fraid not."

"When I met him, his skin was tanned and his hands callused."

"Don't forget there were some numbers of years unaccounted for," Harriet said. "He disappeared from here almost twenty years ago. You told Mavis you'd been married fifteen years ago. How long before that did you meet him?"

Ilsa thought for a moment. "I think we dated for almost a year. And he'd been working for Joris for the year before that. So there must have been three mystery years."

"And you have no idea where he was during that time?" Harriet asked.

"Apparently not. He told me he came to the Netherlands to visit his cousin and decided to stay. He said he lived with them and worked on a farm near Amsterdam until he could save a little money to relocate with. He came to Aalsmeer, where I live, and went to work for Joris."

"Wait," Lauren interrupted. "You work at a flower shop and Gerald was a farm hand and you can afford to dress like that?"

"I *own* the flower shop, and flowers are big business in Aalsmeer. Over seven billion cut flowers and one hundred fifty million plants are sold there annually. The flower auctions in Aalsmeer pretty much set the price for the flower trade internationally."

"I stand corrected," Lauren said. "Who would have ever thought flowers were such big business." She got up and went to the counter to get her drink refilled.

"Please excuse Lauren's lack of tact," Mavis said.

"She obviously can't help herself," Ilsa said with a small smile.

"So nothing out of the ordinary happened for fifteen years?" Robin said, bringing the group back to the time line.

"Not that I can think of," Ilsa said. "I mean I could second-guess every pensive moment he had, but really, looking back I can't point to anything out of the ordinary until he got the phone call and said he was going on a trip."

"Did he go on solo trips often?" Connie asked.

"No, that's why it was so strange, why I followed him here. Neither one of us had ever taken a trip alone. I figured it was because it was his son—that is, the reason he lied about it. He didn't want to upset me."

Robin looked at her tablet. "Well, kids, we're going to have to come up with more than this."

"Isn't investigating Gerard's death a job for the police?" Ilsa asked.

"Of course," Harriet said. "I'm sure they will figure out a cause of death and even eventually who killed him, but for Mavis's sake, we need to know why he left here, why he stayed gone and, most of all, why he came back. I'm not sure the police care about that, or they won't, if they catch the killer first."

"Are you about ready to go, mija?" Connie asked. "I have to take care of my granddaughter tonight, and I need to get a few things done before then."

"Sure," Harriet said and picked up her bag. "Could you drop me off at Carlton's office?" she asked when they were in Connie's car. "I want to see if they have an employee badge book."

"You mean like our yearbook at school? They give us a new badge every year with an updated picture."

"Yeah, something like that."

"Who are you looking for? If it's someone at the factory, can't you just ask Carlton?"

"I tried that—he didn't recognize the name I was looking for. I just want to be sure." She quickly told Connie who she was looking for and why.

"I'll come in with you. Two people can work faster than one, especially a one-handed one." She smiled and patted Harriet's good hand.

The two women spent an hour and a half at Foggy Point Fire Protection, poring through the badge books. To be Terry's father, the man couldn't have worked there in the last ten or twelve years. Terry had said his dad died when he was young, and since he couldn't be more than thirty and probably was younger than that, they concentrated their efforts on the books from the nineteen-eighties. When that didn't yield anything, they checked the first few years of the nineteen-nineties, but to no avail.

"This just confirms what I already believed," Harriet said. "Terry is here for some reason, but finding friends of his dead father isn't it."

"You're worried about Carla, aren't you?" Connie asked.

"Aunt Beth keeps telling me Carla's a big girl, but I have a bad feeling about this. Young people just don't come to hang out in Foggy Point."

"*You* came back," Connie reminded.

"Yeah, but I had a reason. I have a relative here, one who really exists."

"Shall I drop you at your house?"

"Yeah, thanks. I need to think about what this means."

Chapter 16

There was a car parked in the circular driveway when Connie dropped Harriet off.

"Oh, joy," Harriet said, "that looks like Lauren's car."

"Come on, honey," Connie said. "Think positive."

Harriet gave her a half-smile and thanked her for the lift.

"It took you long enough to get home," Lauren greeted her as she came through the quilt studio door.

"I didn't know I was on the clock," Harriet said.

"You asked me to do some research, and I got some results. I thought you were anxious to hear any news regarding Gerald."

Harriet knew there was no winning with Lauren. However, the woman did know her way around a keyboard, and Harriet appreciated the fact that she'd taken the trouble to deliver the news privately.

"This took some work. You owe me big time."

"Okay, already, I owe you. I'll name my firstborn child after you. Better yet, I'll *give* you my firstborn child."

"Eww," Lauren groaned.

"I've got to take my medicine—you're going to have to come to the kitchen to impart this earth-shattering news."

When Lauren got up without further argument it piqued Harriet's interest.

"You want some lemonade?" she asked as Lauren plopped down on a bar stool.

"Sure," Lauren said, and pulled a folded sheet of paper from her pocket.

Harriet filled two glasses from a pitcher in the refrigerator, handed one to Lauren and then used hers to down two pills. She opened a plastic bag of chocolate chip cookies and put half a dozen on a plate then set it in front of Lauren. She finally sat down at the bar, one stool between herself and Lauren.

"Okay, I'm ready. Amaze me."

"You certainly know how to take the thrill out of things," Lauren groused, and twisted a strand of her blond hair around her finger. "I searched for everything I could find on Gerald and didn't turn up much," she said without waiting for Harriet to react to her accusation. "But when you gave me the Gerard Van Auken name, things started getting interesting."

"How so?"

"Hold your horses, I'm coming to that." She looked at her paper again. "Gerard surfaced in Amsterdam the year after he left here. He wasn't exactly hiding. He gave a paper at a small conference that had something to do with industrial products. I'm not exactly sure what—I had to use a language translation program, so it's a little rough. He definitely delivered a paper. He seems to have attended a number of conferences that year. Nothing too big, but it seems like he was networking in his field."

"Is that the wow news?"

"No, that's not the big news. It is interesting, though, don't you think? He obviously wasn't concerned about hiding from everyone—just Foggy Pointers, or maybe just Americans."

Harriet gave her an impatient look.

"Okay, already," Lauren continued. "The big news is that he took out a patent on a fiber formula then sold it for lots of money to a company that makes body armor. So, I guess he could afford to work as a simple peasant. He's got a few mil in the bank. Double-digit millions."

"Wow," Harriet said in spite of herself. "You're right, I owe you for that."

"Don't worry," Lauren said. "You *will* pay."

She stayed until she'd finished her lemonade and cookies. Harriet asked her a few polite questions about what she was working on for her ongoing class at the Angel Harbor Folk Art School. After a few smart remarks, she offered to show Harriet her latest project samples. Harriet followed her to her car, where Lauren pulled out a pizza box filled with ten-inch-square samples in a variety of techniques. Her final project would be a three-dimensional vine-covered cottage. She was trying out stitch combinations to make a thatch roof, vine-covered walls, wooden doors and windows and a rose bush. Harriet was amazed by the intricacy of the detail as well as the density of stitching.

"We had to dye our own thread and ribbon, too."

"These are really cool," Harriet said and realized she actually meant it.

"I gotta go," Lauren said and got in her car.

"Thanks for the info."

Lauren waved and drove off down the driveway.

Harriet went back into the studio where her aunt was still working on the show quilt.

"Mavis called while you were outside with Lauren," Aunt Beth said.

"What did she want?"

"She wants you to call her. I told her you would call as soon as Lauren left."

"Do you know what she wants?"

"Her boys are all coming to town for the funeral service. She's going to talk to Ilsa about going forward with whatever plans they need to make. The boys decided they're coming to support their mother no matter what happens, and if nothing else, they'll have a small private memorial of their own."

"And that has what to do with me?"

"You know she only has two bedrooms in the cottage. She was wondering if you'd be willing to let a couple of the boys stay in your spare bedrooms."

"I'm guessing that me calling is a mere formality," Harriet said and tried to look serious. Her aunt didn't deny it, and Harriet ended up laughing in spite of herself. "You two are impossible."

"You know you wouldn't have said no."

"Of course I wouldn't say no, but it makes me feel like such a grown-up when I get to say yes, or heaven forbid, offer before I'm asked. And I would have as soon as she told me they were coming."

"I know, dear," Aunt Beth said, and patted Harriet's good arm.

"Do I at least get to pick which sons I get?"

"Call Mavis."

Harriet went into the kitchen and called Mavis. After reassuring her it was okay with her to have the boys stay at her house, she listened while Mavis went into a detailed analysis of which of her sons would be the best house guests.

"Mavis, it'll be fine. Send whoever you want. I've got plenty of room…Send all three of them if you want. It'll take the pressure off you and your house…Okay, I'll await their arrival." She hung up. "Get ready for company, Fred. The Willis boys are coming."

Chapter 17

So let me get this straight," Aiden said when he stopped by Harriet's on his way home from work. "You're hosting a house full of testosterone-fueled men?"

"Don't be ridiculous," Harriet said. "I'll probably have the youngest boys."

"From what I hear, they were the worst of the lot. And they're not that young—a couple of aging troublemakers. If they step a toe out of line, they'll have me to contend with."

"You're such a tough guy," she said and pulled him into a hug made only slightly awkward by her right arm being strapped to her chest.

"How much longer do you have to wear this iron maiden?" he asked with a smile.

Harriet used the fingers of her good hand to sweep a strand of hair out of his eyes. "The doctor said it could be six weeks—sooner if I heal more quickly."

He caught her fingers in his hand and pulled them to his lips. "That seems an eternity, m'lady."

"You'll live."

"Can I take you to dinner?"

"I told Aunt Beth I'd make her dinner, since she's been doing all my work. I've got chicken in the oven. Want to join us?"

"Of course."

"Wait a minute. Aren't you supposed to be babysitting Wendy tonight?"

"I was, but dinner got cancelled; and before you ask, Carla didn't tell me any more than that."

✂ ✂ ✂

With Aiden's help, Harriet made a cold cauliflower salad and a tossed green salad to go with the chicken.

"Honey, this is wonderful." Aunt Beth proclaimed.

"You're only saying that because you didn't have to cook," Harriet said.

A knock on the door interrupted the conversation, and Aiden got up to see the guests in.

"Hi," said a tall, thin red-headed man. "Hey, aren't you Marcel's little brother?"

Aiden didn't say anything.

"Dude, you gotta know those eyes give you away every time."

Harriet came up behind Aiden.

"Hi, I'm Harriet," she said. "Are you Harry or Ben?"

"I'm Harry. Ben's parking the car. He sent me to check things out. We're pretty sure my mom and your aunt volunteered your house. We just wanted to give you a chance to bail. If it isn't a good time for you, we can go get a hotel room."

Aiden started to speak, but Harriet poked him hard in the back and whatever he'd intended to say came out as a cough.

"You'll do no such thing," Harriet said. "I would have offered in any case."

Harry Willis turned back and waved to his brother to park the car.

"We're in," he called.

✂ ✂ ✂

Aunt Beth stayed until the two youngest Willis boys were settled in their rooms then returned to the peace of her own cottage.

"I better go, too," Aiden announced. "The feral cat people are bringing a group of females in, and I got spay duty. We're starting early in the morning, so I'll need my beauty rest. I'll check with you later in the day and make sure you're surviving."

Harriet kissed him lightly on the cheek, and he pulled her to him in a gentle hug. He tilted his face to the ceiling.

"This brace thing is killing me," he muttered.

"You've made that clear," Harriet said with a rueful smile. "I'm sorry."

He kissed her then held her for another minute before turning and going out the door.

✂ ✂ ✂

Harriet was still in the studio a few moments later, when she heard a soft knock on the outside door.

"Hey, did you forget something?" she asked as she opened the door. Her smile faded when she realized it wasn't Aiden.

"Sorry," the man on her porch said. "I hope it's not too late to come by to see my brothers.

"Oh, Gerry, hi," Harriet said, recognizing him. "Aiden just left. I thought maybe he'd forgotten something. Come in."

He looked at her arm strapped to her side.

"How's the arm?" he asked. "Mom told me what happened."

Gerald Willis Junior was the only one of Mavis's sons who actually lived in Foggy Point. He was already working when his father disappeared, and according to Aunt Beth, he'd been the one who felt most responsible for taking care of Mavis.

"Sorry you're stuck with my brothers. If we weren't in the middle of a remodel, Katy and I would have had room. As it is, we have two teenagers and a ten-year-old living in three rooms."

"Don't give it another thought. Come into the kitchen. I'll call your brothers."

But Harry and Ben had heard their brother's voice and were already waiting when she ushered him through the door.

"Hi, guys," Gerry said, and took a seat between his brothers at the kitchen island.

"Can I get you something to drink?" Harriet asked. "I've got lemonade or I can make coffee."

The trio decided on coffee, and Harriet loaded the coffeemaker while the brothers made small talk about their day's travel. She laid out mugs, sugar, milk and spoons, and when the coffee was finished, she poured the steaming liquid.

"Would one of you turn off the pot when you're done?" she asked and started for the stairs.

"Actually, could you stay and talk with us for a little while?" Ben asked. "Gerry told us what Mom said, but you were there. And Mom said your…" He pointed at her shoulder. "…injury happened when you went back to look at the place where you found our dad."

"There's really not a lot to tell," Harriet said. "I was watching the main battle with your mom. We were sitting high enough in the bleachers to see the far side of the field and the edge of the forest. I noticed someone lying there, and thought it was one of the re-enactors. The battle took place, and when people got up to take their bows, the man at the edge of the forest didn't move. Your mom and I went over there, and unfortunately, it turned out to be your dad."

"He was already on the ground when you first saw him?" Gerry asked.

"Yes. I didn't look over there at first because, of course, everything was going to be happening on the main field, but I think he'd been lying there for a little while."

"This is all too weird," Harry said. "I mean, our dad has been dead for more than half my life. Is there any possibility it isn't our father? Could it be someone who looks like our dad—maybe a cousin of his or something? Did they do a DNA test?"

Ben looked at Gerry. "You *are* sure, right?"

"It's our dad," Gerry said. He'd gotten up and was pacing the length of the kitchen, his back to his younger brothers.

"You seem awfully sure," Ben said. "Did you see his body?"

"I didn't need to."

Harry stood and grabbed his brother by the arm, turning him.

"You knew." he stated. "All this time, you *knew*."

"Gerry," Ben said, "is that true? Have you known all these years that our father wasn't dead?"

A muscle in Gerry's jaw twitched. "It's not that simple."

Before anyone could react, Harry reared his arm back and threw a solid punch at his brother's jaw. The blow landed with enough force to stagger Gerry, who grabbed at the edge of the counter before sinking onto his rear end.

Ben pinned Harry's arms behind his back. "Stop." he said. "Just stop."

Harriet helped Gerry to his feet.

"Are you okay?" she asked in a quiet voice. "Do you want me to call anyone?"

He brushed her concern aside. "I'm fine," he said. "And I deserved that."

"Let me at least get you some ice." She dug in a drawer for a sandwich bag then opened the freezer and filled the bag with ice cubes. She wrapped the bag in a dish towel and handed it to him.

"I'm calling James," Ben said. "He should be in on this."

James, Mavis's second son, was an attorney in Port Townsend.

"We don't need to drag James over here this late," Gerry said around his ice bag.

"You don't get a vote," Ben said. "You didn't think we needed to know about Dad, either."

Harriet thought about calling Mavis but decided it wasn't her place to tell the boys' mother. She also didn't want to draw attention to the fact she was still there listening.

"Dad is dead. Just because he wasn't dead for the last twenty years doesn't change the fact that he's dead now," Gerry said.

"Things are going to get crazy when everyone finds out. We need to understand the implications," Ben said. "We need to prepare."

"Prepare for what?" Gerry shouted.

"If Dad wasn't dead, Mom's been falsely collecting his insurance." Ben ticked his points off on his fingers. "And maybe getting Social Security payments. And we still don't know why he left." He looked at Gerry. "Do we?"

Gerry shook his head indicating they didn't.

"We don't know if Dad was involved in something shady—I mean, he left suddenly. People don't leave like that unless they screwed something up."

"Ben, everyone already knows this stuff," Harry said, rubbing the knuckles on his right hand.

Harriet noticed for the first time how red and swollen it was. She prepared another bag of ice and handed it to him.

"The police have Dad's body," Harry continued, "all the old timers in town know Dad died twenty years ago. What's new?"

"If Gerry knew Dad was alive, other people probably did, too. This changes *everything*," Ben said.

"Ben," Harry said, "I agree we need to tell James—and Pete, too," mentioning Mavis's middle son for the first time. "But not tonight. Gerry's 'secret' changes things for us, but *only* for us. Not for Mom, not for the police. Two and Three are coming tomorrow anyway." He used the number nicknames he had invented when he was a toddler, trying to master his four brothers' names.

"Have you been in touch with Dad all this time?" Ben asked, putting his cell phone back in his pocket and finally asking the question Harriet wanted answered.

"No, I haven't." Gerry got up from the floor and started pacing again. "It's not like Dad and I made some plan together. He called me to his office one day. He gave me a piece of paper with the address of a post office box and a polymer formula. He said he was leaving on a business trip the following day. He said no matter what I heard after that, I shouldn't believe it. He told me not to tell anyone else what he'd said. Then he told me that if I ever started seeing orders for that polymer come across my desk, I should send a postcard to the address. A blank postcard. That's it."

"And you didn't hear anything else all this time?" Harry asked.

"I heard nothing for almost twenty years. When Dad left, I was a clerk in the purchasing department. When I became manager of the department, I made a habit of reviewing all chemical purchases, just in case. For nineteen years, nothing out of the ordinary happened. I caught a few counting errors by my own employees, but no sign of the polymer.

"Then, about two and a half months ago, someone ordered a small quantity of the stuff. I didn't do anything right away, because the product development people order small quantities of all sorts of chemicals, and besides, I wasn't sure Dad was still out there." He picked up his ice bag and held it to his jaw again.

"Sorry," Harry said, and hung his head momentarily.

Gerry put the bag down and took the two ibuprofens Harriet handed him.

"I decided to check out who was using the chemical and what they were using it for," Gerry continued. "I went down to the production area, and I got the run-around on who had placed the order. The best I could get was that a new project was coming up, and they were preparing for it. Brett, one of the production managers, said he'd heard Carlton had purchased a new product from a company that was closing. He said they were relocating their own managers and technical people. He said they had probably ordered the stuff under Carlton's account number because they aren't set up here yet."

"So, you sent the postcard." Ben said.

"I did. And to tell you the truth, I didn't think anything would come of it. The first couple of years, I thought Dad would show up with some explanation so all this would make sense. Then, for a few more years after that, I told myself he probably did have an accident, or a heart attack or something. If he'd really left us behind, no one would know to notify us."

"Did you ever try to find him?" Ben asked

"How was I supposed to do that?" Gerry protested. "Don't forget, it was twenty years ago. Everything wasn't a computer keystroke away. He was supposed to have died in Malaysia, but other than that, he could have been anywhere. I couldn't leave my job and go searching the world. Besides, I couldn't afford to go anywhere."

"So the first thing we need to do is hire an investigator and figure out where he's been," Ben suggested.

The brothers bickered for a minute about how to go about hiring and paying for an investigator. It was clear Mavis hadn't told them about Ilsa yet. Harriet didn't want to be the one to break the news, but it couldn't be helped.

"Guys," she said, and held up her good hand to silence them. "I can save you some time and money."

"Do you know something?" Harry asked.

"Of course, she knows something," Ben said, "Why do you think she said that?"

"Does anyone need more coffee?" Harriet stalled.

"Let me do that," Ben said, and took the coffeepot and refilled their mugs.

When everyone was settled again, Harriet took a deep breath and began.

"There's no easy way to tell you all this, so if you could, let me get it all out before you ask any questions." She proceeded to tell them about Ilsa and the Netherlands, and then Lauren's discovery about their dad's sale of his invention and the resulting money.

"Dad remarried?" Harry said.

"Dad's a millionaire?" Ben said at the same time.

"What do we know about this woman?" Gerry asked.

"I don't think we know anything about Ilsa, except for what she told us," Harriet said. "She claims to have followed your dad here. I'm not sure how else she would have ended up here unless she got the information from him in some way, or followed him. I know it doesn't mean anything, but I've spent a few hours with her and she seems sincere. From listening to her talk to your mom, she either knew your dad for some amount of time or did really thorough research."

"We should be able to call Dad's cousins in Holland. At least we could verify that much," Gerry said.

"Lauren did find the information about the fiber formula under Gerard Van Auken, which is the name Ilsa knew him by, so that must mean something, too," Harriet said.

"I can't believe our dad left us and married someone else," Harry said in a hollow voice.

"This is *all* pretty unbelievable," Gerry agreed.

"There's one more thing," Harriet said. "I'm not sure if this was a coincidence or if it's connected, but your mom was called to go babysit for your brother Pete during most of the re-enactment. She got back just before we saw your dad lying at the edge of the forest. She told me she thought something was off about the request. Pete told her their babysitter had to attend an out-of-town funeral, and then Mavis ran into the girl at a coffee shop. She fled when Mavis recognized her."

"You're not trying to say Pete's in on this, are you?" Gerry asked. "Why would Dad ask Pete, of all people?"

"I don't know what I'm trying to say. It just seemed weird. It came up all of a sudden, and then the girl was in town when she was supposed to be gone. I think that's a pretty big coincidence."

Gerry stared at the ceiling. "This just keeps getting better," he said.

"What's so important about that particular polymer?" Harry asked. "Is it poisonous or environmentally dangerous?"

"No more so than any of the other chemicals we use to make the fireman's turnouts. None of the stuff we use is without its dangerous properties, but nothing radical. But I'm a business guy, what do I know. We can ask one of the chemists tomorrow, if you want."

"Speaking of tomorrow, it's going to be here before we know it." Harriet took her cup to the sink and rinsed it before putting it in the dishwasher. "I'm going to bed. Can I trust you not to tear the place up?"

"I'll behave," Harry said. "I'm sorry I over-reacted. This has been a lot to take in."

"I'll take responsibility for the coffeepot," Ben offered.

Harriet thanked him, called Fred and went up to bed.

Chapter 18

Mavis was drinking tea in the kitchen the next morning when Harriet and Fred came downstairs.

"How's the shoulder, honey?" she asked.

"It's getting better each day. I'm really tired of this tie-down though." Harriet wiggled the fingers on her injured side.

"I'm sorry the boys misbehaved last night. They confessed as soon as I got here this morning."

"Where are they?"

"Harry is out running, and Ben went to get doughnuts."

"Did they mention what we talked about last night?"

"Yes, and I'm sorry you had to be in the middle of all this, honey. I'm sure it was no picnic telling them about their dad's new wife."

Harriet looked away. "I wasn't sure if I should be the one to break the news, but they were getting worked up about hiring an investigator. I felt like I had to stop them before they actually did something."

"Well, I'm sorry, honey." Mavis reached over and patted Harriet's good arm.

"Have you decided what you're going to do?"

"About what?"

"Ilsa, the funeral, all of this?"

"There's not much I can do. Ilsa's the one whose husband just died. Gerald Willis has been dead a long time. Ilsa seems pretty sensible. I thought I'd see what she wants to do about a memorial. If she doesn't want to do anything public, then the boys and I will do something private ourselves."

"Have you talked to James yet?" Harriet asked. "You need to find out where you stand legally. We're assuming Ilsa is the widow here, but if Gerald was never dead, than you were still his wife when he died. It doesn't matter if he changed his name or married a second time or anything."

"Honey, I'm trying to avoid thinking about the insurance money I've been getting all this time. I suppose there's nothing for it, though. James has to be in court this morning, but he said he'd come over when he's finished and see what he can figure out."

"What a mess this all is. I wish we knew what was so important about that polymer. It doesn't make sense. If something made Gerald leave, what about a polymer could make him come back?"

"I think I hear Aunt Beth arriving," Harriet said. "I'm going to check in with her, and then I'm going to Pins and Needles. The needle I'm using for my hand-piecing doesn't feel right. I realize it could be the fact that I have to hold my work at a weird angle, but my hand gets a cramp if I work for very long. I thought I'd try a short needle."

"I'm going to wait here with the boys until James arrives," Mavis said. "Could you check and see if Marjory has that extra-wide backing fabric in a pale yellow while you're there?"

"Sure," Harriet said, and went through the connecting door into the studio.

✂ ✂ ✂

Driving was a little harder than Harriet had anticipated, and she had to park three blocks away from Pins and Needles in order find a spot big enough to lurch her car into.

"Hey, Carla," she said as she came into the quilt store. Her young friend was behind the counter. She explained her needle problem, and Carla showed her the array of needles Marjory stocked. Harriet ended up choosing a Jean Lyle big-eye quilting needle. It was short and should prove easy to thread.

"I heard one of the teachers in Angel Harbor say we should try quilting thread for our hand-piecing. She seemed to think it was easier to use," Carla offered.

"I'll try anything. It's hard to keep my thread from tangling when I use sewing thread, so maybe this will be the answer."

"Mavis told me to cut my length of thread shorter and it wouldn't tangle so much." Carla looked at her feet. "She said it didn't pay to be lazy."

"Threading a needle every five minutes isn't my idea of fun, so I guess I'm lazy."

"Mavis showed me how to wax the end of my thread on a candle and then load a whole package of needles onto my spool. You tie a knot in the end of the thread and then each time you want a new needle, you grab it and pull some thread out, then clip the thread and needle from the spool and retie the end of the spool piece."

"She's been holding out on me," Harriet said. Carla blushed. "That technique could really help me now. I think I'll get two packages of needles. My aunt can thread them on for me, and then I can stitch for quite a while without having to bug her."

Carla followed Harriet to the checkout counter, carrying the thread and needles for her. She rang up the purchase then hesitated as she put the items into one of the flowered bags Pins and Needles used for that purpose.

"Can I ask you a question?" she asked, looking everywhere except at Harriet. "About men," she added, her face turning the familiar red color.

"Sure," Harriet said, not sure she knew much more than Carla did where men were concerned.

"It's about the dinner I made the other night."

Harriet's mind immediately went to the practice meal Aiden had dumped her for, and wasn't sure if she'd be able to talk about it without her anger being obvious.

"I cooked dinner for Terry, my friend, the other night," she started then faltered. Of course—she was going to talk about the main event, Harriet thought with relief. Why would she give the practice dinner a second thought?

"And?" she prompted. "What happened?"

"He cancelled. I'd already prepared the do-ahead stuff and everything. What did I do wrong?" Carla pleaded.

"What did he say?"

"Nothing. We'd been talking about food. He said his mom wasn't a very inspired cook. I can't think of anything we talked about that would have scared him away."

"It probably wasn't anything to do with you," Harriet said. She put her good hand on Carla's shoulder. "Sometimes things happen that have nothing to do with us," she added, thinking that little bit of wisdom applied to most of her childhood.

"He had come over for coffee and we were talking about food. I was getting him warmed up so I could ask him, and then his phone made a noise and he looked at it."

"Could you see his phone screen?"

"I saw it light up, but I couldn't see if he got a text or what. I asked him if he could come to dinner that night, and he said no, so I said how about tomorrow and he said no, and I was afraid to ask anymore."

"Something must have come up. Someone contacted him, and he had to meet them or do something for them. Have you seen him since?"

"He stopped by here, but he made excuses for why he can't come to Aiden's house at night, and he did it before I could even try to invite him again. I'm starting to wonder if he's a vampire or something."

"It's daytime that vampires don't like, not night. Besides, you said he eats, right? And drinks coffee?"

"Just because they live on blood doesn't mean they can't eat food. They just don't need to. And they have to hunt at night."

"You don't seriously believe in vampires, do you?" Harriet couldn't believe she was having this conversation with Carla, of all people. If there was anyone acquainted with the real world, it was Carla.

Carla pulled a thick book with a black cover from under the counter, one of a popular teen vampire series.

"Come on, you know that's fiction."

"It sounds so real, though, the way the young man protects her."

"Oh, Carla, it's a nice fairy tale, but he's just like your knight when you were little and your mom locked you in the closet. He helped you through a rough time, but he wasn't a real person.

"I know," she said with a crooked smile. "But sometimes when people do weird stuff it's easier to believe in fairy tales."

"Do you think Aiden said something to him?" Harriet asked, pulling the conversation back to reality.

"Not that I know of. He's always been really friendly when Terry is there, and he usually goes to some other part of the house when Terry visits."

"Terry said he's trying to find people his dad worked with. Maybe he did."

"I don't think so. He doesn't like to talk about his dad."

"I'm not putting Terry down," Harriet said, "but there's something strange about his search for information about his father."

"What?"

"I'm not sure. He seems like a smart guy, but he's trying to find out about his dad by just asking around in a town they lived in once. It would make sense if his dad was still alive, but he isn't."

Carla leaned against the back counter and picked at her lip.

"I'm sorry I don't have better answers. I'm not that great with men myself." Harriet picked up her bag and started to leave. "Oh, before I forget, Mavis asked about extra-wide quilt backing." She described what Mavis was looking for, and Carla showed her the options, two of which seemed like possible choices.

"Tell you what," she said. "I'll talk to Aiden tonight and see what he thinks. He's a guy, maybe he can enlighten us."

Carla busied herself straightening a stack of postcards telling about an upcoming guild show.

"I could cook dinner for you," she said in a quiet voice.

"What?" Harriet asked, not hearing her clearly.

Carla looked up.

"Could you come to dinner tonight? I can try out another recipe your aunt Beth taught me."

"I think that would be delightful," Harriet said with an encouraging smile.

She left the store, heading for her car. Going home wasn't an appealing option right now, with the Willis family reunion going on, so she pointed her car toward Foggy Point Fire Protection. Like Gerry, Carlton had been a newly minted college graduate who had just joined the company twenty years ago. Now he owned the company—if anyone had answers, Carlton would.

She pulled into the visitors section of the parking lot and was relieved that the other spaces were empty.

"Hey, Lynn," she said when she entered the small reception area. Foggy Point Fire Protection was not the type of business that hosted a lot of customers onsite, so their waiting room had an industrial quality to it, with gray indoor/outdoor carpeting and two groupings of molded plastic chairs arranged around a stern mannequin wearing the company's signature fire protection gear.

"Oh, hi, Harriet. Do you need to see Carlton?" Lynn asked. Carlton's lack of cooperation during the lead-up to the reenactment had necessitated so many trips to his workplace Harriet had sworn she would never come here again, yet here she was for the second time in a week. "Did you find the man you were looking for?"

"Yes, I'd like to see Carlton, if he's in and no, I haven't found Mr. Jansen yet. By the way, has anyone else come by asking about my mystery man?"

"No, you're the only one's who's looked in those books in years. The way the economy's been, we haven't hired anyone in ages, so we haven't even added any new pictures."

"And you're sure no one else has asked to see the pictures or asked about anyone who used to work here?"

"Trust me. I'm here every day, eight to five. And on the rare occasion I leave my desk for lunch, I put the phones on automatic and lock the office. If someone called or came in, I'd know it."

"Okay, well, thanks," Harriet said, and Lynn flipped a switch on her phone and announced Harriet's presence into her headset.

"He'll be right out," she said.

Her phone rang, and she became engrossed with a customer placing a sizable order, or at least that's what it sounded like on

Lynn's side of the conversation, which she was broadcasting to the whole room. She was obviously used to having the place to herself.

"Harriet," Carlton boomed a few minutes later as he entered from the hallway. "Come in." He held his arm out, gesturing for her to precede him back into the hallway. "What's up?" he asked.

Another man might have asked "How can I help you?" but it wasn't in Carlton's nature to think of others.

"Are you making a new product?" she asked him when they were both seated in his office, him behind and her in front of his desk.

"Well," he said, and stopped twirling the pencil he'd been toying with. "Why do you ask?"

Good question, Harriet thought. "I heard someone say they thought you were going to start a new product line, and I wondered if that meant you would be hiring. I know someone who's looking for work." It sounded lame even to her, but Carlton didn't seem to notice.

"Carlton, baby, let's get out of here," Bebe said as she sauntered into the office. She was wearing a pale-pink tube top and dark blue denim skirt that was almost conservative, falling only six inches above her tanned knees. "We have lunch reservations at Bella Italia in Port Angeles."

"I didn't think they were open for lunch," Harriet said.

"Oh, hi, Harriet," Bebe said. "They aren't open to the *public* till four, but they're opening early for us." She looked at the pink-faced, gold Juicy Couture charm watch on her left wrist. "Say bye, Carlton, we gotta go."

Carlton got up and grabbed his linen sport coat then plucked his car keys from a ceramic ashtray on his desk.

"Sorry, Harriet, I've got to run," he said, and left through a back door to the outside.

"Don't worry, I'll show myself out," Harriet said but didn't move. As long as she was here, she might as well have a look around.

She stood and glanced through the open door. Lynn was still sitting at her desk and talking on her headset. Harriet went around the desk and sat in Carlton's chair. There were stacks of papers and files on both sides of the center blotter. The first folder she opened contained a flyer from a company that supplied premium items with the company logo on them. A note clipped to the flyer instructed Carlton to pick his two favorite colors for the insulated cup holders the company would be handing out at the annual picnic.

The next folder contained his credit card bill and a stack of receipts that looked like they matched the charges. The third folder was the information she'd asked him for—a list of projects Gerald had worked on. She wasn't sure how it was going to help, but she took the list from the folder, folded it in half and tucked it into her sling.

A quick glance through the remaining files and papers revealed more of the same—busy work. The company managers obviously gave Carlton just enough to keep him busy the few hours he was in the office but kept him far away from the actual running of the business.

After another quick check into the hallway, she returned to Carlton's desk and tried the drawers. They were locked, all of them. She yanked on the handle of what should be a file drawer. Not only was the drawer locked but it appeared to have more than the usual flimsy device that was standard issue on most office furniture.

Carlton's bookshelves held a few titles on business subjects that appeared to have never had their spines cracked. The rest of the shelves were filled with framed pictures of Carlton and his parents, Carlton and Bebe, and Bebe standing by an array of pink cars and boats, wearing an assortment of pink nautical outfits.

Harriet took one last look around the office then stepped quietly into the hallway and left through the same back door Carlton and Bebe had used twenty minutes earlier.

✂ ✂ ✂

Aiden was standing on the porch to the vet hospital stretching his arms over his head then reaching down and touching his toes when Harriet drove past. She pulled into the next driveway she came to and turned around.

"Did you finish your surgeries?" she asked when she'd parked and gotten out of her car. He met her on the sidewalk.

"Yeah, I just finished. Do you have time for a cup of coffee?"

"Sure," she said. "I wanted to ask you something anyway."

"Let me tell them where I'm going," he said with a nod back toward the clinic.

"I'll drive," he said when he'd returned. "I can't believe you're safe tooling around with that thing on your arm."

"Lucky for me there's no traffic to speak of this time of day."

He helped her into the car and then drove them the dozen blocks to Annie's Coffee Shop on Ship Street. Harriet sat at a table while he ordered their drinks. He was still wearing blue surgical scrubs, and Harriet couldn't help but admire how well he filled them out.

"What are you staring at?" he asked when he came back and sat down opposite her at the dark wood table.

"I was just noting how well your scrubs fit," she admitted.

"You do know what we wear under these, don't you?"

"You're going to make me blush if you keep talking like that."

Aiden twined his fingers in hers. "Is that a bad thing?" he said with a roguish smile.

She was saved from answering by the arrival of their drinks—Aiden's cafe Americano her tamer hot cocoa.

"I had an interesting morning," she said when Annie had returned to the coffee bar. She recounted her talk with Carla and her visit to Foggy Point Fire Protection.

"I know you like Terry, but I still think there's something going on with him, and I think Carla's starting to suspect something, too. She didn't quite say it that way, but she knows something isn't right."

"I hate to say it, but I'm starting to wonder myself. I didn't want to say anything to Carla, but it seems weird to me he was at the house night and day for a couple of weeks and now all of a sudden he's only around in the morning. But he claims he's on vacation, and he says he hasn't found anything out about his dad. If that's true, what's he doing at night that's keeping him from seeing Carla?"

"That's what I was wondering. And I have an idea."

"Now I'm afraid."

"It's not dangerous or anything. I think we should follow him. Tonight."

"I knew I should be afraid. We aren't detectives. You're a quilter and I'm a vet—we don't follow people."

"But we could. I think Carla knows where he's staying. We follow him, and when we find out he joined a bowling league and is practicing his game every evening, we can tell Carla and then she won't be worried that she's done something wrong."

"What if we follow him and he goes to the docks and picks up a drug shipment? What then?"

She didn't say anything.

"Didn't think of that, did you? We might find out things we don't want to know."

"If he's a drug dealer or worse we do need to know that. It might break Carla's heart, but she needs to know if it's something like that."

"I can't believe I'm saying this, but okay, say we're going to follow Terry. Do you have any idea how to do that without being detected immediately?" he asked.

"I have a few ideas," she said with a smile. She picked up her cup and took a sip.

"Since I did early surgery I can be off by four." He took a drink from his cup.

"Carla invited me to dinner at your house tonight. She wants to do another practice dinner. I'll call her and see how early we can do it."

"Shall I pick you up on my way home?"

"No, my plan requires us each to have a car."

"You're starting to make me nervous."

"It's going to be fine. We're going to find out where Terry goes at night, and he'll be none the wiser."

Aiden glanced at his watch. "I better go. I need to make sure everybody woke up okay after their surgeries. I hate to leave you on your own when you're like this."

"I think I've just been insulted."

"You know what I mean. When you're trying to help one of your friends, you take risks—it scares me."

"I'm not taking any risks!"

Aiden tugged on the edge of her sling with his fingers. "Says the woman with the broken collar bone."

"I was not taking a risk when this happened. I was walking in a public park."

"Yeah, which just happens to be the scene of a crime."

"It was broad daylight," Harriet argued, her voice rising slightly.

"I don't like to see you hurt," he said softly and stood up.

She stood up, too, and leaned into him as he put his arm carefully around her shoulders.

"I won't get hurt again. You'll be with me, remember?"

He guided her past the dirty cup station and out to the car.

"I'm going to go back home and see what the Willis gang is up to," she said as they drove back to the Animal Hospital.

"I hope they're keeping their hands to themselves."

"They've got bigger fish to fry. They're waiting for James to arrive."

"He's the lawyer?"

"Yeah, and unfortunately, it's not hard to imagine more than one reason Mavis could need one."

"She'll be alright. She's a tough old bird."

"Not this time. You haven't seen her like I have. She cried when she found that quilt in her house. Have you ever seen her cry?"

"I'm sure with you helping it will all be sorted out."

"I wish I had your confidence."

"See you tonight," he said when she was once again behind the wheel of her car. He leaned in the open window and kissed her. She smiled when he started to pull away, and pulled him back for seconds before she raised her window and drove away.

✂ ✂ ✂

Aunt Beth was working on the long arm machine when Harriet came into the studio.

"Hi," she said and then realized her aunt wasn't alone. A tall red-head Harriet didn't recognize was sitting at her computer. The presence of Harry and Ben on either side of the man meant that this had to be Mavis's second-to-oldest son, James the attorney.

"I hope you don't mind," Aunt Beth said. "I told James it would be okay for him to use your computer."

"Sorry," James said from behind the monitor. "Your wifi is password protected, so I couldn't use my laptop."

"It's no problem. If it will help your mom, use it all you need. Where is she, by the way?"

"She went to see that woman," Harry said.

"Ilsa?" Harriet asked. "Why is she seeing Ilsa?"

"The woman called and wanted to talk about the funeral. They decided to meet with Pastor Hafer to help figure things out."

"So have you found out anything interesting yet?"

"It's really weird," Ben said without looking up. James was furiously clicking the mouse.

"Mom might not be cheating the insurance company after all." Harry offered.

"What do you mean?" Harriet put her purse down and went over.

"He means the company issuing the payment checks to our mom doesn't seem to exist." James stood up and held out his hand. "I'm James, by the way. I'm assuming you're Harriet."

"I am," Harriet said, and took his hand awkwardly in her left one. "Nice to meet you. Your mom is very proud of you."

"That's embarrassing," James said. "Usually Mom just apologizes for the misdeeds of our youth."

"She quit including you in that when you passed the bar," Harry said.

"So, tell me about the insurance payments," Harriet said.

"Something very strange is going on," James explained. "She is supposedly receiving widow's benefits from Dad's company insurance. I use the term *supposedly* because I can't find any record of the insurance company that's issuing the checks. As near as I can tell, the checks are being auto-drafted from a bank account. Gerry told me the name of the insurance carrier the company uses now, and they have no record of any type of payout to my mom."

"Where does that leave her?" Harriet asked.

"It could mean several things. It might simply mean we didn't find the insurance company. It's not unusual that a company the size of Foggy Point Fire might have changed insurance carriers more than once or twice in a twenty-year period. That being said, it *is* unusual that we couldn't find the company.

"Mom's checks are no help, as they don't have a company name, only a numerical ID. Even with her power of attorney, I got nowhere on the phone with the bank. They won't tell me who the account holder is. It's possible Foggy Point Fire chose to carry their own paper."

"So?" Harriet asked.

"It means they didn't have a policy through a company. They simply set aside a large pot of money that could be used if needed but otherwise belongs to the company. Remember, the company was pretty small back then. The rules change when you get bigger."

"So, now what?"

"I'm going to hire an investigator; I know a guy who specializes in this type of search. We can't begin to assess where Mom stands until we can talk to whatever entity has been providing the money."

"It's not like Mom was trying to defraud the insurance company," Ben said. "She really thought Dad was dead."

"Unfortunately, as far as the law is concerned, ignorance isn't considered a valid argument in most proceedings."

"What about Social Security?" Harriet asked.

"I was in law school when Dad died." James said. "Gerry worked at the company, but he had just started and the rest of the boys were still in school. Mom didn't talk to any of us about her financial situation. Mom says Carlton's dad Marvin advised her not to apply for Social Security for herself or the boys at that point. I'll have to do a little research to find out why he would have said that, but frankly, right now, I'm glad she didn't."

He leaned back in the chair and rubbed his hands over his face and then his head. "I haven't looked at the second wife and Dad's estate yet. That could be a real can of worms, given that his second marriage was in a foreign country." He pulled a small notebook out of his shirt pocket and made a note. "I'll get someone to research that for me. If we're lucky, Mom's marriage will be the valid one."

"What a mess," Harriet said.

"Dad must have known how this would wreck Mom's life," Harry said. "Why would he just disappear?"

"Don't even go there," James said. "Dad's dead. We may never know why he left. We need to concentrate on Mom."

"I agree we need to take care of Mom, but I need to know who killed Dad and why," Ben said.

The outside studio door opened, and Mavis entered. Harriet couldn't help but notice the new-looking black shirt-style jacket that had replaced her usual man's plaid flannel shirt. In her mind's eye, Harriet imagined Mavis in her back yard burning a pile of similar flannel shirts she had been wearing and carefully repairing for almost twenty years; her personal shrine to the husband she'd thought she'd lost.

"What was the old saying when you guys were all at home? Any time you see three Willis boys together in one place, trouble is sure to follow." Mavis crossed the entry area and stood in front of her offspring.

"Mom, I'm injured," James said with a hint of the boyish smile that had helped him charm his way out of trouble. Harriet wondered if he used it on juries.

"Yeah," Harry added. "Cut us to the quick."

"We're trying to keep you out of jail, if you must know," Ben said.

"And just how are you doing that?" Mavis asked, and poked a finger into his chest.

"Well, technically, I guess you could say I'm not, but I'm helping James."

"That's what I thought. He always has been able to get you to do his dirty work."

"Seriously, Mom," James said. "We're trying to figure your widow's benefits out. If you can remember anything else about that time, it could help."

Mavis returned to the sitting area and settled in one of the wing-back chairs. Aunt Beth joined her, taking the chair opposite her friend.

"Your mom has thought about this all she can," Beth said. "Your dad had just died then, and he's just died again now. Let her be until she can catch up with herself. Harry, you go put the water on for tea. Ben, put some of those chocolate chip cookies on the cooling rack on a plate and bring them in here."

"You made cookies while I was gone?" Harriet said, but no one was listening to her.

"James, take a break."

The attorney looked like he was going to protest, but one look at Aunt Beth changed his mind.

"I'll go make some calls in the living room," he said. "Mom, I'll talk to you later."

"You just sit back and relax," Aunt Beth ordered.

"I need to make some calls myself," Harriet said, and followed James through the connecting door into the kitchen. She went to the refrigerator and took out a can of foul-smelling cat food and scooped out a portion for Fred. "Don't eat it all in one bite," she said as he flew off his strangers-in-the-kitchen perch on top of the hallway bookcase and dove at his dish.

"Don't mind my aunt," she said to the collected Willis men. "She's protective of her friends."

"You don't have to apologize for your aunt," Ben said. "We've lived it."

"Our mom probably taught your aunt her best tricks," Harry added.

Harriet offered a few directions about where to find additional snacks and went to her bedroom to place her calls.

She came downstairs a half-hour later and strode across the kitchen and into the studio.

"I'm going out for a little while," she told her aunt and Mavis as she picked up her purse and headed for the door. "I'll be back shortly."

She was out before either of them could ask any questions. Aunt Beth appeared in the doorway, but by that time Harriet had backed her car up and turned it down the driveway toward town. She knew her aunt wouldn't approve of her planned evening's activities.

✂ ✂ ✂

Connie was speaking in rapidfire Spanish to Jorge when Harriet came into Tico's Tacos a few minutes later.

"Hola, chiquita," Connie said and pulled Harriet into a bear hug. "I filled Jorge in on the plan. He can't leave here, but he's preparing snacks for each team."

"Thanks, Jorge."

Jorge tipped his ball cap to her in acknowledgment. She took a deep breath. He was roasting peppers, and the smell permeated the room.

"I'll have to have a snack after smelling the wonderful aroma in here."

"I pulled a couple of tables together in the back room," he said, and indicated a doorway near the kitchen. "And I packed a container of guacamole with roasted peppers for you."

Harriet thanked him and crossed to the door he was now holding open for her.

She had never been in that part of the restaurant. Woven serapes in pinks, greens and yellows were draped on the walls with ornately embellished sombreros in complimentary colors positioned between each pair. Two square wooden picnic-style tables had been pushed together. Robin and DeAnn sat on benches opposite each other, sipping icy glasses of lemonade, a pitcher and additional glasses between them on the table.

Robin was dressed in her usual capri-length black yoga pants, but this time her customary pastel sleeveless top had been replaced by its black counterpart. DeAnn had on black shorts and a black T-shirt.

"We're ready," Robin said.

"Well, we think we're ready," DeAnn amended. "We haven't heard the plan yet."

"Did I miss a memo?" Lauren asked as she entered the back room and poured a glass of lemonade. She indicated her khaki shorts and pale blue T-shirt.

"We don't have a dress code, if that's what you're asking," Harriet said. "We're going to be in cars."

"Oh, my gosh," Lauren said as a realization hit her. "Did you think we were going to be skulking around in the bushes?" she asked DeAnn. "Did you think black shorts would make up for your fluorescent white legs?"

"Okay, Lauren, we're all a little nervous. You don't need to settle yours by picking on DeAnn or anyone else," Connie said in her teacher voice, which was less accented than her casual one.

Lauren took her glass and sat down at the end of the table. Jorge opened the door and held it for Jenny, who had also come dressed in black—knee-length shorts and a sleeveless hooded tunic. Her silver hair was pulled back in a low ponytail.

"Here is another conspirator." He laughed and went back to work in the kitchen.

A few minutes later, Sarah let herself in.

"This better be good," she announced. "I canceled a hot date for this." She was dressed in a creased navy blue cotton blazer and gray slacks. Harriet hoped she'd been planning on changing before her date.

When everyone was seated and had drinks, Harriet cleared her throat, then waited until everyone stopped speaking.

"Thanks for coming on such short notice."

Sarah started to reply, but Connie clamped a hand on her wrist and she closed her mouth.

"I'm sorry I was so mysterious on the phone, but I decided it would be better to talk about this in person. As you all know, Carla's been seeing a new fellow. He's a stranger in town, but that's not necessarily a bad thing. He's been very kind and attentive, and he's a natural with Wendy."

"That all sounds good," Jenny said. "What's the problem?"

"I'm not sure there is a problem, but that's what I want your help to find out. All of a sudden, Carla's friend Terry is unavailable at night."

Several started to talk at once, and she held up her good hand to silence them.

"There could be any number of valid reasons for Terry to be otherwise occupied at night."

"But you don't think so," DeAnn said.

"I don't know. Maybe I'm being paranoid, but there's something off about his whole story. He's supposed to be here finding people who knew his dad, who he says worked at Foggy Point Foggy Fire Protection when Terry was little. The trouble is, I've talked to Carlton and looked in their employee picture book, and there are no Jansen's. He looks like he's military, but Carla said he was in the SEALs and *he* said he was an army paramedic in Iraq. Those are two very different things."

"If he's not looking for his dad's past, why is he here?" Connie asked.

"That's what I'm hoping we're going to find out. Listen, Terry's been going somewhere every evening, and I intend to find out where."

"What do you want us to do?" Jenny asked.

"First, I'd like to say that if anyone is uncomfortable with the idea of following someone or, for that matter, meddling in Carla's business, feel free to exclude yourself. No hard feelings."

"For crying out loud," Lauren said. "We're all here, aren't we? Let's get on with it."

"Okay, I've broken us up into teams. Most of us won't start until later, but I'd like one group to sit down the street from his motel—he's at Pine Villa over at Smuggler's Cove. I dialed for dollars among the cheap motels and got lucky on the third try.

"The rest of us will wait for a call from that team." She took a sip from her glass of lemonade. "There aren't that many routes he could take and still be in Foggy Point, and until I learn different, I'm going to assume his target is here."

"So, one of us will pick him up when he commits to a route?" DeAnn asked.

"That's the idea. Then the other teams will circle around to the next forks in the road. Each time he turns onto a road, the other cars will position themselves along his possible routes and pick him up. That way, he won't see a particular car following him."

Jorge came into the room again. He carried a stack of folded maps.

"Here, you can have these," he said, and handed them to Harriet. "The Business Association had these printed up for the tourists. They have all the streets in Foggy Point."

She looked at him with amazement. He laughed and pointed to a speaker mounted near the ceiling in a corner of the room.

"Intercom," he said, and left the room with a laugh.

"You didn't sweep the room for bugs before we started?" Lauren asked in disbelief.

Harriet laughed. "Somehow, I never guessed Jorge had the place bugged for his own purposes."

"Don't forget I can hear you," said a disembodied voice, followed by a maniacal cackle.

"Now, one more thing," Harriet said. "Does everyone know how to use conference call and speaker phone on your cell phone?"

She waited while everyone pulled out their phones.

"I'm not sure I know how to do conference calls," Connie said.

"Me, either," Jenny said.

"Okay, let's see what kind of phone we all have."

Lauren and Jenny both had the style with a segment that flipped up and spun around. Connie had an iPhone. Robin and DeAnn had the same brand of smartphone, and Sarah had one that was similar.

"Come on, Jenny," Lauren said. "I can see where this is going. Let me show you how to make a conference call."

They divided up by phone style and began making calls to each other, practicing until each one could quickly initiate a conference call and add in the rest of the members, using speaker phone or not at will.

"Okay," Harriet said finally. "Is everyone comfortable with our communication plan?"

"We get the phones," Lauren said, "but let's run over the plan."

"Who wants to sit outside the motel until he moves?" Harriet asked. "I would, but I'm supposed to eat at Carla's first. I told her I needed to eat early, so we should be done well before dark. I'm making an assumption about him waiting until dark, based on when he's visited Carla, but I could be wrong, so I'd like to have someone there pretty much as soon as we're finished here. We can take one- or two-hour shifts. It doesn't have to be the same person the whole time."

"I took the rest of the day off," Sarah said. "I can go sit there. I don't need a copilot until close to dark when we think he's going to move. I have a new Carola Dunn novel to read."

"That's good," Connie said. "I can join her around seven."

"Everyone needs to keep their phones close to them and turned on. If he moves early, we'll have to react quickly," Harriet cautioned. "Let's get our maps out and mark the intersections where we'll place the follow cars."

They spent the next half-hour marking their maps and deciding who would do each part of the plan. When they finished, Jorge came in with bags marked with each of their names. Sarah's was the fullest, and in addition, Jorge instructed her to choose the drinks of her choice to go along with it. He had packed Harriet's guacamole in a plastic bag with ice.

"Thank you so much," Harriet told him as the women filed out.

"De nada," Jorge said. He hugged her, being careful of her shoulder, and sent her on her way.

✂ ✂ ✂

Mavis and Aunt Beth had moved into the kitchen and were sitting at the island bar with mugs of hot tea in front of them.

"What have you been up to?" Aunt Beth demanded.

"Oh, just checking up on Carla's new boyfriend," she said, trying to maintain a casual tone in her voice.

"What did you find out?" Beth asked.

"Nothing yet," Harriet said. "I'm just having trouble believing his story about why he's here. I'm not going to give up until I find out the truth, either." She reached between the two women and grabbed a cookie from the plate on the bar. "Mmm, these are good."

"And you should be snacking on fruit," Aunt Beth scolded.

"What have you two been up to?"

Mavis sighed. "Ilsa and I met with Pastor Hafer and planned a funeral for Gerard. He's an amazing preacher.

"The service will be divided to address the two parts of Gerard's life, then he'll talk about how we may never know how or why this one man had two lives, but that both parts were, in fact, one man fulfilling God's plan for him."

Her tone of voice let Harriet know she wasn't fully buying it yet, and she couldn't help but notice she was calling him Gerard instead of Gerald now.

"When will it be?"

"We have to wait until the police release his body, but they told Ilsa they expect to be able to do that in another day or so. Given a day or two to notify people, it will probably be early next week."

"If there's anything I can do, just say it," Harriet said.

"I wish there *was* something you could do. I need to know what happened twenty years ago and what happened this last week. Until I know that, there's nothing anyone can do."

Harriet grabbed a second cookie and retreated to her bedroom, where she called Aiden's cell phone and left him a message, letting him know there had been a change in her as-yet-unrevealed-to-him plan and he would now be required to pick her up. When she'd finished, she called Carla to see if she needed them to bring anything to dinner. Carla said she thought she had everything and was anxiously awaiting their arrival.

✂ ✂ ✂

"Where is everybody?" Aiden asked an hour later when he came into the studio. Harriet was sitting alone at her computer.

"Aunt Beth finished the show quilt she was working on and went home. The Willis group is having a family dinner later at Mama Theresa's. They've all scattered to points unknown in the meantime, so me and Fred are all you get."

"I'll take it," he said and crossed the room quickly, scooping her into his arms and kissing her. He kept his arms around her as he looked into her eyes. He sighed. "Something tells me we aren't going to be late to dinner because we're taking advantage of your empty house and making out."

"That would be a good guess," Harriet said and stepped away from him. "Not because I don't want to, but we've got a mission tonight and we need to get started."

"Okay, the suspense is going to kill me before dinner's over. What's the plan?"

"Actually, the plan is already in motion. We're following Terry to see where he's going at night."

"We who? We you and me? What have we already started?"

"I realized Foggy Point's too small for the two of us to follow Terry without him noticing, so I called the Loose Threads." She started pacing between her desk and the long arm machine.

"I knew I wasn't going to like this."

"Wait until you hear the plan," Harriet said, and explained how the Threads would position themselves at successive intersections, the last cars leapfrogging ahead based on Terry's moves and the lead car dropping off as he turned onto new roads. "He won't have a single car following him more than a few blocks at a time. We'll communicate with our cell phones."

"Okay, I hate to admit it, but that could work, and I like that you're working in teams. But say you follow him and you find him…" He paused. "…somewhere. What then?"

"I don't know, I'll have to see where he goes. If he meets up with other people, we could follow them, or if he's obviously dealing drugs or some other criminal activity, I'll call nine-one-one. I really don't know what the next step is. I just have to do something, and this is all I can think of."

Aiden grabbed her good hand as she came back toward her desk. He pulled her into his arms again.

"You know what I like about you?" he said. "Your loyalty to your friends—even the ones you don't like, you still defend."

"You're going to make me blush, talking that way," Harriet said. "But seriously, Carla's life has been so hard. I can't stand the idea that this guy is just using her. She deserves better. And who knows—there's always the chance that I'm wrong."

"But you don't think so, and like I said before, I'm starting to think you're right."

"So, what are we hanging around here for? Let's go eat with Carla so we can get on with tailing Terry."

"Your chariot awaits, madam." Aiden bowed low at the waist and ushered her out.

Chapter 19

Carla's dinner went by in a blur. Her baked chicken was moist and her corn on the cob was tender and sweet. Wendy climbed into Harriet's lap with her book about a bunny that lived in a tree right after they arrived. No matter how distracted Harriet was by the upcoming events, her heart melted a little when the toddler put her arms around her neck and hugged her when they'd finished reading.

Aiden and Harriet both assured Carla her cooking was wonderful, and that she'd set a beautiful summer table. They helped clear the dishes while Carla cut slices of apple pie. The crust had been patched in places, but the apples had a caramel flavor that was incredible. Harriet decided she'd ask about the recipe when she had both the time and the attention to actually retain the answer.

"Would you like some more coffee or tea?" Carla asked when they had finished their pie.

"I hate to eat and run," Harriet said, "but I have to go to a meeting."

"You have to go to a meeting?" Aiden repeated when they'd said their goodbyes and were walking from the porch to the car.

"It *is* a meeting. We're just all in different cars," she said with a smile. "What did you want me to do? Tell her we had to go so we could spy on her boyfriend?"

"Where are we supposed to go?"

Harriet was spared having to answer by the ring of her cell phone.

"It's Sarah," she said, and put the call on speaker phone.

"This is Silver Needle reporting. The stitch is running. Repeat, the stitch is running."

Aiden started laughing.

"What?" Lauren said in the faraway voice created by the conference call and speaker phone combination.

"Terry's moving," Sarah said in disgust. "He's headed into downtown Foggy Point, just like we expected."

Terry had not moved early, so the other two cars would be in place along two of the three main roads leading out of downtown. Aiden turned up a steep side street that would allow them to drop down onto the third option before Terry got there, should he choose that route.

"Good work, Silver Needle," said Harriet, getting into the spirit of things. "Roll toward town, and as soon as he commits to a route, we'll let you know where to go next."

"Silver Needle?" Aiden said when Harriet had disconnected.

"Hey, whatever works. Besides, what's wrong with having a little fun along the way?"

"This isn't a laughing matter," he said, serious again. "You have no idea what this guy is into." He pulled to the curb and parked just before the through street, leaving the engine running.

Harriet's phone rang again. She pressed the talk button followed by the speaker phone option.

"Silk Thread here," came Jenny's voice. "He turned toward the strait. Lauren's got one car between him and us."

"Good job," Harriet said. "Robin?"

"We're here," Robin answered. "That is, Cotton Thread here," she corrected, and Harriet could hear the laughter in her voice.

"You two go down the beach road a little way. Aiden and I will be parallel and three blocks over in case he goes inland."

"Sarah?" There was no acknowledgment. "Silver Needle?" she tried.

"Silver Needle here," Sarah said. "Can you go back into town and then take the shortcut through Fogg Park to the spot we marked in yellow on the map?"

"Will do. Thimble, over and out."

"You ladies are nuts," Aiden said as he drove to their next position.

Once again the phone rang.

"Harriet?" said Jenny. "You've got him. There's a small red truck in front of a yellow van and then he's the gray sedan."

"Everyone get that?" Harriet asked.

"Okay, we know where to go next," Robin said.

"We're still aiming for the yellow spot," Connie said.

Harriet spotted the red truck as she disconnected the call. Aiden let another car pass before he pulled out into the flow of traffic. They drove up a long curving slope that had transitioned from planned housing developments to single houses and then to grassy fields interspersed with sections of forest on both sides of the road.

"Hello," Aiden said as they came up a slight rise and drove past the gray sedan, parked at the side of the road.

Harriet picked up her phone and dialed the others.

"Listen up, everyone," she said. "Our subject has left his car and is traveling overland. He's headed into the woods on the back side of Miller Hill. Aiden and I will follow on foot. Robin and DeAnn, you two stay on the beach road in case he goes over the hill and keeps going. Silver Needle, you take the west side of Miller Hill, and Lauren, you two take the east side of the hill. Go up to that little park near the top that has the mineral water well and wait for Aiden and I to show up on foot. I'm assuming he won't stop before the top, since there's nothing between here and there."

"I hate to rain on your parade," Lauren said, "but other than the park, there's nothing *anywhere* on Miller Hill. He's either meeting someone in the woods or he's on to us."

"I guess we're going to have to follow him to find out, then, aren't we?"

"Over and out," Lauren said and disconnected.

Less than a quarter-mile past Terry's gray car was the wide mouth to a gated drive that was set back from the road. Aiden parked several car lengths past the gate, got out and went around to the back. He rummaged around and pulled out a pair of binoculars and a gallon jug.

"What are you doing?" Harriet asked.

"Props," he said. "When we run into Terry and he asks what we're doing, I want to have some crumb of credibility. I'm birdwatching and you're getting some of that famous Miller Spring mineral water. Let's go."

He led the way back along the shoulder of the road and then into the knee high grass that bordered the forested top of Miller Hill. They reached the parking area adjacent to the well and its pump without encountering Terry. Lauren and Jenny pulled into the lot right after Aiden and Harriet arrived.

"I'm going to make use of the restroom as long as we're here and he isn't," Harriet said.

"You're not going alone," Lauren said. "Not after last time," she added, referring to Harriet's kidnapping from a restroom at the Angel Harbor Folk Art School a few months earlier.

"Fine, come on, then."

Aiden walked to the far edge of the clearing and put the binoculars to his eyes.

Jenny joined the trek to the restroom. She flipped her hood up to cover her silver hair. Aiden was standing outside the small building when they came back out.

"Did you see anything?" Harriet asked. It wasn't dark yet, but the sun was almost down, so it wasn't likely he could see much, but he might have gotten lucky.

"I can't see him clearly, but he's sitting on a big rock on a slight rise with his back to us, as near as I can tell. From the position he's in, my guess is he's using binoculars. The angle is wrong for me to see what he's looking at."

"You could have just asked me," said Terry as he came out of the forest.

"What are you talking about?" Harriet asked.

"Could we please not waste both of our time? Since you're here and insisting on sticking your nose into my business, maybe you can help me."

"I'm sure I don't know what you mean," Harriet insisted.

"Harriet," Aiden said. "You're busted. Let's hear the man out."

"How did you know we were following you?" Lauren asked.

"I didn't know *you* were. I spotted the car that sat in front of my motel all afternoon almost immediately—the plates belong to some kind of senior living center. I didn't know how that fit, but when I passed Aiden and Harriet parked on the side street, it started to come together."

"So, get to the part where you tell us why you're spying on someone else," Lauren demanded.

"Let me show you. Stay behind me and stay low when we crest the rise," Terry said. "And you..." He indicated Lauren. "Do you have something dark you can put over your shirt?"

"I've got a navy windbreaker," she said, and went to her car to get it.

When Lauren was properly dressed, the group set off down the path through the woods, and then through the grass and up the small rise. Terry signaled them to stop before they reached the rock.

"Come and look, one at a time," he said.

Harriet followed him up to the rock. Below them was Foggy Point Fire Protection. She looked at him, and would have asked a question if he hadn't held his finger to her lips.

"Just look," he whispered. "We can talk back at the park." He handed her a set of low-light binoculars.

Foggy Point Fire Protection was bustling. Garage-style doors stood open at one end of the main building. Light poured out, and she could see people moving about inside. A forklift carrying a pallet of boxes came around the end of the building and went inside the open doors. Harriet sucked in her breath, and Terry once again put a finger to her lips. He took the binoculars and led her back to the others. He took Lauren next and then Aiden and Jenny.

Everyone started talking at once when Jenny and Terry got back from the rock.

Terry held up his hand.

"Please," he said. "Am I correct that the fire turn-out company doesn't run a night shift?"

"They don't," Jenny said. "And haven't for a long time."

"Have any of you heard anything about them renting out the company to someone else to make a different product?"

They all shook their heads.

"I *have* seen a few new people in town who didn't look like they belonged here," Lauren said. "Besides you, that is."

"That doesn't mean anything," Jenny said. "We do have a small seasonal work force this time of year. They work at the organic farm out past Smuggler's Cove."

"Okay," Aiden said, and took a step toward Terry. "It's time for you to tell us why you're spying on the factory and why you're in Foggy Point. The real reason this time."

At six-foot-three, Aiden could look imposing when he wanted to. Harriet didn't know what had happened to him during the three years he'd spent doing animal research in Uganda, but there was an underlying toughness to him she guessed hadn't been there prior to his trip to Africa.

"I have to get down there." Terry looked at the black Luminox watch on his wrist. "I'm meeting a guy. It's almost his break time. I'll know more after I talk to him. I promise, I'll tell you what this is about later."

Aiden started to grab Terry's arm, but Harriet stopped him.

"Let him go," she said.

Terry gave her a grateful look and took off through the woods.

"What now, Mata Hari," Aiden asked.

Jenny pulled her hood off and repositioned her short ponytail.

I'll call off the others," she said. "Shall we meet back at Tico's?"

"I'll call Jorge and make sure no one else is using spy central," Lauren said.

"They're right," Harriet said. "We need to get together with the Threads."

✂ ✂ ✂

Harriet called Aunt Beth on the ride back to Tico's Tacos. She knew that, even though her aunt would have nixed the idea of following Terry, she'd want to be in on the results of the enterprise.

"So, let me get this straight," Aunt Beth said when the Loose Threads and Aiden were all seated in Tico's back room and Jorge had supplied iced tea and lemonade for all of them—minus Sarah, who had presumably gone to salvage her hot date. "You followed Terry because you were suspicious about where he went every night. You discovered he's following someone else for reasons unknown."

"That pretty much sums it up," Aiden said. "I wanted to squeeze it out of him, but your niece wouldn't let me."

"He said he'd tell us everything as soon as he met with his source," Harriet reminded him.

"And of course you believed him because you trusted him so much. He's so trustworthy you had to follow him all over Foggy Point tonight."

"He had official binoculars," Connie offered.

"And of course that means he's legit," Aunt Beth said.

"It doesn't mean he's legit," Harriet said. "But the important part isn't what he's doing. it's more what he's not doing."

"We were trying to see if he was doing something that would be harmful to Carla," Lauren said. "I didn't see anything we should worry about."

"What kind of person skulks around at night following other people who are probably doing something perfectly legitimate?" Aunt Beth said. "I don't think you've proved anything. In fact," she continued, "from where I'm sitting, you've raised more questions than you've answered."

Jorge brought a platter heaped with cheese-drenched nachos and set it in the middle of the picnic table.

"Dig in folks, it'll help you think more clearly," he said.

Aiden had just scooped a tortilla chip dripping with cheese into the beans and salsa on the edge of the platter when his pager sounded. Harriet took the gooey bite from his hand and ate it as he called the animal clinic.

"Gotta go," he said. "Can you get a ride?"

"Of course she can," Connie said. "You go save the animal world."

"Let's talk about what we know," Robin said, and pulled the yellow tablet and a pen from her purse.

"Terry is following someone," DeAnn offered.

"Not following," Lauren corrected. "He's spying on someone at Carlton's factory. I take that back. He's spying on the factory. We don't have any evidence he is spying on a particular person."

"Good point," Harriet said grudgingly. "He was spying on the activity taking place at the factory. Right now, we don't know if there is anything unusual about what's going on there. Just because we don't know about a night shift doesn't mean there isn't one."

"So, that's the first thing we need to figure out," Robin said. "If Terry is spying on the ordinary operation of a factory, then we have to wonder what he's up to and if he's planning some criminal activity. If, as he tried to lead us to believe, there is something wrong with what's happening at the factory, then we have to wonder why Terry's involved in spying on that wrong activity."

"He said he was meeting someone there, so we can't really say he was spying on the factory," DeAnn pointed out. "He could have been verifying that his friend was there before he went down."

"You're quite the spies," Aunt Beth said with a laugh. "You've just concluded that after all that following, you really don't know anything."

"We learned that Terry has some interest in Foggy Point Fire Protection and whatever is going on there at night," Harriet told her.

"At last," Aunt Beth said. "That is a fact."

"What do we do next?" DeAnn asked.

"I should be able to find out what's going on at Foggy Point Fire," Harriet said. "Two of the Willis boys are staying at my house, and Gerry's been coming over to talk with them. They're all trying to sort out what happened with their dad. If Gerry is at my place when I get home, I'll ask him. If not, I can ask him or Carlton tomorrow."

"That'll be a good start," Robin said.

"Speaking of the Willis boys and the questions about their father," Connie said, "do you suppose there is some connection between Terry and Ilsa? I mean, they both came to town at the same time and they both were following someone."

"Whoa," Lauren said.

"Could he be her son?" DeAnn wondered.

"If you're asking whether he could be *Gerald's* son," Aunt Beth said, "I don't think so. At least, not if he was born after he and Ilsa were married. He was gone not quite twenty years, and Ilsa says they've only been married fifteen. But of course that assumes everyone is telling the truth."

"That's a slippery slope to go down," Harriet said. "If we're questioning everything, Ilsa and Gerald might have had a relationship before he left. He did travel, didn't he?"

"You all aren't old enough to really know the man. I'd bet my life he wasn't having an affair on Mavis," Beth said. "Unless Terry is fourteen, he's not Gerard's son. That doesn't preclude the possibility that he's *Ilsa's* son."

"And that might give him a good motive for killing Gerard," Harriet suggested. "What would he have against Carlton that would have him sizing up the factory?"

"It's not a perfect theory yet, but it does seem to be a bit of a coincidence that Gerard comes back, followed by Ilsa and then it turns out Terry showed up at the same time," DeAnn said.

"I think you guys are way off track, but let me dig on the internet about Terry," Lauren said. "I'm not holding out a lot of hope, though. He seems kind of sharp, which means he's probably not using his real name and has probably lied about everything else, too."

"I've got to check up on Carla tomorrow," Aunt Beth said. "I'll probe a little and see what Terry has disclosed to her. Who knows? He might have told her something useful."

"Call if you get anything," Lauren said and stood up. "I've got to go." She pulled a few bills from her purse and left them on the table.

"I better go, too," Robin said. DeAnn left with her.

The remainder of the group stayed until the nachos were gone.

"I had Lauren swing by my house on our way here so I could get my car," Jenny said. "I can drop you both off on my way home."

"Thanks, that would be great," Harriet said, and Connie nodded agreement.

With that settled, they left the back room and threaded their way through the dining area.

"Oh, hi," came Bebe's girlish voice from a booth by the door. "What are you gals doing here?"

"Eating Mexican food," Harriet replied. "What about you?"

"Me and Carlton are having dinner. He's in the little boy's room."

"Are you ladies leaving me?" Jorge said as he set two plates on the table. Each was covered with dark-green torn lettuce pieces with two thin strips of chicken breast laid in a cross through the middle.

"You didn't cook these in oil, did you?" Bebe asked.

"Never," he said and turned his back to her. He rolled his eyes to the ceiling and mouthed a prayer for salvation. "You need picnic lunches again, you let me know," he said to the Loose Threads, and went back to his kitchen.

"Is that all you're eating?" Connie asked.

"Carlton and I are going to Hawaii in a week and we need to be in swimsuit shape," she said.

They all knew she'd been born in swimsuit shape—Carlton was the one being whipped into it. It was equally clear, to everyone but Bebe, that no amount of starving and exercising was going to erase his Humpty-Dumpty shape.

"Were you having a picnic in the dark?" Bebe asked.

Connie looked at Jenny and Harriet.

"We all went up to Miller Hill Park to get mineral water. Nadene at the Beauty Barn told us it would soften our calluses if we soaked our feet in it."

"That's funny, she didn't tell me that. She told me to rub olive oil on my feet and then put on clean cotton socks before I go to bed."

"You're probably not old enough to need the mineral water," Jenny said smoothly.

"Hi, ladies," Carlton said. "Are you here for dinner, too?"

"No, we were just leaving." Connie ushered the other two out the door.

"Didn't we want to ask Carlton about what we saw at the factory tonight?" Jenny asked.

"I want to try Gerry first," Harriet said. "Somehow, I'd feel more confident in what he said. Not that I have any reason to think Carlton would lie to us."

"I know what you mean," Connie said. "You get the feeling Carlton is probably the last to know a lot that goes on at that company."

Chapter 20

Four of the Willis brothers were assembled in Harriet's kitchen when she got home. An empty pizza box full of greasy, wadded-up paper napkins lay discarded on the island bar.

"Hi, guys," she said as she came through the connecting door. Fred jumped from the counter to weave through her legs. "What's wrong, Fred? Wouldn't anyone feed you?"

"That cat is a con artist," Harry said. "Each one of us fed him as we arrived. He's got a great starving cat shtick."

"He does know how to work it," Harriet agreed and smiled.

"We've found out a few things while you were out," Ben said.

"You mean James found something out," Harry corrected.

"Let me put my purse down and get a cup of tea," Harriet said. "I've learned a few things, too. Or at least, I've learned enough to have a few more questions."

Harry jumped up and put the kettle on. Ben opened the dishwasher and pulled Harriet's newly cleaned mug from the rack. Harriet took an Earl Grey tea bag from a box in the pantry closet. She sat down, and when the water boiled, Ben poured for her then made himself a cup.

"So," she said as she dunked her bag up and down. "What did you guys learn?"

"No fair," Harry said. "Ladies first."

"Hey," Ben said and playfully slapped his brother's shoulder. "It's her house. She gets to go whenever she wants."

"Grow up, you two," James Willis said. "Sorry, Harriet. "I've been investigating my mom's widow's benefits," he explained.

Harry and Ben joined Harriet at the table while Gerry sat with James at the island bar.

"The first thing I did was obtain a copy of Dad's death certificate. Or, I should say, I *attempted* to obtain a copy. Since we now know he wasn't dead, I wondered how thorough the set-up had been. Of course, there is none on file, either in Washington State or in Malaysia."

"You called Malaysia?" Harry said.

James glared at his younger brother then continued. "I got the death certificate Mom received with Dad's..." He made quote-mark motions with the first two fingers of both hands. "...ashes. A simple internet search and comparison quickly demonstrated it was a fake."

"Didn't we already know that, pretty much as soon as Dad turned up dead again?" Ben asked.

"Good question," James said. He got up and started pacing between the island and the table as if he were pleading a case in court. "We knew his certificate had to be a fake, but what this tells us is that it wasn't a sophisticated fake. A child could have made Dad's death certificate. It would have failed under any scrutiny."

"So, again, what does all that tell us?" Ben asked, his voice rising at the end of the sentence.

"It tells us that Mom's widow's benefits were not through an insurance company. Any insurance company would have recognized the certificate was fraudulent. That means her benefits must be coming from a private annuity or something similar."

"Not to sound like your brother," Harriet said with a smile at Ben, "but didn't we already know that?"

"We knew her checks came from a numbered account. I submitted a request to the bank for the identity of the originator of the account. It was set up in a way that would insure Mom would always get the money no matter what happened to the original account holder, the original administrator or even the bank itself.

"Annuities are set up for minor heirs all the time, but this had some unusual features. I'm taking the position that Mom is the ultimate owner of the account and therefore has a right to all the account records and history. Banking is not my area of law, so I'm basically blowing smoke and hoping they will go for it."

"You sly dog," Harry said.

"I'd almost guarantee Dad didn't set up that account. We need to know who did, and I'm hoping the identity of that person will get us a step closer to finding out what the heck is going on," James said. "My investigator will try to get a name if he can, but he needs time. Look, I know you were all hoping for more, but it's like any case—you have to build it step by step."

"You're right, it's a step—a baby step," Ben said. "I guess."

"Did you find something?" Harry asked, looking at Harriet.

"Wait," James said. "I'm not finished."

"Do you actually have some *real* information?" Ben demanded.

"Not about the banking, but I went to the police station earlier to find out what's happening with Dad. They told Mom and that woman they'd be releasing his body days ago, and then they kept dragging it out. It turns out that, originally, they were leaning toward the idea Dad's death was some kind of accident. Closer examination showed that, in addition to the blunt-force trauma wound to Dad's chest, it's kind of burned, which would indicate a gunshot wound, except there's no bullet and no exit wound."

"So our dad was killed with an invisible bullet?" Harry asked.

"Dad was murdered?" Ben asked at the same time.

"That would be why they haven't released his body," James said. "They're running out of things to test for. The only thing they'll say is that Dad received a lethal blow to his heart by object or objects unknown, and that it doesn't appear to be self-inflicted."

"Do they have any idea who killed him?" Ben asked.

"Ironically, Mom could be at the top of their list. Dad was killed while she was on her way back from babysitting for our dear brother Pete," James said. "They have no evidence against her—only her lack of alibi. His other wife is in the same boat—no one saw her at the critical time, but there is no evidence to imply she had anything to do with it."

"If we could figure out why your dad left and then came back, that might help us identify other suspects," Harriet suggested.

"How are we supposed to do that?" Ben asked. He took an orange from the fruit bowl on the table and started peeling it.

"Follow the money trail," James said. "Someone set up the account that's paid Mom all this time. Our dad didn't have that kind of money. Or if he did, Mom didn't know about it, so someone else must have been involved."

"Maybe someone he worked with would know something," Harriet said. "I can talk to Carlton tomorrow. I've already talked to him about trying to find the father of a guy one of our quilters is dating. He supposedly worked there around the same time."

"I'd appreciate that," Gerry said. "Carlton being my ultimate boss makes it difficult for me to ask too many questions."

"I think Mom and that woman are planning on having a memorial service whether they get Dad's body or not." Ben said, changing the topic.

"They might as well, since we're all here," Harry said.

"Mom said the cousins from the Netherlands are coming," James said.

"Good," said Harriet. "Maybe they can tell us something useful."

"So, did you say earlier you found out something that can help us?"

"Not directly, and I'm not sure it connects to your dad at all." She explained her concern about Carla's new boyfriend and the resulting surveillance by the Loose Threads. "We ended up at the park on Miller Hill, looking down on Foggy Point Fire Protection."

"Is this guy some kind of domestic terrorist?" Gerry asked. "Maybe we should be talking to the police."

"I'm not sure what this guy is, but he claimed he was going to talk to someone. He was definitely doing surveillance. He didn't say anything to indicate he wanted to blow the place up or anything." Harriet sipped her tea. "He was interested in what the night shift was doing."

"We don't have a night shift," Gerry said.

"Somebody does," Harriet told him. "There were people driving forklifts in and out of the big doors at the end of the building."

"Oh, that. We rented out warehouse space to another company. Since we're doing zero inventory management, we don't need a lot of storage space anymore. Materials come in daily on trucks and finished products leave at roughly the same pace. Japanese companies call it just-in-time manufacturing."

"What does the other company make?" Harriet asked.

"I have no idea. We advertised we had X number of square feet of storage space available and someone contacted us and rented it. It's not my area, so I don't really know the details."

"Would Carlton know?"

"If you'd asked *should* he, the answer is yes. Whether he *does* is anyone's guess."

"You implied there might be a connection between this guy and our dad," Harry prompted.

"Nothing I can put my finger on," Harriet said. "The Threads and I were talking, and we think it's a bit of a coincidence that he showed up skulking around town around the time your dad returned and right before Ilsa showed up. We even speculated about whether he was related to Ilsa. But we couldn't come up with a good reason why he would be spying on the factory, if that was the case."

"Oh, that's good," Harry said, "I hadn't even thought about the possibility that Dad might have had more kids." He looked serious for once.

"Don't go off the deep end," Harriet cautioned. "We were just speculating and trying to make connections. We have no reason to believe your dad has other children."

"Yeah, but it would make sense," Ben said. "Dad obviously loved kids, I mean, he had all of us, didn't he? And Mom said his other wife looks younger than her."

"That's a big leap, from liking kids to having more and younger," James said. "Dad seemed kind of relieved when we got big enough to drive ourselves."

"Speak for yourself," Harry said. "He left before I got my license."

How sad, Harriet thought. The boys measured their dad's absence by their milestones he'd missed.

"I'll let you know if I learn anything, but your brother's right. We don't have nearly enough information to jump to any conclusions."

She heard a rhythmic tapping on the outer door to her quilt studio. She went through and let a very tired-looking Aiden in. He was once again dressed in scrubs, and his hair had the flattened ridge that was a result of wearing a scrub cap.

She led him into the kitchen, where he sat beside Gerry at the island.

"Tough night, huh?" Gerry said and clapped him on the back.

"Yeah, something like that."

"I was just leaving." Gerry got up and put his empty cup in the sink. "Are you ready?" he asked James.

"Where are you guys going?" Ben asked.

"Relax, tag-along, I'm just dropping James at Mom's—he's sleeping on her couch tonight. And then I'm going home."

"We could go have a beer on your way home," Ben suggested.

"I'm tired," Gerry said. "When you two get married and have real jobs you'll understand. The only thing I'm doing tonight is sleeping."

"Come on, Ben" Harry said. "Harriet has cable. We can watch old sci-fi movies in her TV room." He headed for the stairs.

Ben glanced at Aiden and Harriet, and his face turned pink under his freckles.

"Good idea," he said and followed his brother.

"Rough night?" Harriet asked when she and Aiden were alone.

"Dog fight," he said. "Multiple victims. I hate seeing young, irresponsible pet owners getting unaltered male pit bulls."

"Were they purposely fighting them?"

"No, it was actually a group of friends meeting on a street corner. The dogs got into it, and the kids couldn't control them. A couple of the kids ended up in the emergency room with bites, too."

"That's too bad," Harriet said. She massaged his neck with her good hand. "Sorry I can't give you a decent massage."

He turned and pulled her into his arms. She ran her hand through his silky hair, and he tilted his head down and kissed her gently on the lips.

"Can I sleep over?" he asked.

She pulled away.

"No, you can't sleep over," she said. "We aren't that kind of friends."

"Yet," he said. "We aren't that kind of friends yet. Say it."

"Even if we were that kind of friends, you can't stay over when there are children in the house."

"Children?" he said loudly, and she hushed him immediately. "They're all older than me," he finished in a loud whisper.

"I rest my case," she said.

"You're killing me here," he said. He pulled her back toward him and wrapped his arms around her again. "They do seem younger, though, don't they."

"I think Harry is in graduate school, and Ben works as a research assistant for a save the some-kind-of-crustacean group. They both spend a lot of time with college students."

"Did you learn anything from the guys?" Aiden smoothed her hair away from her face with both hands.

"Not really. James says he's sure his mom wasn't getting insurance money. And the police are sure Gerard, or Gerald or whatever we're supposed to call him, was murdered, but they're not sure how."

"I guess that's good for Mavis," he said. "The insurance part, I mean."

"Someone said the cousins from the Netherlands are coming for the funeral, which is apparently going to happen whether the body has been released or not."

"So, what's on tap for the great detective?" he asked.

"Not much. I'm going to ask Carlton about who works at his company at night and also if he knows who is around from twenty years ago who might have known what was going on back then. Other than that, I'm at a loss."

Aiden slid his hands under the back of her shirt and rubbed the knotted muscles of her back as she leaned into him.

"I'm sure you'll think of something," he said.

Chapter 21

I've been thinking," Aunt Beth said as she poured hot water over her orange spice tea bag. She dunked the bag up and down several times in the blue hand-thrown mug she had selected from the shelf then let it fall back into the liquid.

"This must be serious," said Harriet.

Aunt Beth had arrived early with a bag of doughnuts clutched in her hand along with her purse. Something big must be on her mind for her to bring something other than fruit to Harriet. She'd bake cookies until the end of time for the Willis boys; Harriet always got the fruit.

She got up from the island, sipping her own tea, and got a plate from the cupboard and a handful of napkins from the drawer next to the dishwasher.

"I'm trying to figure out what the right thing to do is," Beth said, leaving Harriet to scramble for a topic. "Having two wives makes things complicated."

"Throw me a bone here. What are you talking about?"

"Oh, I'm thinking out loud," Aunt Beth said and unbagged the pastries. She'd brought a large apple fritter, two raspberry-filled raised doughnuts and a pair of cinnamon twists. Judging by the quantity of sweets, she was very troubled. "Hand me a sharp knife."

Harriet complied, then came back around the bar and sat on her stool. Beth cut the apple fritter into bite-sized pieces.

"You know how we always make blocks for a person when someone dear to them dies? I was thinking we should be making blocks for Mavis."

It all became clear.

"And you don't know what to do about Ilsa."

"That, and the fact I'm not sure how Mavis is feeling about Gerald right now."

Harriet had a thought about that, but didn't want to throw it out there too soon for fear Aunt Beth would pack up her doughnuts and go.

"It seems like Ilsa should be included. I mean, she *is* a quilter. I realize we aren't her friends, but she's alone here and far from her home. And no matter what the final explanation is for Gerald/Gerard's actions, both women are grieving." Harriet popped a piece of fritter in her mouth and put a doughnut on her napkin. She took a sip of her tea. "Mavis may be at the anger stage of grief, but she's still grieving."

"I don't want to add to her burden," Aunt Beth said. "And I don't want Mavis mad if we make something for Ilsa." She picked up a cinnamon twist, tore the end off and ate it.

Harriet bit her raised doughnut, marking it as her own. "I think we should make blocks for Mavis, but not have a theme related to Gerald/Gerard. You know, maybe make something purely for comfort and as feminine as Mavis could stand."

"That's not a bad idea," Aunt Beth said and took another bite of her twist.

"As for Ilsa, let's ask Mavis what she thinks. If she absolutely hates the idea, then we'll find something else to do for her." Harriet took another bite of fritter, and as she put it to her mouth, Aunt Beth slid the plate just out of her reach. "My guess is Mavis will say we should make blocks. You can figure out whether we should let her know we're making blocks for *her* or not."

"Probably not," Aunt Beth said. "She's going to be busy today anyway. Gerald's cousins from the Netherlands are arriving."

"Won't they be with Ilsa?"

"I think Mavis and Ilsa are going to pick them up from the airport together."

"Are they coming in to Sea-Tac?" Harriet asked, referring to the Seattle/Tacoma airport..

"Yes. I think Mavis volunteered to drive."

"It must be kinda of weird for her, though."

"Well, the whole thing is weird. In a way, I think Ilsa gives Mavis a way to hang on to Gerald even though she's mad at the same time. And Ilsa is learning about a whole part of Gerald's life she never knew existed."

"I'm not sure I could be so buddy-buddy if I were Mavis." Harriet rose off her stool to reach the plate with the fritter. Aunt Beth slapped at her hand as she reached for another piece.

"Don't you think you've had enough?" she scolded. "You need to keep your girlish figure if you're going to keep that man of yours."

"Aiden is not 'my man,' and furthermore, if he cares that much about my weight, he's not going to *be* 'my man.'"

"I'll save you," Harry said and reached for the doughnut plate.

"You help yourself," Aunt Beth invited warmly.

"Thanks." He took the plate to the counter and began filling Harriet's coffeemaker.

"I'll start calling the Loose Threads. Shall we see if we can meet at Pins and Needles in an hour?" Harriet asked.

"Thanks, honey, that would be good. We're all caught up in the studio, so I was going to slip one of my own quilts onto the machine and get it started," Aunt Beth said. "I'll call Connie and Jenny, if you want."

"It's a plan," Harriet said and went upstairs to get dressed and make her calls.

✂ ✂ ✂

Aunt Beth and Harriet drove down the hill to Pins and Needles an hour later in Aunt Beth's new Volkswagen Beetle. She had ordered it weeks ago and had just picked it up at Fogg Volkswagen and Saab the day before.

"This thing is tiny," Harriet said as she settled in the passenger seat. "Did you have to special-order this vase?" She referred to a flower vase attached to the dashboard.

Aunt Beth rolled her eyes.

"I don't need to be driving a tank around Foggy Point, getting single-digit gas mileage," she said. "And I kept the pickup. I'll drive that if I need to go to Seattle." She parked easily at the curb in front of Pins and Needles. "See? It may be small, but it's much easier to park than my old tank."

"Whatever," Harriet said as she crawled out and onto the sidewalk. She took her quilting bag from the back seat and Aunt Beth did the same.

"You'll be in the small classroom today, if that's okay," Marjory informed them.

"That's great," Harriet said. "Thanks for accommodating us on such short notice."

"Glad I could be of help. Carla is in there right now showing Bebe how to braid grosgrain ribbon to attach to her suitcase so she can identify it easier at baggage claim at the airport, but they should be done in a few minutes."

"No problem," Aunt Beth said.

"There's coffee and hot water in the kitchen," Marjory added. "Let me know if you need anything else."

"Thanks," Harriet told her and went straight to the kitchen. "You want anything to drink?" she asked Aunt Beth. Her aunt shook her head and went on into the classroom. Harriet made herself tea and followed.

"How's it going?" she asked Carla. Aunt Beth had taken over the task of trying to teach Bebe how to braid with four ribbons. They were sitting at four eight-foot tables that had been pushed into the center of the room to form one large island. More tables were pushed against one wall with mats for cutting fabric on top. The other walls had six-foot-by-eight-foot foam core boards that had been covered with flannel leaning up against them, providing quilters a place to pin their cut out fabric pieces and plan their arrangement before sewing them together.

"Okay," Carla said and looked at the floor.

"Just okay?"

"Terry and I were supposed to have coffee this morning, but he canceled."

"Does he do that often?"

"Not at first, but lately, yeah."

"It might not have anything to do with you," Harriet said. "I think he might be distracted by his search for information about his dad."

"How do you know? Did you talk to him?" She looked so hopeful Harriet had to tell her something. She ended up telling her everything.

"You followed him?" Carla asked, sounding amazed at her daring.

"We did," Harriet said. "He said he would explain what he was doing in Miller Hill Park after he met a guy at Foggy Point Fire Protection. That was last night, and I haven't seen him yet to hear the explanation."

"Someone was at Carlton's company last night?" Bebe asked, looking up from her braiding.

"I was going to ask Carlton about that," Harriet said. "Do you know anything about the people who are leasing warehouse space?"

"No, I don't know anything about what goes on out there. All I know is it takes a lot of Carlton's time, running that company."

As near as Harriet could tell, Carlton barely spent any time at the company, and he certainly wasn't the one running it, but she wasn't about to tell Bebe that.

"Pay attention," Aunt Beth ordered, and Bebe picked up the four strands of ribbon again and tried to follow the pattern Aunt Beth had drawn on a piece of paper. A quick glance in that direction showed it wasn't going well.

"Has Terry said anything to you about how his search for information about his father is going?" Harriet asked Carla.

"Not really. He said he was trying to find a man someone else had suggested might be able to tell him something, but he didn't tell me who."

"That must have been who he was going to meet last night."

"He's not really looking for his father, is he?" Carla asked with a sigh. She'd had a lifetime of disappointment and could recognize the signs, Harriet thought. She could have spun a tale, but then looked at Carla and knew she deserved better.

"No, he probably isn't. But don't jump to conclusions. That doesn't necessarily mean he's doing anything illegal or immoral."

"I don't need any more lying, cheating men in my life," Carla said, and her eyes filled with tears.

"Come on. Let's get you a cup of tea," Harriet said, and felt like she was channeling Mavis or her aunt. She led Carla to the kitchen. "Let's not make any assumptions," she continued.

She couldn't believe what she was saying. If it was her own life, she'd kick him to the curb, no questions asked, but she knew Carla didn't need to hear that right now. Besides, she was curious about what was going on at Foggy Point Fire Protection and wanted to keep Terry around until he found out.

"I'm not saying you shouldn't confront him, but give him a chance to explain."

"My momma always said men are trouble," Carla said.

"You're way too young to be that jaded. Remember your knight in shining armor?"

When she and Carla had been locked in a basement together, Carla had told her how she'd imagined being rescued by a knight when her mother locked her in a closet, as a way of keeping the bogey man at bay.

"He's still out there somewhere."

Carla dried her tears and sipped her tea.

"We better see if your aunt needs help," she said with a sigh. "She had her lips pressed together real tight when she was watching Bebe try to braid."

"It can't be easy with those inch-long plastic sabers she calls fingernails," Harriet said.

Carla laughed and led the way back to the classroom.

Connie and Jenny had arrived while they were in the kitchen. Jenny looked cool in a crisp white sleeveless blouse and pale-blue linen knee-length shorts that were belted at the waist. Connie, by contrast, wore stretchy black pants, and her sleeveless top was a pink, orange and black floral print in a jersey-type fabric.

"Hi, Bebe," Connie said. "What are you doing?"

Bebe giggled and explained she was trying to make embellishments that would make her and Carlton's new luggage easier to identify on their upcoming trip to Hawaii.

"Do you want me to do it for you?" Connie asked.

"Oh, could you?"

"I would be happy to." Connie sat down, and in a matter of minutes had created four colorful markers that could be attached to the handles of Bebe's luggage.

"Oh, thank you," Bebe gushed then jumped up and hugged her, almost knocking the older woman over.

"De nada, de nada," Connie said, and forcefully disengaged herself. "You run along now. I'm sure you have things to do."

"I do," Bebe replied, clearly grateful Connie understood. She tucked the ribbon markers in her oversized pink hobo bag and left.

"She's so frightfully busy," Connie said, and then laughed.

"Why did you indulge her?" Beth asked. "I was making her do it herself."

"Because nothing you were doing was going to change who she is. And did you want her here for the next hour?"

"Who her?" Robin said as she came in. Today's sleeveless yoga top was pale pink. Her pants were their usual black Lycra.

"Oh, Bebe was here trying to make those braided ribbon thingies that you put on your suitcase handle so you can find your bag more easily at the airport," Harriet said.

"Connie was just explaining why she made them for her instead making her struggle through doing them herself," Beth said.

"You wanted her out of here?" Robin guessed.

"See, she understands," Connie said. She went toward the kitchen. "Anyone want anything?

Robin joined her in the kitchen, and they both returned with cups of coffee.

"Lauren is in the middle of a work project and might join us later, and Sarah was on front desk duty at the senior center, so we can start as soon as DeAnn gets here," Harriet explained.

"DeAnn's here," the missing woman called from the hallway. "Marjory is cutting some backing fabric for my dot-on-dot quilt," she said, referring to the product of a class she had taken a few months earlier. The quilt top was a circular pattern made completely from dotted fabrics.

She came in tucking her new purchase into her quilting bag as she went to her usual spot at the table. Like most groups, each person had a favorite place.

"As I told you all on the phone, I asked everyone to come in today so we can plan a comfort quilt for Mavis," Harriet went on. "We also need to discuss what to do about Ilsa, who also lost her husband."

"Oh, that's a tricky one," Robin said.

"Let's think about that while we decide what we're going to do for Mavis," Connie suggested.

"Good idea," Harriet agreed. "Suggestions?"

"I like the idea you and I were talking about," Beth said. "Something different enough that she can't associate it with Gerald in any way."

"That's a new twist," Jenny said. "Usually, we're struggling to make our comfort quilt bring out memories of the lost loved one."

"How about soft florals?" Connie suggested. "We could do pale versions of the colors she likes."

"That sounds good to me," Robin said. "And I think we should use a simple pattern so the fabric print shows more."

"Corn and Beans?" Jenny suggested, referring to a block made from three different sizes of triangle formed into squares.

"How about shoo-fly?" Carla suggested. "We've been using that with the young mothers group."

"I like that idea," Aunt Beth said. "It's nice and simple."

"If we choose the fabric pretty quick, we can start cutting our blocks while we're here," DeAnn said.

"Mavis usually buys rust colors and dark blues and greens," Carla offered.

"So, let's try for lighter, softer versions of those colors," Beth said.

"And maybe some peach," Connie offered.

Robin and DeAnn laughed, and Jenny smiled.

"What?" Connie asked. "Peach would go nicely with those colors."

"And you would have suggested it even if it hadn't matched," Robin pointed out.

Connie smiled. "It does go with everything," she said in defense of her favorite color.

"Come on, ladies, everyone grab a bolt and meet back here," Aunt Beth said.

"I could carry yours," Carla offered Harriet.

"That would be real nice," Harriet said. "Now, you've been working here for months. Where is the best match for Connie's colors?"

"We just got a new shipment from Hoffman. There's a floral print that has all those colors. I could check it in real quick," Carla said with a devilish grin Harriet hadn't seen before.

"Lead the way," she said.

They were sitting at the table again when the remainder of the group began to filter in with their fabric choices.

"That's perfect!" Robin said as she set her bolt of pale-blue batik on the table. "Where was that?"

"Yeah," DeAnn said and put her pale-yellow floral on top of Robin's batik.

"We cheated," Harriet said with a laugh. Carla had carried in three bolts of coordinated print from the new line.

"Hey, it's not cheating if it works," Robin said.

The group spent the next fifteen minutes rejecting and then replacing various bolts of fabric until they had a grouping everyone was sure would coordinate with Mavis's color palette. Carla took the bolts to the cutting table by the cash register to cut fat quarters of each for each quilter.

"Now, what about Ilsa?" Jenny asked.

"Aunt Beth and I were thinking we need to ask Mavis before we give anything to Ilsa," Harriet said.

"But we could make them, and then if Mavis objects, which I think she won't, but if she does, we could use them for the raffle quilt next month," Jenny said.

"All right, what are we going to do?"

They discussed and then rejected an Americana-style quilt with folk art imagery. They decided to stay away from the traditional blue and white associated with Dutch motifs and finally settled on shades of brown with dark and light blues and an accent of yellow done in a log cabin pattern.

Aunt Beth suggested they pull colors from their own stashes and go for a scrappy look. The rest agreed then got out their cutting mats to start working on the block for Mavis.

"Red alert," Carla said as she brought in the stack of fat quarters. "I saw Mavis out the front window. She was down the block but headed this way."

The women stuffed their fat quarters in their bags and quickly tucked their rotary cutters back in their tool kits.

"Mavis," Robin said when she came in. "Can I get you some tea?"

"No, but does Marjory have any cold water in her refrigerator?" Mavis's face was pale, and her lipstick had worn away.

"I'll get it," Carla said and left the room.

"Did you get the cousins?" Aunt Beth asked.

"Yes, we did, and they had a little surprise package with them," she said.

"Surprise package?" Harriet said.

"That's what I said," Mavis stalled as she accepted a frosty bottle of water from Carla. "Keep in mind I've met Theobald and Uda," she went on after taking a drink. "And their two daughters. Well, I think they were planning on claiming the child with them was their granddaughter."

"They brought a child with them?" Harriet said.

"They must have lost track of the fact that I have five boys with Gerald. Either that, or they hadn't taken a good look at the Christmas pictures I've been sending them, because the little girl they brought is a dead ringer for my Harry. At least, for what he looked like when he was twelve." Mavis took another drink of her water.

"Gerard had a daughter with Ilsa?" Aunt Beth asked.

"Looks like it."

"How do you feel about that?" Connie asked.

"Compared to finding out Gerald has been alive for the past twenty years? It's just one more thing. And besides, I couldn't think about how I was feeling when that little girl is devastated."

"Wow," Harriet said. "This just keeps getting more complicated, doesn't it?"

"Have you told the boys yet?" Connie asked.

"No," Mavis said. "I dropped the Dutch bunch off at the bed and breakfast at Smuggler's Cove and took Ilsa back to her cottage at DeAnn's and then I came here." She sipped her water. "Ilsa and I figured we'd give the cousins a day to recover from the trip and then do the funeral on Saturday. I need to get the boys and their families together to meet the cousins and spring the surprise on them as soon as possible. I want everyone to have whatever reaction they're going to have and then have time to calm down before we go to church."

"Would you like to have a family dinner at my house tonight?" Harriet asked. "I mean, half the tribe is there already, and I have plenty of room."

"I'll come cook," Connie offered.

"I could make a couple of desserts," Jenny added.

"I'll prepare a big green salad," Beth said. "Carla, you could make the potato salad recipe."

"Do you think I do it well enough?" Carla asked.

"You make it just fine, honey," Beth said, and reached over and patted her hand.

Robin said she'd make a fruit salad, and DeAnn volunteered to provide drinks for them.

"What do you think?" Harriet asked.

"That would be wonderful," Mavis said. "I was trying to figure out where I could take them that would be private and could be gotten on short notice. I will owe you big time."

"Nonsense," Harriet said. "What time would you like to have dinner?"

"They're going to be jet-lagged," Mavis said, "so we probably should make is as early as we can."

Aunt Beth looked at her watch. "How about five-thirty?" she said. "That would give the cousins some time to rest before they have to go out again."

"Sounds good," Mavis said. "I better go call Pete and James. Pete was already planning on coming to town tonight to see the cousins, so the time should work for them. James went back to Port Townsend for a couple of hours, but he was planning on being here, too. The rest of them were going to be at Harriet's."

✂ ✂ ✂

Mavis, Harriet and Aunt Beth were standing outside on the sidewalk talking after the rest of the group had left when a Foggy Point Police car pulled up to the curb.

"Mrs. Willis?" the officer asked when he was out of his car.

"Officer Nguyen," Mavis said. The young Asian policeman had come to question Harriet at Mavis's cottage earlier in the year when Harriet had been hit in the head and left unconscious. "What do you need?"

"Detective Black asked me to see if you would come in and answer a few questions."

"Is he going to arrest me?"

"I don't know what his plan is, ma'am."

"Can I lock my car?"

"Do you want me to come with you?" Harriet asked.

"No, I have nothing to worry about. I haven't done anything."

"I'm calling Robin and asking her to meet you there," Harriet said.

"I'm telling you, it's unnecessary," Mavis insisted before she walked down the block and locked her car then returned and got into the back seat of Officer Nguyen's unit.

Harriet pulled her cell phone from her bag and pressed the speed dial number for Robin's cell phone. Robin answered on the second ring, and Harriet quickly filled her in.

"I'm still in my car," Robin said. "I'll turn around and head for the police station. I'll probably get there before Mavis does."

"Thanks," Harriet said. "Tell Mavis I'll call her sons for her."

"Will do," Robin said and rang off.

"I'll help you get the house ready," Aunt Beth said and put Harriet's bag in the back seat of her little car. Harriet angled herself into the front seat, and Aunt Beth drove them back home.

Harry was in the kitchen, rummaging through the refrigerator, when they came in from the studio.

"Can you give me your brother's phone numbers?" Harriet asked.

"Sure," he said, and pulled his cell phone out. "What do you need them for?"

Harriet explained about the dinner that would be happening later that day.

"Do you want me to just call them?" he asked.

"Sure. Tell them the Dutch cousins will be here."

"No prob," he said, and started dialing. "Yo, bro. Dinner, Harriet's house, five-thirty, Dutch cousins will be here—be there, be square." He paused a minute. "See ya."

He then repeated the process twice more.

"They'll be here," he said. "I'll go tell Ben. He's upstairs video chatting with his girlfriend."

Harriet laughed when he was out of earshot.

"Not quite how I would have gone about it, but he got the job done."

"That's all that counts," Aunt Beth said.

"By the way," Harry said a few minutes later when he'd come back downstairs. "Why are you calling my brothers? Why isn't Mom?"

"She's busy," Harriet said.

"Too busy to call her sons? Hello, we're the lights of her life. She's never too busy for us."

Harriet looked at Aunt Beth.

"Your mom is at the police station tying up a few loose ends," Aunt Beth said.

"Mom's been arrested?" Ben asked as he joined them. "We need to help her."

"Just calm down a minute," Aunt Beth said. "She isn't being arrested and she doesn't need you two going down there causing her more trouble."

"Then you admit she's in trouble," Ben said.

"No," Aunt Beth said. "I only know what I just told you. The officer said they wanted to ask her a few more questions. Harriet called Robin from the Loose Threads. She's a lawyer, and she was meeting your mom at the police station."

"While we're waiting to hear something, you two boys can make yourselves useful," Aunt Beth said. "Harry, you take the blue-handled broom from that closet over there and go through the dining room and out the French doors. When you reach the patio, start sweeping."

She looked at Ben. "You go out to the garage and go upstairs and get the two white coolers down and bring them outside. If they need it, hose them out. Then you can take my car and go get enough bags of ice to half-fill both of them and two cases of bottled water. You can put the ice in the freezer in the garage until closer to dinnertime."

"Yes, ma'am," Ben said.

"No fair," Harry said. "You get to drive Aunt Beth's new car while I have to sweep the patio."

"Harry," Aunt Beth said and handed him the broom. "Life is tough."

"Tell me about it," the youngest Willis said, and headed for the dining room with his broom.

The weather man had predicted comfortable evening temperatures, so Aunt Beth had Harry and Ben out on the patio an hour later, setting up tables and planting bamboo Tiki lights she had left behind in Harriet's garage in the soft dirt of the flowerbed that separated the patio from the grass of the back yard.

"We won't light the Tikis until we see if anyone is still sitting out here when it starts to get dark. You two keep an eye on things and light them if we need them. There are matches in the drawer to the left of the stove."

"Yes, ma'am," Ben said.

Harriet came out with an armload of table cloths that had been hanging in the upstairs linen closet, waiting for just such an occasion.

"Do you want these on the tables now, or should we wait until closer to dinner?"

"Let's wait a bit longer, so the trees don't have as much time to drop debris on them," Beth replied. "How'd it go?" she asked as Mavis stepped out on the patio.

"Are you okay?" Ben asked.

"Aunt Beth wouldn't let us come help you," Harry said at the same time.

"Boys," she said and held her arms out. "As you can see, I'm fine." The two boys closed in on their mom. Mavis put one arm around the waist of each. "Beth was right. She and Harriet shouldn't have to do all the work for our family."

"Harry," Harriet said. "There are folding chairs in the garage attic. Can you and Ben go get enough to go around the tables?"

The boys fetched chairs, and Harriet brought out a pitcher of iced tea and glasses and set them on the table closest to the house. Mavis and Beth sat down, and Harriet poured tea for everyone.

"So, what did the police say?" Ben asked when he'd set up enough chairs for everyone.

"They said a lot, but I can summarize it in one sentence—they don't have a clue."

"Why did they make you go to the police station?" Harriet asked.

"As near as I can tell, they are trying to go over everything one more time and they were trying to shake us up by making us come to their place."

"Us?" Harriet asked. "Who us?"

"Oh, didn't I mention it when I came in? They had Ilsa in there too."

"Wow," Harriet said. "She must have been terrified." She thought a minute. "At least if she didn't do it," she added.

"Was she by herself?" Beth asked.

"Robin called her husband's law partner and he came down. She said the partner had done some international law when he graduated from law school. He called the Dutch consulate in Seattle."

"Do they have any idea why Gerald/Gerard came back?" Harriet asked.

"I'm telling you they don't have anything," Mavis said and shook her head in disgust. "Detective Black did say they had been in touch with detectives in Amsterdam. If they learned anything they weren't sharing."

"Dios mio," Connie exclaimed as she came through the house when she caught sight of Mavis. "Are you okay? Did the Federales beat you?"

"Connie," Mavis said with a smile, "as you can see, I'm fine. Everyone needs to stop fussing about the police. We've got more important things to talk about."

"Like what?" asked Ben.

"I can't think of anything more important than your freedom," said Harry.

Harriet felt sorry for the boys.

"There's a reason we wanted to get all you boys together tonight, before the funeral on Saturday and before you have a chance to accidentally happen on the information. I was going to tell you all at once, but this might be better."

"You're scaring me, Mom," said Ben.

Harry sat up in his chair, closed his eyes and took a deep breath, then let it out slowly. "Okay, lay it on me," he said.

"You have a sister," Mavis blurted out without preamble.

"What!" Harry screeched.

"No way," Ben said.

"Dios mio," said Connie, as if she, too, were hearing the news for the first time.

Every one fell silent for a moment. "Geez, Mom. Don't sugarcoat it or anything," Ben finally said. "A sister? How?"

Mavis laughed. "The usual way, I expect."

"Ben, your father was gone for a long time," Aunt Beth said. "He apparently remarried fifteen years ago. It's not a giant leap that he might have had more children."

"Are there more?" Harry asked.

"I'm not sure I know the answer to that," Mavis said. "Ilsa didn't say there weren't more, but if there are more kids, she didn't talk about them. And only her daughter came for the funeral."

"Are you sure she's Dad's daughter?" Ben asked.

"Yes," Mavis said, "I think so."

"I suppose she has red hair?" Harry said. Mavis and Gerald were both red-heads, and while their sons had a variety of hair textures and shades, they too were all ginger-haired.

"She does."

"What else?" Harry pressed.

"You'll see when you meet her," Mavis said. "Now, let's get busy and help get this dinner going."

Chapter 22

All five Willis boys and the wives and children of the older three were present and accounted for before the Dutch contingent arrived. Harry had been pacing the kitchen and was the first down the hall and to the front door when Ilsa rang the bell. He opened the door and stood in stunned silence, leaving the new arrivals on the porch.

Mavis came up behind him. She gently nudged him to the side.

"Welcome," she said to Gerard's cousins. "Come on in."

Theobald, his wife Uda and Ilsa came in. Ilsa's daughter stood frozen, staring at Harry.

"Don't be rude, Marit," Ilsa said, and pulled her daughter by the hand into the house.

Mavis poked Harry in the back.

"Sorry," he said. "I'm Harry."

"Hello, Harry. I'm Ilsa, and this is my daughter Marit." Ilsa held her hand out, and Harry took it.

"Is this my brother?" Marit asked Mavis in nearly unaccented English.

"This is one of them."

"He's very old," Marit said, staring at Harry's face.

"Would you like to meet the rest of your brothers?" Mavis asked with a glance at Ilsa. Ilsa smiled encouragement.

Mavis took Marit by the hand and led her into the kitchen. She completed the introductions, and although Marit wasn't very impressed with her grown brothers, her face lit up when she realized she was an aunt and that she had a niece who was just two years her junior. The two girls were shy at first, but Gerry's daughter Elfie was a talker, and soon the girls were chattering as if they'd known each other for years.

Connie stayed in the kitchen until dinner was served.

"Can you handle things, mija?" she asked Harriet when the rest of the guests were out on the patio filling plates with pollo con chipotle, fruit and potato salads and the rest of the delicious food the Loose Threads had delivered. "Any leftover salads and the chicken can go into the refrigerator in the containers they're in, so clean-up shouldn't be too hard." She took her apron off. "If you get a chance, grill the little girl," she advised. "Kids that age are more observant then people give them credit for."

When Connie was gone, Harriet circulated among the people seated on the patio, refilling glasses, first with iced tea and then lemonade. Theobald was talking with Gerry and James, both of whom had visited the Netherlands and stayed with their dad's cousins after high school, before their dad left.

"I never could understand why Mavis would divorce Gerald. And his story about you boys not wanting to see him anymore seemed unlikely, too," Theobald said. "He insisted he'd been thrown out and needed to be far away so he could start his life over. I saw the way he studied the Christmas pictures your mother sent us every year, like a hungry man with a fish." He made a dismissive wave with his hand. "I never believed it."

Harriet moved on to the cluster of women.

"We raised her to speak both Dutch and English. And she studies English at school," Ilsa said. She was wearing a blue seersucker skirt with a sleeveless white shirt, a pale yellow sweater draped loosely over her shoulders. James and Pete Willis were both married to women who dressed to impress and both were outclassed by Ilsa.

She moved on to the children. Mavis's older grandchildren had gone upstairs to Harriet's TV room to watch music DVDs they'd brought with them. Marit and Elfie sat side-by-side on the patio swing.

"Where is your bathroom?" Elfie asked Harriet, who directed her to the half-bath off the kitchen.

"This must be a little overwhelming," she said to Marit. The girl shrugged. "Did you have any idea you had brothers?" Harriet pressed.

The girl's face turned pink, and she squirmed in her seat. Harriet let the silence grow.

"Vader used to keep sweets in his office at home. He would hide them, and then I would find them and he would move them again." She paused.

"And?" Harriet finally said.

The girl's blue eyes filled with tears.

"One day I opened a drawer, and there were no sweets. I began to shut the drawer, but then something fell from the surface above and it dropped into the drawer."

"What was it?"

"It was a picture. It had been taped to the board above the drawer, and the tape came loose." She sighed. "It was a picture of five boys, and one looked very like me."

"What did your father say? I assume you asked him."

"Vader said it was his cousin's children."

"But you didn't believe him?"

"Uda and Theobald are his cousins, and they have girls, and they have blond hair. And at Christmas, Uda would get a picture card from her friend in America, and there were five men with ginger hair. I asked Moeder, but she said all only children imagine secret brothers and sisters."

Harriet felt mean grilling a child, but she continued anyway. "Did your father tell you where he was going when he came here?"

She tilted her face away. "He told me not to tell anyone. He said especially not Moeder, because she would worry."

"I don't think he would mind your telling me. I'm trying to figure out what happened. I think he would want that."

Marit turned her wide, blue-eyed gaze onto Harriet and then sighed.

"He said there was a man who was doing something bad, and he could stop him. He told me he would be back before I knew it." Her tears welled again.

"What are you guys talking about?" Elfie asked, and when Marit held the swing still, she hopped back to her place beside her new aunt.

Harriet was saved from having to answer by Aiden's arrival.

"Hi," he said, and kissed her on the top of her head. "I thought I'd come by and see if I could help with the clean-up." He looked around at the clusters of people. I guess I'm a little early."

"Your eyes are very strange," Elfie said. "Are you wearing contacts?"

"No, I'm not wearing contacts, and my eyes are just like yours, I just don't have quite as much color as you do."

"Can you see the same as me?" Elfie pressed.

"How do *you* see?" Aiden asked. Harriet could tell he was fighting to keep from smiling.

"I see the regular way," Elfie answered.

"Me, too."

"I've got to continue my rounds," Harriet said, and tugged awkwardly on Aiden's sleeve as she walked away with her pitcher.

"Give me that," he said and took the lemonade from her. "How's it going?" He gestured toward the assembled Willis clan.

"I think the boys were a bit shocked to find out their father had another child, but everyone is being civil. Marit was just telling me her father was coming to 'stop a man who was doing something bad.'"

"That covers a lot of ground, approximately half of the world's population being male."

"Can you help me bring a garbage can from the garage to the edge of the patio?" She needed to think about the implications of what Marit had said, and working was a good way to think. She began gathering paper plates and crumpled napkins from the tables. Aiden brought the can then helped her.

"Would anyone care for dessert?" she asked.

Everyone but James's and Pete's wives nodded or murmured assent.

"What are we having?" Aiden asked.

"Jenny made two pies and a chocolate cake." She'd also brought two half-gallon cartons of vanilla ice cream.

"How do we know who wants what?"

"We're going to cut pie and cake and put it on plates and put the plates on a tray and then carry the ice cream and scoop with us. We will offer cake or pie and then add ice cream if they want it. You think you can handle it?"

"I think my two hands will handle it better than your one," he said with a smirk.

Harriet, however, surprised him with her show of one-handed scooping, and they quickly served the dessert and returned to the kitchen.

Aiden's phone trilled with the low tones of Blake Shelton's rendition of the song "Home." He pulled it from his pocket and pressed the green answer button.

"Calm down, I can't understand what you're saying…No, don't go anywhere…Don't do anything until I get there." He turned to Harriet. "I gotta go."

"Trouble?"

"Carla needs me," he said.

"Oh, well. You better go then."

"I'm sorry," he said. He put a finger under her chin and tilted her face up, then kissed her gently on the lips. "She's really upset about something, and I need to go see what's going on."

She put her good arm around his shoulder and leaned into him, twining her fingers through his silky hair. "Of course you do—go. You can tell me all about it tomorrow." She said this last with false enthusiasm and hoped he was distracted enough not to notice.

He stepped away.

"I'll call you tomorrow," he said as he headed for the door. He glanced back at her, and she tried to convince herself it was a look of regret she saw on his face.

"Where's he going in such a hurry?" Mavis asked. Harriet hadn't noticed her enter the kitchen.

"Carla called. He said she was upset, so he had to go find out why."

"You do know she's not a threat, don't you?"

"That knowledge doesn't excuse his behavior," Harriet complained and sat on a stool at the bar.

"That youthful lack of finesse is one of the things that attracts you to him, isn't it?"

Harriet didn't want to think about that, so she got up and started loading silverware into the dishwasher. She could justify the use of paper plates for a group dinner—they tended to start the bio-degrading process before dinner was over. Plastic silverware was a whole different thing, though. She imagined post-apocalyptic scenes with all living things gone and plastic forks sticking their tines skyward out of landfills everywhere, silent reminders of man's stay on earth. Because of this, she avoided them and opted to use her stainless flatware, even when the meal was eaten outside.

"I have to wonder what Carla's so upset about," Mavis said, and Harriet realized she had missed out on the whole "spy on Terry" mission.

"Aiden didn't say, but my guess is it's something to do with her new friend, Terry."

"Why would she call Aiden about man troubles?"

"She's not having typical man troubles. Terry has proven to be a bit unreliable, which by itself might just mean he's a flake, but in reality, he's a man with an agenda. His claim that he's looking for people who knew his father doesn't ring true, especially in light of our recent discovery that he's sitting on a hill using binoculars to spy on Carlton's company."

"That doesn't sound like the usual genealogy search, does it?" Mavis said.

"No, I think he's investigating something else. It's not clear if the something else has to do with his father at all. He could be working for a person or persons unknown, or even an organization. He said he'd explain it all, and now he's playing hard to get."

"What do you mean?"

"He was supposed to meet Carla this morning for coffee, and he didn't show up. That alone makes me want to wring his neck. But if he's working for someone else, I'm sure his work, whatever it is, has to take priority over everything."

"Something else must have happened," Mavis said and took over the dishwasher loading process. "Move over, it's going to take you all night, working with one hand. Our Carla gets resigned and dejected, but she's had too much experience with disappointment to become agitated over a missed date. And to call Aiden, she must have been real upset."

"I don't think so. They've become pretty close since she's been living there. You're right, though, she's not the hysterical type."

Mavis shut the dishwasher and turned it on. "Well, we aren't going to be able to figure it out until one of them tells us something, and that's not likely to be tonight." She glanced at her narrow gold wristwatch. "Goodness, look at the time. I'm going to run my bunch out of here so you can get some rest. I can't tell you how much I appreciate your letting me use your house like this."

"After all the times you've helped me? Don't give it a second thought."

True to her word, Mavis went outside and encouraged her guests to call it a night.

Chapter 23

Harriet's hand was caught in the drive chain of the conveyor belt at Foggy Point Fire Protection, and she was being dragged toward two giant rollers that compressed two layers of fiber into one. She tried to scream, but no sound came out of her mouth. She thrashed from side to side, but the belt kept moving. She awoke tangled in her sheets with Fred biting the knuckles of her good hand.

"Stop that," she said and batted him away. "I left food in your dish last night after you were sawing logs, so at the very least, you've eaten that. I'll just bet at least one Willis boy has fed you, too."

She got up, showered and dressed, and went down to find her kitchen empty. She ate a bowl of cereal and fed Fred again before grabbing her purse and heading for the door to her studio. Aunt Beth arrived as she unlocked the door to the outside.

"Good morning. I hope I'm not being presumptuous, but since we still don't have any jobs pressing, I thought I'd work on my own quilt again."

"It's your machine."

"I gave it to you, though, and I'm trying to honor that."

"Oh, Auntie, what's mine is yours, literally." Harriet smiled and gave her aunt a one-armed hug.

"So, where are you off to?" Beth asked. "You checking up on Carla and Aiden?"

"I guess you talked to Mavis."

"We had tea this morning. She said things went well with the family dinner."

"Yeah, it seemed to, after everyone got over the initial shock of finding out Gerald/Gerard had a daughter."

"Mavis said Carla called for Aiden at the end."

"She did. I've thought about this, and I think what bothers me is not that he goes to her, but more the way he does it."

"You need to tell him that," Aunt Beth said.

"This gets back to the same old problem. I'm just not sure I want to 'train' someone…another someone. Look how that turned out." She was trying to leave Steve and his lies in the past, and she truly believed she was doing better, but it still sneaked up on her now and then.

"He's not a dog," Aunt Beth said. "Any relationship requires communication by both parties. He's not a mind reader, and for that matter, neither are you. If you need him to act different before he goes to help someone else you need to tell him. Your uncle Hank and I were learning things about each other right up till the end."

"Well, in any case, Aiden's at work, so I'm not going to visit him. I thought I'd go talk to Carlton and see if he can tell me who Gerard/Gerald was working with twenty years ago and who is still around. Marit told me her father came back because a man was doing something bad and he could stop him. It has to relate to something that was going on twenty years or more ago. Our only other clue is the postcard he had Gerry send to the post office box about the chemical use."

"Don't forget what you saw from Miller Hill," Aunt Beth reminded. "That has to fit into the picture."

"I think it's obvious the chemicals are being used to make something other than firemen's turnouts. And Carla's friend Terry has something to do with it. I just don't know what."

"Whatever is going on, someone cares enough about it to kill Gerald to keep it secret," Aunt Beth said. "And you be careful, missy. Whoever killed Gerald is serious about protecting their business."

"I'm not doing anything dangerous, I promise. I'm going to talk to Carlton. I may go by Pins and Needles and see if Carla's there on my way home."

"I'll probably go by the church later and see if Jenny and DeAnn need any help arranging the flowers. The Dutch people are all in the business, so they called home last night and apparently have arranged for a lot of flowers to arrive this afternoon."

"I'll have my cell phone on if you need any help," Harriet said and left.

July through September were among the warmest months in Foggy Point, but they also are the months when morning fog returns, and such was the case as Harriet drove down her driveway and headed for Foggy Point Fire Protection. Wisps of white mist clung to the Muckleshoot River and curled toward the roadway as she drove to the factory.

Lynn was in her customary place at the reception desk when Harriet came into the lobby.

"Is the big man in?" Harriet asked.

"Yeah. Want me to see if he's receiving this morning?"

"Please."

But before Lynn could carry out her offer, Carlton emerged from his office.

"Hi, Harriet," he said "What can I do you for?"

"Gerald's funeral is going to be tomorrow at the Methodist Church. We're trying to get the word out, so I thought I'd come by and see if there are any people here that knew him and might want to be notified." She mentally patted herself on the back for her brilliant ruse.

"I can post a notice in the lunchroom," Carlton offered.

"I was hoping to be a little more pro-active than that. You know—I thought I could personally invite them."

"I'm sure they appreciate your concern, but that's what we have Human Resources for. They handle this type of thing. Lynn, have HR call Pastor Hafer at the Methodist Church and get the details. Thanks again for stopping by, Harriet." He put his arm around her shoulders and guided her toward the entrance.

Harriet planted her feet before he could get her out the door.

"A couple of us went up to Miller Hill Park the other night to get mineral water," she said. "We realized we were looking down on your factory."

Carlton didn't say anything.

"I didn't think you ran a night shift," she said finally.

"We don't."

"*Someone* was working. The lights were on, and a big door was open on the side toward the end of the building."

"We rent that section to an outside company for warehouse space. Maybe they were shuffling their goods around. That wouldn't be a shock, if you think about it. Now, I've got to get back to work. It was nice seeing you, and thanks for the information about Gerald's funeral. We'll be sure and let anyone who plans on attending have the time off."

He turned his head at the sound of a door opening somewhere down the hall. Bebe appeared dressed in a bright-pink flower print mini-dress.

"Gosh, Harriet, are you here again? Seems like every time I turn around you're here bothering Carlton."

Harriet could feel her shoulders tensing, and it hurt. "I was telling Carlton about the funeral arrangements for Gerald. I thought since Gerald had worked with Carlton's dad for so long, he'd want to know."

"So what did that have to do with what's going on in our warehouse? That's what you were talking about when I came in, wasn't it?"

"Darling, it's okay. Harriet was at Miller Hill Park the other night and noticed the lights, that's all."

Bebe gave Harriet a mother-lioness-protecting-her-cub look then pivoted on her pink spike heel and went back down the hall.

"Don't mind Bebe," Carlton said. "She's helping me manage my stress."

Harriet had no choice but to leave. She wasn't sure what else she could ask if he wouldn't acknowledge the basic fact that people were doing work at night. She got in her car and drove back to downtown Foggy Point.

✂ ✂ ✂

Marjory was at the cutting table when Harriet walked into Pins and Needles.

"Did you come for a look at the new Christmas fabric I just got in?" she asked. "Connie beat you to it if you were hoping to be the first."

"I haven't given Christmas a thought yet. It's still summer."

"Exactly. Summer is when you should be thinking about those Christmas projects, especially if you plan on making bed quilts."

"I suppose it couldn't hurt to look."

"That's my girl," Marjory said with a smile. "Can I get you a cup of tea?"

Harriet smiled back and nodded then continued on into the small classroom, where Marjory had set up a temporary display of all the new fabric. She'd arranged the bolts of material around the room, draping lengths from some across chair backs while others were stacked on tables against the wall. All of them were placed for easy access and viewing. Once they went onto the shelves with all the other bolts of fabric, only their edge would show, like books on a shelf.

An hour passed before Harriet even thought to ask where Carla was.

"She asked if she could rearrange her schedule today. She said she was worried about her friend Terry and was going to look for him." She checked her wristwatch. "She should be here in just a bit."

"Did she say where she was going to look?"

"She was going to check his hotel room and then drive up to Miller Hill Park and see if he was there."

"Why can't she just stay home and wait for him to resurface?" Harriet asked.

"Maybe she's been watching her mentor a little too close. Or maybe she wants you to know how your aunt feels."

"In any case," Harriet said, not ready to admit Marjory may be onto something, "I think I'll go by Aiden's on my way home and see if she's back."

She tried to pick up four bolts of Christmas fabric with her one arm but could only manage two.

"Here, let me help you," Marjory said. "How much do you want?"

"I think I'll have two yards of each." She didn't have a plan for the fabric, but with two yards of each she should be able to do something. "And maybe I better have a yard of the cream-colored print that goes with them." Harriet was trying to adhere to an article she'd read that pointed out most quilters didn't have enough light-colored fabrics in their stash and should therefore make it a point to pick up a neutral light color with every purchase, whether they needed it at the time or not.

Marjory unrolled several rotations'-worth of fabric off the first bolt and smoothed it out on her cutting table, measuring and moving it until she had two yards of the maroon-and-gray tree print to her right. She made a small cut on the fold of the fabric to mark the two-yard point then slid that point to the middle of her cutting mat and used her plexiglas ruler and rotary tool to cut the fabric in a straight line.

"You were here twenty years ago when Mavis's husband disappeared, weren't you?" Harriet asked.

"I've lived in Foggy Point my whole life, so yes, I was here when Gerald Willis died—the first time. I didn't own the store, of course, but I was around."

"Can you think of anyone who worked with Gerald back then and is still around now?"

Marjory thought for a moment. "You know, I can't. Remember, Foggy Point Fire Protection wasn't called that, and it was much smaller. Let me think again." She tapped her forefinger against her upper lip. "You know, my brother worked there around then. What I remember is that there was a big layoff. I remember it because the unemployment in Washington State had been improving for a number of years and was at one of its lower points, so it was weird that Carlton's dad laid off almost the whole work force.

"My brother found another job within a week. I think most of the other people did, too. FPFP actually had trouble a few months later when they started making the fireman's turnouts. They had a big job fair in the middle of town. *I* even worked for them for a few years. They offered signing bonuses and everything, but my brother didn't trust Carlton's dad and refused to come back."

"That's weird," Harriet said.

"Well, that's the Brewsters for you—or haven't you noticed that Carlton's not the sharpest knife in the rack? His dad wasn't as slow as Carlton, but he was always strange."

Harriet paid for her purchases and headed for Aiden's house to check up on Carla. She could see the road to Mavis's cottage coming up on her right, and in a last-minute move, she turned.

Mavis's powder blue Town Car was parked in front, and she opened the front door before Harriet could knock.

"Your asters are beautiful," Harriet said, referring to the lavender daisy-shaped flowers that covered two large plants in the flowerbeds on either side of the path leading to the cottage porch.

"Yes, they are, but I'm sure you didn't come to admire my asters. Are you staying for tea?" She held the door open, and Harriet stepped into the cozy living room.

"No, I was just at Pins and Needles, and Marjory said Carla took some time off to search for Terry. I thought I'd go by Aiden's and see if she's back."

Mavis waited patiently for her to say more.

"I swung by Carlton's office before I went to the quilt store. He insists nothing is going on at night other than warehouse work. I tried to get him to tell me who still works there that worked there during Gerald's time. He was kind of evasive, but it was hard to tell if he was trying to avoid telling me or if he was just being Carlton."

"I lost touch with those people after Gerald die—" She stopped and corrected herself. "…disappeared."

"Marjory said they had a layoff around the time Gerald left."

"Yeah, but that wasn't unusual back in those days. Until they started making the fireman's turnouts, things were real up and down. Products came and went, and the work force came and went with them."

"This is so frustrating," Harriet said. "I feel like we're so close to knowing what happened. If only we could figure out how the pieces fit together. Actually, that's why I stopped by. I was hoping you'd let me borrow the mystery square and Gerald's quilt. I'd like to get as many of the Threads together as we can on short notice. If everyone could look at the mystery square, it might jog a memory or create a connection or something."

Mavis went into her sewing room and returned with the quilt and the square.

"Do you need a bag?" she asked. "I tried to pin the magic square to the quilt, but my pin bent."

"This is fine," Harriet said and took the two pieces.

"You want me to start calling people?"

"I don't want to impose on your time."

"I need the distraction. Everyone is busy working on the funeral, and I'm just sitting here stewing. Where do you want to meet?"

"Tico's, if it's okay with Jorge."

"You go check on Carla, and I'll call around and let you know what people say."

"Thanks." She gave Mavis a one-armed hug.

"Thank *you*, honey. You're the one doing *me* a favor, figuring this thing out."

Harriet went to her car hoping she wasn't going to disappoint her friend.

Aiden's mother had left him her house and her collection of cars. It had been one of her few indulgences, apart from quilting fabric. The stately Victorian had a matching carriage house that had been turned into a five-car garage complete with servant's quarters on the second floor.

Carla didn't own a car of her own, and Aiden had been happy to share his fleet with her. It was anyone's guess which one she was driving today.

Harriet pulled around to the back of the house, as she generally came and went through the back porch door when she visited. There were no other cars visible, but she parked and went up to the door anyway, looking around the groomed back yard and the landscaped grounds leading to the woods beyond. She was reminded again of just how isolated the house was.

She heard the crunch of gravel behind her and was relieved to see a familiar Mercedes sedan pull in behind her car.

"Hi, Harriet," Carla said as she got out. "Aiden's at work."

"Actually, I came to see you."

"What's up?" She went around to the passenger side and got Wendy out of her car seat in the back.

"I heard you went to look for Terry this morning."

"I did," Carla said.

"And you took Wendy with you?" Harriet asked without thinking about how it would sound.

"No, I didn't take Wendy." Carla's face burned red.

"I'm sorry," Harriet said. "Of course you didn't."

"I took her to the drop-in day care at the Methodist Church."

"Did you find Terry?"

"No," Carla's shoulders drooped. "His car wasn't at his motel, and it wasn't at Miller Hill Park either."

"Well," Harriet said, trying to brighten her voice. "We know he's good at sneaking around. A whole group of us were following him, and four of us followed him all the way into the park, and he still was able to get the drop on us. He could very well be right here in town and doing just fine."

"He's not trying to hide from me on purpose, though," Carla said defensively. "He told me he was taking Wendy and me to breakfast. And he wanted to take Wendy to toddler time at the library. He wouldn't have made all those plans if he didn't want to see me anymore."

Let's hope not, Harriet thought. "Did he say anything about what he was doing?"

Wendy ran to the grassy back yard and plopped down on her rear end, laughing as she did so. Carla followed and handed her a brightly colored plush chicken. The toy made a cackling noise in response to the motion, which caused Wendy to giggle.

"He hasn't told me anything except that he's trying to find people who knew his dad. He said he was meeting a guy the other night. And he went to the library, but mostly he doesn't like to talk about it."

"Assuming he's not a big jerk—and at this point we don't have any evidence that he is—I'm starting to get worried."

Carla's eyes opened wide, and she sucked in her breath, but she didn't say anything.

"We're trying to get the Loose Threads together this afternoon to talk about things. Can you come?"

"What time?"

"Mavis was going to start calling people while I came here to check up on you," Harriet said. "She said she'd call and tell me the time when she had one."

"Do you want some lemonade?" Carla asked. "I made some from scratch this morning. Maybe Mavis will call while we're drinking it."

"Okay," Harriet said. "Tell me everything you saw at Terry's motel."

Carla picked up Wendy and swung her onto her hip, then led the way into the kitchen. She poured lemonade for herself and Harriet and poured apple juice into Wendy's sippy-cup. The toddled insisted on sitting on a "big-girl" chair at the kitchen table instead of her high chair, and Carla indulged her.

Harriet made Carla retrace her steps over and over again, but the only significant observation she made was the absence of Terry's car. He wasn't at his motel.

Carla had gotten up to refill their glasses when Harriet's cell phone rang. Mavis had arranged a meeting of most of the Loose Threads at Tico's Tacos at four that afternoon.

"I better go," Harriet said when she'd hung up. "Can you come to the meeting?"

"I think so," Carla replied. "I have to see if I can find someone to watch Wendy."

"I don't think anyone would mind if you brought her with you."

She thanked Carla for the lemonade, which really was the best she had ever tasted. They agreed they'd see each other in a few hours.

Chapter 24

Aunt Beth was still stitching her quilt when Harriet returned to her studio.

"You aren't overdoing it with your shoulder, are you?" Harriet asked.

"No. I've been taking it slow today, taking lots of breaks."

"Did Mavis call you?"

"Yeah, she told me about the meeting. I don't know what you think you're going to accomplish."

"We're right on the brink of knowing what happened to Gerald. I'll bet you anything that whoever killed him will show up at the funeral."

"And just what makes you think that?"

"All those detective shows on TV. They always say the killer comes to the funeral just to feel superior because no one knows who they are."

Aunt Beth shook her head. "Don't you think criminals watch television? If you know to expect him to show up, then he knows not to show up."

"Well, then, we'll pay attention to who isn't there and should be. And I can tell you, unless something happens overnight, Carla's friend Terry is going to be at the top of the absent list."

"Okay, I said I'd be there," Aunt Beth said. "I'm going to go home and put my feet up for a while before meeting time, and I suggest you do the same. You know your collar bone will heal faster if you rest a little now and then."

"Yeah, yeah, yeah."

"Don't get smart with me," Beth said, but she was smiling.

"I promise I'll lie down."

With that promise, Beth left.

Harriet did intend to lie down, but not until she had a snack. Her refrigerator was filled with leftovers, and she quickly found the potato salad. The lid was the sort that automatically released air as it sealed making it a sturdier seal than its cheaper competitors. This also made it impossible to open with one hand.

"Here, let me do that," Harry said. He'd come downstairs as Harriet was trying to use the edge of the counter to pop the lid. "I don't want to see a grown woman cry."

"And you would have, too."

He fetched two bowls and scooped potato salad into them. He handed one to Harriet and took the other one himself, returning the storage bowl to the refrigerator.

"Have you figured out who killed my dad yet?"

"I wish I could say yes," she said, looking at Harry's serious face. "But so far, I have more questions than answers. Carlton's father is dead. The people who worked with your dad are no longer at the company, and Carlton isn't being very forthcoming with names. But Carlton is generally not a helpful guy, so that in and of itself doesn't mean anything. Carla's friend Terry has been snooping around and spying on the factory, and now he's gone missing."

"Don't forget the magic bullet that wasn't a bullet," Harry added.

"How could I forget the magic bullet? Like I said—lots of questions, not so many answers."

"I might have one little answer," Harry said and paused for dramatic effect.

"Come on, my heart can't take the suspense." She was only half-joking.

"Well, my friend Nick's dad worked with my dad back then. And he's still in town. In fact, he'll be coming to the funeral tomorrow."

"So how long were you going to wait to tell me?"

"Geez, you sound like my mom. I just found out. Nick heard about Dad's funeral and told me he was going to be there with his dad."

"Sorry," Harriet said. "I've been badgering Carlton Brewster to give me names and he hasn't, so it's been a bit frustrating."

"Nick only called me last night to offer his condolences."

"It's all right, Harry, really." She finished eating her potato salad. It was true what they said about potato salad benefiting from a day in the refrigerator. It was always better the second day. She rinsed her bowl and put it in the dishwasher while Harry went for seconds.

"I'm going to go lie down and rest my collar bone," she said and went upstairs.

Chapter 25

It was déjà vu when Harriet walked into the back room of Tico's Tacos just before four o'clock. Jenny and Lauren were at the picnic table sipping iced tea. A pitcher and more glasses sat on a smaller table off to the side. Jenny had shed the black spy look and was dressed in silver cotton pants and a pale pink shell. Lauren wore denim capri pants and a yellow T-shirt that brought out the highlights in her pale hair.

Connie came in from the kitchen where she explained she had been talking to Jorge about a recipe for barbacoa. She'd come from her volunteer job reading stories to preschool children at the library, and was still wearing a floral shirtwaist dress in her signature sherbet tones. She knew the current crop of pre-school teachers dressed in jeans and sometimes even sweatpants, under the theory that a teacher needed to crawl around on the floor to relate to her students; but she had made it clear to Harriet on more than one occasion she didn't believe rolling around on the floor on the teacher's part was an integral part of learning.

Harriet filled a glass and, after a nod from Connie, one for her friend. She carried them to the table one at a time.

"Has anyone had any insights since we last talked?"

"Aren't you supposed to be the hot-stuff crime solver around here?" Lauren asked.

"Only if the rest of you won't step up to the plate."

The room went silent.

"Look, right now, Mavis is suspect number one as far as the police are concerned. I'm not willing to sit back and watch her get arrested for something she didn't do."

"Are you certain she *didn't* do it?" Lauren asked. "I mean, she doesn't have an alibi for the time of the crime."

"Well, it's nice to know I have one person on my side," Mavis said. No one had heard her arrive.

Jenny and Connie started talking at once, assuring her of their belief in her innocence.

Lauren cleared her throat. "I don't think you killed your husband," she said in a subdued voice."I stayed up until three o'clock this morning doing computer searches." She pulled her shoulder-length hair into a ponytail and slid the Scrunchi that had been on her wrist onto her hair to hold it in place. "Carla's friend doesn't exist. There are plenty of Terry Jansens but no one that comes close to any of the information he's given us. And believe me, I dug."

"Are you a hacker?" Connie asked.

"I have a master's degree in computer science, I don't hack." She started to say something else but was interrupted by the arrival of Robin and DeAnn. Robin was wearing flared black Lycra pants and a pale blue baby tee that flashed her well muscled abs when she reach for an iced tea glass. DeAnn had on knee-length khaki shorts and a dark green T-shirt with the Foggy Point Video logo on the chest.

"So, what did we miss?" she asked.

"Lauren did some research about Terry Jansen, and she couldn't find him." Connie said.

"Is that all?" DeAnn asked.

"No, that's not all," Lauren said. "I was trying to finish reporting on my findings when you came in and interrupted."

"Well, excuse me," DeAnn said.

"What else did you find out?" Harriet asked before the conversation could deteriorate any further.

"I was about to say that when I couldn't develop anything about Terry, one of our potential suspects, I decided to see what I could find about Mavis's lack of alibi. I mean, if she hadn't been called away, she would have been in our booth at the critical moment. I started to wonder if she was being set up right from the get-go."

"And?" Mavis said.

"I started looking at funerals that took place in Portland on the days you were gone. Fortunately, there weren't that many. Now, we're assuming people accurately report who the survivors are in the obituary, but if that's true, then the only way Pete's babysitter was at her grandfather's funeral would be if she's really a grandson, a great-granddaughter or under twelve years of age."

"I knew there was something fishy about that girl," Mavis said.

"Unfortunately, nothing I found tells us who did the set-up," Lauren said.

"Thank you for looking," Mavis said.

Aunt Beth arrived carrying a basket of chips and a dish of salsa Jorge had handed her as she passed the kitchen door.

"Jorge said this would help us think," she said, and set the treats on the table. "Is anyone else coming?" she asked Mavis.

"Sarah couldn't get off work, and Carla was looking for a babysitter. If she's not here by now, she must not have been successful," Mavis replied.

"So, what are we here for?" Robin asked.

Aunt Beth sat beside Mavis, and Harriet stood up and moved to the end of the table.

"I feel like we're getting close to figuring out what happened, but a few pieces of the puzzle are missing. First, I'd hoped we could list everything we know and see if anyone can see a pattern. Second, I'd like to make sure we get all the information we can at the funeral."

Robin pulled out the yellow tablet she always kept in her shoulder bag. Once again, she listed Gerry's postcard, Mavis's sudden babysitting job in Portland, Gerald's reappearance, Gerald's second family, Terry's appearance in town, his night-time absences, his surveillance of Foggy Point Fire Protection, the night work and now Terry's disappearance. She put them in neat columns—Gerald/Gerard information in one, Terry information in another.

Harriet had her add the information about the layoffs at the time of Gerard's disappearance, the contradiction in Terry's report of his military service, and the magic bullet.

"Ideas anyone?" she asked.

"What they're doing at night at Foggy Point Fire Protection is why Gerald came back," DeAnn suggested.

"But why did he leave in the first place?" Lauren asked.

"Wait." Harriet reached into a canvas bag bearing the Quilt As Desired logo and pulled out Gerald's plaid flannel quilt and the black mystery material. "Exhibit one," she said, and placed the two items on the table. "Mavis found this quilt in her sewing room just before the re-enactment. It appeared out of nowhere after twenty years. It was Gerald's."

"So, obviously Gerald put it there," Lauren said.

"But why?" Robin wondered.

"Let me see that," DeAnn said. She bent the square, corner to corner, tugged at the edges and then smelled it. "Does anyone have a scissor?"

Several people rummaged in their purses. Connie won, triumphantly holding a pair of Gingher shears up.

"I was going to drop these off at Pins and Needles to go to the sharpener."

"Is it okay if I cut the mystery square with them?" DeAnn asked.

Connie agreed, and DeAnn began a series of attempts to cut the fabric. She tried snipping with the scissor tips. She pulled the piece deep into the blades. She laid the fabric on the table and stabbed at it with the scissors held in her fist.

"Anyone else want to try?" she asked.

Lauren held her hands out for the piece. DeAnn passed it to her, and Lauren repeated the experiment.

"So, this is some sort of thin, protective material?" she said when she'd run out of methods to try.

"That's weird," Harriet said. She glanced at Mavis and Aunt Beth.

"We all three saw Mavis's appliqué scissors poke a hole in that square," Beth said.

"So, how did you do it?" Robin asked.

"I was holding it while Mavis held a match to it," Harriet explained. "She got the flame close to my hand and I dropped the square, bumped my teacup and knocked the scissors off the table. The tea slopped onto the square and the scissors fell point down into and through the material. The square didn't protect my hand from the heat, by the way."

"Hand me the tea," Lauren said.

DeAnn was closest to the small table and passed it to her down the table, where Robin handed it to Lauren. Lauren laid down her napkin, put the black square on it and poured iced tea onto its surface. She took Connie's scissors into her fist, raised her arm and stabbed down into the material. The scissors slid sideways and skittered off the black square and into the scarred top of the picnic table.

She looked at Harriet. "So tell us again how you poked a hole in this thing."

"Don't look at me. Feel the center, my hole is still there," Harriet said.

Lauren tried her experiment again with similar results. "So, what gives?"

"It was hot tea," said the disembodied voice of Jorge over the intercom speaker. Moments later he appeared in the back room with a steaming water kettle. "Try this." He laid a thick cotton dishtowel on the table. Lauren reached up for the pot, and he pulled it away. "Hey, it was my idea. At least let me pour."

"Knock yourself out," Lauren said, and put the square on top of the towel.

Jorge carefully poured steaming water onto the material.

"Okay, hit it," he said, and Lauren stabbed down with the scissors. This time they went through the black square like it was made from butter, embedding the points of the blades in the towel.

"Remind me what this proves, Sherlock," she said.

"It doesn't prove anything," Harriet said. "It gives us more information."

Mavis made a fist and gently pounded it against her forehead.

"I wish I could remember," she said. "Gerald talked about his work a lot, but I'm afraid I was distracted with the boys and trying to get them all pointed to college. He was just perfecting the fire protection cloth, but beyond that, I'm not sure. They were doing something with shoe tops."

"Maybe they were trying to make safety shoes," DeAnn said. "You know, like steel-toed boots only lighter weight."

"That could be a real good deal for people who work in kitchens," Jorge said. The women had forgotten he was still in the room. "You know, in some big kitchens they require steel-toed shoes because of the knives, but those boots were heavy and back then, boots were the only option. A lightweight protective shoe would have been a big deal in the restaurant trades."

"I guess the boiling water thing would be a problem," Connie mused.

"Too bad there's no evidence," Robin said. "Without a prototype or a drawing or a formula linking Gerry's chemical to this material, it's only speculation. I'd be willing to bet Gerald and Carlton's dad made dozens of test fabrics back in the early days. They probably had more than a few chemicals in common, too. I'm sorry, but we need hard evidence."

"At the very least, it would be helpful to know why, out of all the test samples the company made, Gerald as Gerard kept this particular one with him for all these years," Harriet suggested.

Jenny looked at her watch. "I'm sorry, but I'm going to have to leave in a little while. Could we move on to the funeral?"

"Sure," Harriet said. "I'm thinking we have several people we need to watch tomorrow. Ilsa and the cousins, Carlton and anyone who shows up from Foggy Point Fire Protection and Terry, if he shows up. In addition, I want to talk to the father of Harry's friend, and, Mavis, I know this is hard, but I'd like Connie to take a crack at your son Pete." She held her hand up to silence the protest Mavis was about to make. "We need to know why Pete called you to Portland during the re-enactment. I think Connie might be able to get it out of him. Aunt Beth, I thought you could help Connie ratchet up the pressure if needed."

"What do you want me to do?" Jenny asked.

"I penciled you in for keeping an eye on the Dutch people. And DeAnn and Robin, I thought you could cover the Foggy Point Fire Protection group. With two of you, if Carlton splits off to talk to non-company people, one can follow him and the other stay with the employees. Keep track of anyone out of the ordinary who speaks to him."

"Who does that leave me?" Lauren asked.

"I have two things for you. First, if Terry shows up, stick with him. Second, I'd like you to check at regular intervals with Mavis. Mavis, you can keep your eyes open for anyone who seems out of place. Most people should identify themselves to you if they knew Gerald but not you. If you notice anyone who avoids you or in any other way seems out of place, tell Lauren."

"What about Sarah and Carla?" Lauren asked.

"Since they aren't here, all we can do is tell them to keep their eyes and ears open. I know Carla was planning on attending the funeral, but I'm not sure if Sarah's coming."

"Anyone have any objections?" Aunt Beth asked.

No one did, and they finished their drinks with a discussion of the raffle quilt they were going to be starting for an auction benefit-ing the Foggy Point No Kill animal shelter. The group was split over the concept, with DeAnn and Connie pushing for dog-theme blocks, while Jenny and Robin wanted something less cutesy. Lauren said she didn't care and frankly, Harriet thought, neither did she.

"There's a family viewing tonight," Mavis said. "I've been go-ing back and forth about going. But after all this…" She gestured toward the group. "…I'm thinking I should go, just to keep an eye on things. Beth, maybe you and Harriet should come with me."

"I think that's a good idea," Robin said. "I mean about taking Harriet and Beth, if you're going to go."

"Does anyone here speak Dutch?" Lauren asked. The Threads looked at each other, but no one shook her head in the affirmative.

"I know the basics," Mavis said. "We visited the cousins, but they speak English, so I never really had to go too far with my Dutch."

"I was hoping you could tell if they were saying anything revealing about Gerald," Lauren said.

"They're too polite to speak Dutch in a group of English speakers," Mavis said, "so it won't matter."

"Of course, we'll go," Beth said. "If you're sure you're up to it."

"I'm fine," Mavis said. "And no offense, Beth, but I'll drive."

"I'm wounded."

"Thank you, thank you, thank you," Harriet said. "I think we all know who would have been in the back seat."

Mavis and Beth agreed they would all three meet at Mavis's cottage in a half-hour. The rest dispersed after making their various transportation plans for the funeral the next day.

✂ ✂ ✂

With her good hand needed for driving, Harriet had to wait until she was home before she could call Aiden. She left a message on his cell phone telling him about the viewing she was attending in a short while and then called the animal clinic. The receptionist told her he was with a patient and promised to have him call when he was free.

She went upstairs to search her closet for an appropriate black outfit. Her whole wardrobe had been built around black when she was living in Oakland, but at Aunt Beth's urging, she had purged the black and replaced it with other, neutral-colored basics. She awkwardly pulled a suitcase from the overhead shelf above the hanging bar in the closet. Inside, she had secreted her favorite black sheath and a black three-piece suit far from Aunt Beth's prying eyes.

She opened the case, pulled out the sheath and gave it a shake. She would add a black-and-purple print scarf and it would do just fine.

Chapter 26

I wondered what you were going to show up in," Aunt Beth said when Harriet had arrived at Mavis's cottage at the agreed-upon hour. "I was pretty sure you hadn't been shopping."

"She looks okay to me," Mavis said, unaware of Aunt Beth's attempt to ban the black from Harriet's closet.

"You always have been an insolent little twerp," Aunt Beth said with a smile.

She was wearing black pants with a purple rayon blouse and a black hip-length vest. Mavis had chosen black linen pants and a loose-fitting jacket over a cream-colored T-shirt-style linen blouse. Harriet had noticed both her aunt and Mavis were opting for pants more and more often on dress-up occasions to avoid having to wear non-sensible footwear. Today, they both had on their black SAS shoes. Aunt Beth kept encouraging Harriet to try the comfortable shoes, at least while she was working on the long arm machine, but Harriet just couldn't go there yet.

"I guess we better leave," Mavis said. Harriet could hear the reluctance in her voice.

"You don't have to do this," Aunt Beth said.

Mavis squared her shoulders and took a deep breath. "No, I don't have to, but I need to. We may not learn anything new, but we won't know unless we go find out." With that said, she led the way to her Town Car.

Several vehicles were in the parking lot of the Methodist Church when they arrived a few minutes later. Harriet recognized Ilsa's rental car and Pastor Hafer's mini-van. She assumed the rest belonged to the Willis brothers.

"Welcome," Pastor Hafer said as they approached the open door to the church, and pointed them to their left. They walked down a hallway that led away from the sanctuary and toward the fellowship hall, a smaller public room that adjoined the kitchen area and could be configured with tables for dining or with rows of chairs for smaller meetings. Today, the chairs were arranged in a horseshoe shape, with three rows of chairs in the curved section and Gerald's casket at the open end of the shoe. The half-lid of the dark wooden casket was open, but a standing spray of flowers was strategically placed to prevent premature viewing.

Ilsa stood with the Dutch cousins and nodded to the trio when they came into the room. Harriet noticed Marit had been left elsewhere for the evening. Gerry and James were in front of the pass-through window to the kitchen. Their wives were on the other side with two women who looked familiar to Harriet. She assumed they were involved in the after-funeral food for tomorrow.

Pete was sitting in a chair by himself on the far side of the room.

"Could you all take a seat please?" Pastor Hafer asked as he ushered Harry and Ben in and shut the door. "I won't keep you long.

"This is a time for family to come together and support each other. We have a rather unusual situation here, so I'd like to do something before we move on to the actual viewing.

"Gerald Willis left his family nearly twenty years ago. We can only guess why. He began a new life in the Netherlands, and again, we can but speculate about why he never told his new family about his life in Foggy Point. God knows, and that has to be enough.

"Everyone here has suffered a loss, some more recently than others." He went on to suggest they set aside any anger they had over the situation for a few minutes and share a few stories of life with Gerald…or Gerard.

It sounded like a terrible idea to Harriet, but Pastor Hafer started the group out with a story one of the ushers had told him about the time Gerald was helping out during a Christmas Eve service and accidentally lit the manger on fire when he dozed off and dropped the candle he was holding. The organist had a pitcher of water, and had gotten up and dumped it on the manger, putting out the fire. Gerald had never lived it down.

Before long, both groups were laughing and talking and sharing their memories.

"He's good," Harriet said in a low voice to her Aunt Beth after they had moved away from the group, standing near the now-empty kitchen.

"Who?"

"Pastor Hafer. I was having a little trouble seeing how this was going to be anything but a disaster, but look at them."

"Gerald was a good man. It only stands to reason both of his families would be good people."

"I hope we can give them all some peace by figuring out why all this happened."

A coffee and tea service had been arrayed on the kitchen pass-through counter, and Harriet poured a cup of hot water and selected an Earl Gray bag from the basket of assorted teas.

"Want some?" she asked her aunt.

"No, if I drink anymore I'll be running to the bathroom all night."

Harriet was dunking her bag when the door to the fellowship hall opened a few inches and Aiden gestured for her to come out into the corridor.

"What are you doing here?" she asked, the smile on her face disappearing as she noted his worried expression. "What's wrong?"

"Carla's missing," he said. "The daycare called me at work to say they were closing and she hadn't shown up to get Wendy."

Harriet cracked the door open again and signaled to Aunt Beth. Her aunt came into the hallway, and Aiden repeated his story.

"That's not right," she said. "Carla would never leave that baby."

"That's what I'm saying," Aiden said. "I came here to the daycare then had to go home and get a carseat. I'm just lucky my mom had one at the house from when my nieces were little. I got Wendy and then got hold of Carla's sister to babysit." He was bouncing up and down on the balls of his feet, his left hand rattling the coins in his pocket.

"What about the police?" Harriet asked.

"I called, and she hasn't been gone long enough. They said they would keep an eye out, but without any idea of where she might have gone, they weren't hopeful. If Wendy had been missing it would be different, but for adults they have to consider that the person might have chosen to leave. She has to be missing forty-eight hours before the Foggy Point Police Department will take a formal report.

"I don't suppose there's any sign that her friend Terry showed up, is there?" Aunt Beth asked.

Aiden shook his head. "There's no sign of anything. No note, nothing out of place. I even looked in her room."

"And?" Harriet asked.

"Nothing. I can't even think where to start."

"Let's go talk to her sister," Harriet suggested. "Maybe Carla said something to her that would give us some place to start."

"I'll stay here with Mavis," Beth said. "I'll call when we're out of here and see if you've found her. There's no point calling the Threads for help until we have a starting point." She went back into the Fellowship Hall, and Harriet had to trot to keep up with Aiden as he left the building and went to his Bronco.

"Let's drive by Terry's motel on our way back to your house."

"Okay, but I don't want to leave Wendy with Carla's sister any longer than we have to," Aiden replied. Harriet felt a small twinge of jealousy at the way he spoke of Wendy as if she were his child.

He drove through a series of neighborhood streets where single-story houses nestled among Douglas fir trees and shore pines then onto a gravel roadway, taking a more direct route to Smuggler's Cove. Harriet was pretty sure she'd never been on some of these roads.

"Carla used to leave Wendy with her sister all the time," she said eventually.

"Have you ever met the woman?" Aiden countered. "You might want to before you make any judgments. I'm not sure I'd trust her to take care of Randy."

"You're right, I haven't met her. I think she's a half-sister, not that that should affect her parenting skills."

Aiden guided the Bronco into an empty spot near Terry's motel room. The gray rental car sat at the end of the line of parking spaces that nosed into the sidewalk in front of the ground-floor rooms.

"Isn't that his car?" Harriet asked.

"It looks like the car we followed, but it's a pretty generic model for a rental. I'm sure every motel in town has at least one that looks similar to this one in its parking lot."

Harriet opened her door and jumped out before he could ask what she was doing. She stepped up to Terry's ground-floor room and rapped on the door. No one answered.

"If you're looking for soldier boy, he ain't here," said a balding fat man carrying a bucket of ice cubes. "His room hasn't been slept in for a couple days."

"And you know this how?" Harriet said as she turned toward him.

"I'm the manager here," he said and straightened as much as he could, given his bulging gut. "He ain't used the bed, he ain't left me a tip. Nada."

"Do you know where he is?"

"He don't check in with me. He's friendly enough if he's in his room while I'm cleaning, but he don't tell me his calendar. What he does do is pay in advance a week at a time. So long as his room's paid up, he can sleep wherever he wants."

Harriet found the thought of finding this greasy man, with clean towels over his arm, when you opened your motel room door expecting the maid sort of horrifying.

Aiden started to get out of the Bronco, but she waved him back. She thought of asking the manager to call her if he saw Terry, but she knew it would be a waste of time. Plus, she didn't want him to have her number.

"He's not here," she said as she got back into the car. Aiden immediately backed out of the driveway and headed for his house.

The back door opened before he'd parked the car.

"Here," Cissy said, coming down the porch steps, a bawling baby in her arms. She thrust Wendy into Aiden's arms before they could get into the house. "I gotta work the early shift." She brushed past Harriet and got into her car.

"Her concern for her sister and niece is overwhelming," Harriet said.

"That's what I was trying to tell you. I had to pay her in advance to get her to sit with Wendy while I came to get you."

Wendy began to whimper.

"It's okay, baby," Harriet said in a soothing voice. Wendy reached out for her. She took the toddler and carried her through the kitchen and then up the stairs to Carla's room and the nursery. She bathed her and got her into her pajamas while Aiden fixed a bottle. Within a half-hour, they had the little girl asleep.

"Now what?" Aiden whispered as they tiptoed out of the room.

"We need to find Carla," Harriet said. "My guess is that she's wherever Terry is."

"Any idea where that might be?"

"I'd like to go to Miller Hill Park and have a look at Foggy Point Fire Protection."

"Not by yourself, you're not," Aiden said firmly.

"We can't leave Wendy alone," she reminded him.

"Of course we can't." He ran his hands through his hair and paced across Carla's sitting room.

Harriet pulled out her cell phone and started typing on the keypad.

"I'm texting Aunt Beth to see if she's done with Mavis yet. When she's free, I'll see if she can come stay with Wendy so we can go look for Carla." She finished typing, and they sat in silence waiting for Harriet's phone to signal a return message.

Aunt Beth sent a reply a few minutes later.

"Almost done. Be right there."

Aiden pulled Harriet into his arms. "What would I do without you?"

"If you'd never met me, you probably wouldn't have a missing live-in housekeeper with a baby, for one thing."

"Yeah, but I also wouldn't get to run around in the middle of the night with a beautiful woman at my side searching for her."

"That's not funny."

Aiden kissed her gently on the lips and then let her go to begin pacing again. "I know," he said. "I was trying not to think about it for a minute. I'm really worried about Carla."

"We better go downstairs and wait for Aunt Beth."

Aiden picked up the baby monitor from its base on the table outside Wendy's room.

"I got this thing for Carla because the house is so big, she can't hear it when Wendy wakes up from her afternoon nap." He flicked a switch on the side of the blue-and-white unit and it emitted a static hum. He led the way downstairs.

Aunt Beth arrived a half-hour later, tapping gently on the back door.

"I'm sorry you had to come over here so late," Aiden said.

"Heavens, boy, it's not your fault. We're all concerned about Carla and Wendy. You two go. Find Carla. I'll be fine here. I'm going to go upstairs so I'll be close if Wendy needs anything."

"Thank you," Harriet said and hugged her.

Aiden repeated the sentiment and hugged Beth before guiding Harriet back out to the Bronco.

"Let's go up to the park and have a look, and if we don't see anything, I say we go down to the factory and check it out," Harriet said as she buckled her seatbelt.

Aiden drove down the long driveway and again began the series of turns onto back roads and alleys that cut a direct path across the peninsula and up Miller Hill to the park.

"If Carla or Terry is up here, they must have come on foot," Harriet said as she looked around the empty parking lot.

"Unless they hid their vehicles."

"Somehow, I can't see Carla doing that unless she found Terry and he helped her."

Aiden pulled a camouflaged optics case from behind his seat and got out. "Let's see if we can see anything at the factory from here," he said, and took out a pair of high-powered binoculars. "My dad used to hunt with these."

They crept to the rock they'd hid behind when they had followed Terry. Aiden's father's hunting binoculars were much stronger than the ones Terry had shared with them the last time they'd been up here. Aiden handed them to Harriet after he'd looked, sweeping the lenses from right to left across the whole factory below. Harriet repeated the process.

"Wow," she said. "It almost looks abandoned."

"You'd think there would at least be a night watchman's car in the parking lot."

"Let's go down and have a closer look."

"We can try, but if no one's working, the gate might be locked."

"What gate?"

"The one that's always open. It goes across the road when you first turn onto the property."

They returned to the truck and drove to Foggy Point Fire Protection. As Aiden had feared, the gate was locked.

"Can we climb over?" Harriet asked.

"We could. We could also get arrested for trespassing. Besides, as we saw from above, the place is locked up tight. I don't know about these guys, but the night shift at my parent's factory worked Sunday through Thursday, so I guess I'm not surprised they aren't open."

"Okay," Harriet said with a sigh. "Let's go back to your house and see if Carla has shown up. If not we can figure out where to go from there."

This time he took the usual route home. "Looks like we've got company," he said as they came up the drive and passed three cars parked along its edge.

"Aunt Beth must have cracked and called the Threads," Harriet said. "That first car was Robin's and the one closest to the house is Lauren's. I'm not sure who the other one is."

✂ ✂ ✂

"Apparently, the police won't take a missing person report on Carla until she's been gone forty-eight hours," Aunt Beth was saying to Robin, Lauren and DeAnn, who were sitting around the kitchen table when Aiden and Harriet walked in.

"What car is she driving?" Robin asked.

"One of my mom's," Aiden replied, "One of the Mercedes sedans."

"You didn't give it to her, did you?" Robin pressed.

"I gave her permission to drive it, if that's what you're getting at," Aiden said. A hard edge was creeping into his voice, but Robin didn't back down.

"Report it stolen," she said.

"It's not stolen. I just told you, she has permission to use it while she's working for me."

"Report it stolen," Robin insisted, this time holding out her cell phone.

The muscle in Aiden's jaw twitched as he clenched his teeth in an effort to control his anger.

Harriet put her hand on his arm.

"Aiden," she said, "Listen to Robin. They won't look for Carla till she's missing for forty-eight hours, but if you report that your car has been stolen, they'll start looking for it right away. If we find the car, we'll either find Carla or we'll have a starting point."

He pulled his own phone out of his pocket and dialed the Foggy Point Police Department non-emergency phone number.

"They said they'll start looking immediately," he said after he ended the call.

"I'll call Darcy," Robin said, and started dialing.

By the time Robin clicked the end button, she'd extracted a promise from Darcy to make sure and let the patrol supervisor know this was no ordinary stolen car. Like many of the forensic lab people, Darcy had been a street cop before entering the specialized training that led to her current career, and she still maintained a close relationship with them.

"There must be something else we can do," Aiden said.

"We can ask the Threads to drive the streets before the funeral, but I'm not sure how effective that would be, given that the police are going to be doing the same thing," Harriet said.

"We should all go home and get some rest," Aunt Beth said. "Let's let the police do their job and lets us concentrate on seeing what we can find out at the funeral. I'll stay here with Wendy tonight, and I'll get one of the ladies at church to watch her during the funeral."

"I'm not sitting around," Lauren said.

"Now, honey," Aunt Beth said. "I know you want to help, but…"

"I'm not going anywhere physically. I can get my computer friends on the search. Someone's bound to have access to real-time satellite pictures of Foggy Point. I'll need to know exactly what the car looks like, and the license plate number, too."

"Let me go find that," Aiden said.

"Do you really think you can access satellites?" Harriet asked.

"I can't. I'm saying there's a good chance one of my cyber-friends can. It will take a little time, but we have a couple of heavy hitters in our group, and they're usually up for a challenge."

"Let's hope so," Harriet said.

Aiden came back with the requested information, and the group agreed to meet before the funeral to review their assignments and exchange updates. DeAnn volunteered to call people, and with that everyone but Beth, Harriet and Aiden left.

Harriet took the plastic wrap off a plate of brownies Aunt Beth had brought. She took out three and put them on paper towels she pulled from the dispenser attached to the underside of the cabinet next to the sink. She handed the first one to Aunt Beth and another to Aiden and brought the last one back to her place at the table.

"I thought we needed some chocolate," she said and sat down.

The trio ate in silence.

"I wish I could think of something else to do," Harriet said when her brownie was gone; she began shredding her paper towel, pulling off little pieces and rolling them into balls she then lined up in a neat row.

"Me, too," Aiden said, and leaned back in his chair. "I have to work in the morning, but I took time off to go to the funeral."

"Let's hope Carla's back by then," Aunt Beth said. "In the meanwhile, you, young lady, need to go home and get some rest. And you, too," she told Aiden. "I'm going to go check the baby." She got up and crumpled her paper towel, dropping it in the kitchen wastebasket before going upstairs.

Harriet stood, and Aiden stood with her.

"Come here," he said, and pulled her into his arms. She leaned against his chest, and he rested his chin on her head.

"I don't know what I'm going to do if something's happened to Carla," he said.

Harriet willed her muscles not to tense.

"This house was just starting to feel like a home again. And I can't even think about what will happen to that baby upstairs."

"Let's not go there," she said, and pushed back so she could look into his pale eyes. "We'll find her. Carla's tough. She's survived some pretty hard stuff already. She was the one who led us out of the burning building when we were locked in at quilt camp. She'll figure out a way to get back to her daughter."

"I should have protected her from Terry. You tried to tell me he was bad news."

"I don't think that's exactly what I said. Besides, Carla is a big girl. She can decide who she sees. And we don't know that Terry did anything. Let's not forget that *he* disappeared first."

"I hate this," he said and pulled her back to him. He cupped her face in his hands and gently kissed her. "You better go. I don't want you to, but you need your rest."

Harriet knew he wouldn't sleep. She also knew that, short of finding Carla, nothing she could do or say would make a difference.

She was almost out the door when she remembered she hadn't driven.

"Let me tell Beth I'm leaving, and I'll take you home," he said.

"How about you tell her I'll pick her up at ten, and I'll take her car."

"That's fine," Beth said from the stairs. "I was just coming down for a second brownie."

She might fool Aiden, but Harriet knew her aunt was making sure she went home and got some rest. She took Beth's car keys from the kitchen counter and went out the door.

Chapter 27

Fred exhibited his uncanny ability to wake Harriet before her alarm went off. If she didn't set her alarm, he had his own idea about when she should get up; but if it was on, he would start bothering her fifteen minutes before whatever time she set.

"Would you go away, please," she said, and pushed him to the end of her bed. "I had just finally gotten to sleep."

It had been a restless night. She'd fallen asleep sometime after three. Fred didn't care. She pulled the sheet over her head, and he started pouncing, using just enough claw pressure to ensure she couldn't fall back to sleep.

"Okay, you win," she said, and threw the covers back awkwardly with her good arm.

Gerald's funeral was scheduled to begin at eleven. She had two hours before she needed to pick up Beth. She went downstairs, fed Fred and poured herself a bowl of cereal. There were no signs of life from the Willis boys. She wasn't sure if they were still sleeping or had gone out for an early breakfast.

She picked up her cell phone and could see the telephone icon indicating she had a message. She set the phone on the counter and pressed the buttons to play the message on speaker phone.

"I had to pull in a few favors, but a couple of people are searching real-time satellite photos for Carla's car. Unless they get lucky, it's going to take some time." The message ended as abruptly as it had started. If her associates came through, Harriet decided she could forgive Lauren's brusqueness.

"At least that's something, Fred," she said. Fred lifted his fuzzy face from his dish of kibbles but didn't say anything.

She chose the black pants from her three-piece suit and a charcoal gray sleeveless blouse for her funeral outfit. After showering and dressing, she refilled Fred's bowl then went into her studio to check her stitching schedule to be sure she wasn't expecting anyone to drop off a project while she was at the church. Her next quilt wouldn't be coming until Monday, which was a relief.

Juggling a purse when one arm was strapped to your side was harder than it looked. She pulled her license, debit card, car keys and cell phone from hers and put them in her pants pockets. In a last-minute move, she picked up the black mystery square and slid it into her back pants pocket. Aunt Beth would probably chide her for the bulges, but it couldn't be helped. She took a last look around the kitchen and headed to Aiden's house.

Aunt Beth had a cup of tea steeping for her when she walked into the kitchen. "I heard you coming up the drive," she explained. "Aiden paced all night while Wendy slept like a log. Poor little thing," she added, and looked at the little girl, who was chasing Cheerios around the tray on her high chair. "She has no idea what's going on."

Beth was wearing black jersey pants and a black tone-on-tone blouse. Wendy was dressed in a pink sundress. Beth wet a washcloth at the sink and wiped the child's face and hands.

"I think we're about ready to go," she said. She looked out the window at the driveway. "Oh, good thinking—you brought your own car. It will be easier to put the carseat in yours."

Harriet hadn't thought about it at all. It just never occurred to her to drive her aunt's car again. Beth was right, though. The seat was difficult to install in the middle row of seats in Harriet's Honda SUV. It would have been impossible in the tiny back seat of the Beetle.

The carseat finally settled in, and Aunt Beth lifted Wendy into it, carefully buckling the maze of straps.

"Gosh, you just about need a trade school degree to operate one of those things," Harriet commented.

"Tell me about it," she said. When you were small your carseat was little more than a booster seat and a lap belt."

They carefully avoided mentioning Carla, or their concerns for her whereabouts while her daughter was in the car, even if she was too young to understand.

Connie and Robin were waiting on the steps to the Methodist Church when Harriet guided her car into the parking lot.

"DeAnn's inside finding us an empty room," Robin said as they approached.

"I'm going to take the little one here to the kitchen to meet up with her minder," Beth said. "I'll meet you back here."

"Have you heard anything?" Harriet asked Lauren, when she, too, joined the group.

"Thanks for broadcasting," Lauren said. "I'm sure my friend at NOAA will appreciate everyone knowing what she's doing for us." She was dressed in black twill pants and a silk khaki tank top. A black-and-tan silk scarf was draped artfully around her neck and onto her shoulders.

"Sorry," Harriet replied. "But have you heard anything?"

"Don't you think I'd say something if I'd heard any news?" Lauren turned her back on Harriet.

"I was just asking," she said as Lauren retreated.

"Okay, we can meet in the preschool classroom," DeAnn announced a few minutes later. Aunt Beth had returned, and Jenny and Sarah arrived.

"Mavis is with her sons and their families," Connie said. "Do I need to go get her?"

"No," Harriet said. "I just wanted to review our assignments and talk a little about Carla. Mavis doesn't need to be here for that."

The women squatted awkwardly on the tiny preschool chairs, and one-by-one, they told the group what they would be doing during the funeral. Robin and DeAnn would mingle with the employees of Foggy Point Fire Protection. Robin had done some legal work for the company before she'd gone into semi-retirement. DeAnn rented movies to most of them on a weekly basis, so she, too, would fit in.

Harry had agreed to introduce Harriet to his friend Nick's dad. Pete was likely to be putty in Connie's hands, and Aunt Beth would be there for reinforcement if needed. Jenny had spent time with Ilsa when the flowers arrived, and they had bonded over their mutual love of gardening. Lauren would be watching for Terry, but more important, she would keep her cell phone on silent and let everyone know when she heard anything about Carla's car. In a stroke of genius, Aunt Beth absolved Sarah of any responsibility because of her role as vocalist in the funeral ceremony.

With their assignments clear, the group struggled to their feet and went to lay the groundwork with their subjects.

People were taking their seats when Harriet and Aunt Beth entered the sanctuary and sat down behind Mavis, who was surrounded by Ben and Harry and the rest of her family. Harriet glanced at her watch and realized an hour had passed.

Pastor Hafer outdid himself. He wove the service seamlessly between Gerald's past and present families. He encouraged all the people left behind to embrace each other and make peace with the fact they might never know what caused Gerald/Gerard to live his life as he had. Once again, Sarah sang, and once again Harriet marveled how such an annoying person could have such a beautiful voice. Carlton had insisted on doing a eulogy, and Pastor Hafer managed to keep him from rambling on unduly.

Gerald's Dutch family might be able to make peace with not knowing what had happened before they met him, but Mavis wouldn't rest until she understood what had happened and neither would Harriet.

Pastor Hafer explained that family only would be attending a brief graveside ceremony in the cemetery behind the church. He encouraged the assembled mourners to gather in the Fellowship Hall for a light repast and assured them the family would join them shortly.

"Showtime," Aunt Beth said in a quiet voice. She nodded toward Robin and DeAnn, who were already out of their pews and talking earnestly with Foggy Point Fire Protection employees. "I'll be finding Connie so we can corner Pete as soon as they get back to the Fellowship Hall."

"I'll come with you," Harriet said. "Harry is supposed to introduce me to Nick's dad."

The crowd worked its way from the sanctuary to the fellowship hall, most of the females stopping at the bathrooms and a number of the males sneaking out to the parking lot for smoke breaks. The United Methodist Women had prepared a spread of sandwiches, salads, cookies, juice and coffee and tea, and when Harriet entered, people were clustered around the food tables.

She spotted Lauren partially concealed by a potted tree, tapping the buttons on her cell phone. Robin and DeAnn were mingling, and the rest of the Threads were lying in wait for the family, who were visible through the floor-to-ceiling windows on one side of the room.

"Have you noticed who isn't here?" Aunt Beth whispered.

Harriet looked around. Everyone they needed was either in the room or at the gravesite outside. She looked back at her aunt.

"Carlton's here without Bebe," Beth said. "You don't see that every day."

"I don't blame her for staying away," Harriet said. "She didn't know Gerald, and these people are his friends, not hers."

"I suppose," said Aunt Beth. "Young people don't seem to value funerals anyway."

Harry was still outside when a tall sandy-haired man who looked to be in his early thirties approached them.

"Are you Harriet?" he asked.

"I am."

"I'm Harry's friend Nick. He called me this morning and said you wanted to talk to my father."

"I do, but how did you know who I was?"

"I asked Senora Escorcia. She knows everything." His cheeks pinked slightly. Harriet was once again impressed with Connie's mystique even after all these years.

An older man with short gray hair and a worn-looking blue suit joined them.

"Harriet, this is my dad, Bill," said Nick. "Dad, this is a friend of Harry's mom who is trying to figure out what happened to his dad."

"Nice to meet you," Harriet said.

Bill held his hand out to shake hers but dropped it with an embarrassed laugh when he realized her right arm was strapped down and she had a cup of juice in her left hand.

"Nice to meet you, too," he said. "Nick here tells me you wanted to ask me a few questions."

"I do," Harriet said. She looked at Nick.

"I'll just go get some punch," he said and backed away.

"I wanted to ask you about Foggy Point Fire Protection back when Gerald worked there."

"You probably know it wasn't called that back then," he began. She nodded, and he continued. "Those were some strange times. I'm going to tell you something and ask you not to tell anyone else. If anyone asks me about it, I'll deny it."

"Go ahead."

"Times were tense before Gerald left. Carlton's daddy Marvin was a harsh man. He was struggling to come up with a product that would earn him the kind of money he wanted to be making. Each time one failed, he blamed whoever was working on it. He could never admit that some of his product choices were ill-advised, or even that it was only natural that some of the fibers Gerald invented just didn't do what they expected them to."

He paused and stared out the window. Harriet knew he wasn't seeing the lawn outside.

"Whenever a project failed, Marvin fired someone. Sometimes more than one someone. I had a houseful of kids, and I couldn't afford to lose my job maintaining those pressure machines. I'm not proud of what I did, but given the same circumstances, I'd do it again."

"And that was?"

"Let's just say I built in my own job security switch, deep inside the most complex and expensive machine," he said, not meeting her eyes. "And it did the job. When Gerald left, Marvin started laying everyone off and replacing them with younger people. People who didn't know how to handle complicated machinery."

"And no one ever found it?" Harriet asked.

"If he'd hired a competent machinist they would have found it easily enough, but he fired me, I flipped the switch, and the young man he replaced me with couldn't find it. A week later, I was back. No explanation. I got a call telling me my firing had been rescinded and I should report to work."

"Do you remember what products you were making back then?"

"Gosh," he said and rocked back on his heels. "I know we started making the fireman's turnouts just after Gerald left. I remember that because I had trouble getting the pressure right on the machine, and all we had were Gerald's notes from the prototype run."

Harriet remembered the square of black material in her pocket. She pulled it out and handed it to him.

"Does this mean anything to you?"

"Oh, my gosh," he said. "How could I have forgotten?"

"You recognize it, then?"

"This was supposed to be our big success story," he said, and rubbed it between his thumb and forefinger. "This was our attempt at body armor." He smiled slightly at the memory.

"This was right around the time of the first Gulf War. Maybe a little before, I'm not sure. Gerald had come up with this great lightweight fabric. Many of the early body armors were heavy because you had to have so many layers of the protective fabric. This stuff could stop a bullet with one layer, and for insurance you could use three and it was still half the thickness of the competitor's offerings."

Harriet could see where this was going. "Until it got wet," she said.

He gave her a long silent look. "Bingo. It was great as long as the soldier didn't sweat. It could take cold water. But warm rain or sweat and you might as well have been naked."

"But you said they'd had other products fail," Harriet pressed.

"That they had. Anyway, I can't tell you what happened after that. We made a bunch of prototypes that were sent to DC for testing. Word came back about the warm water problem, and that was that. People were fired. Up to that point, it was business as usual."

"Then what?"

"They laid off everyone who had worked on the body armor. Gerald disappeared. At first we wondered if this time he had gotten the axe, but that made no sense. He was the brains behind the operation."

Bill had slowly edged them toward the table that held the coffee carafe. He poured himself a cup and asked Harriet if she wanted any. She didn't.

He moved away from the drinks table and continued his story.

"We got word that Gerald had been killed in a car accident in Malaysia. The fireman's turnouts took off, and we never looked back. Money was rolling in, we all got raises. They even hired back a few of the old crew to help manage the machinery."

"Why would Gerald fake his own death?" Harriet asked.

"That I don't know," Bill said. "I wish I did."

"Thanks," she said. "You've been very helpful."

"If you think of any questions I can answer, feel free to call," he said and drifted off into the crowd.

Harriet made her way over to Jenny.

"Anything?" she asked quietly. The family had entered the hall while she was talking to Bill.

"So far, they're just talking about how sad they are. They seem genuinely perplexed about what their Gerard was doing here."

"Thanks," Harriet said. "Keep with them, just in case. I'm going to see how Connie and my aunt are doing with Pete."

✂ ✂ ✂

True to form, Connie had worked her magic quickly. She'd confronted Pete and, according to Aunt Beth, he'd cracked like an egg.

"Gerald called him," Connie reported. "After Pete got over his shock, Gerald asked him to keep his mom out of Foggy Point for a few days. He said he wouldn't ask him if it weren't life or death. He swore him to secrecy and said he would tell him everything when he saw him again and promised that it would be soon."

"Pete trusted his daddy," Aunt Beth said, picking up the story. "He doesn't know anything else." She shook her head. "You'd think at his age he would have demanded a few more answers."

"I certainly would have demanded more information before I did something that big for my father," Harriet agreed.

Aunt Beth gave her an exasperated look.

"Okay, so maybe I'm not typical," Harriet said with a sigh. "By the way, have either of you seen Aiden? He had to go to work this morning, but I thought he meant to be here before the ceremony started."

"Maybe he got hung up at work," Beth suggested.

Harriet scanned the crowd and stopped when she noticed Lauren nodding at her.

"Have you got something?" she asked without preamble when she'd worked her way through the people to Lauren's side.

"Carla's car is in the middle of a forested area down below Miller Hill Road." She turned her phone toward Harriet. The display showed a small aerial photo. A dark spot that must be the car sat inside a ring of trees. "From the ground, it's probably well hidden."

"What's that?" Harriet pointed at another car-sized blob. This one sat out in the open between the ring of trees and the roof of a building.

Lauren punched a series of buttons and magnified the area containing the other car. "Looks like an SUV, maybe a Bronco," she said.

"Aiden's car," Harriet said, a knot forming in her stomach.

"Come on," Lauren said. "My car's closer."

Harriet was too shocked to answer. She followed Lauren out a side door that led to the parking lot.

"I think we should go up to the park and see if the hill is high enough to see where the clearing in the trees is. It doesn't look like there's a road through that part of the forest. Someone must have done some off-roading," Lauren said as they drove. "Have you called Aiden?"

Harriet pulled out her phone and punched in his number. His phone rang then went to voice mail. "Nothing."

Lauren pulled into the parking lot at Miller Hill and got out, but she had to hustle to keep up as Harriet all but ran up to the rocky outcrop that overlooked Foggy Point Fire Protection. The outbuildings were between them and the main plant.

Harriet scanned the woods around the factory. There were several small buildings that could be the one in Lauren's picture. She carefully studied the trees around each one.

"Look," she said, pointing to a windowless tin shed. See the area of trees right down there?" She pointed to a spot below them. "Doesn't it look like there could be a gap there?"

"One way to find out," Lauren said. She pressed the electronic door lock on her key chain, pocketed her keys and followed Harriet to the path that led toward the forest.

The black flats Harriet was wearing weren't the best choice for descending a steep rocky trail. Lauren's black sandals were even worse. The two women slipped and slid to the edge of the woods.

"I think we need to go to the right," Harriet said and left the trail, picking her way through the tall grass and working toward a break in the undergrowth that would allow them to enter the stand of trees she hoped hid the gray Mercedes.

The going was easier under the dense canopy of trees. It was difficult for underbrush to grow, given the sparse sunlight, and that worked in their favor. They picked their way through the trees for ten minutes, trying to walk as silently as they could and not talking for fear the distraction might cause one or the other to fall. Harriet led the way.

"I think I see the car," she whispered finally, and waited for Lauren to come alongside her. "You wait here," she continued, "just in case someone else is here. I'll go up to the car and see if Carla's inside. If she isn't, and no one appears, come out and we'll go whichever way the car came in."

Lauren was punching buttons on her phone. "FYI, we have no cell reception," she said. Harriet wasn't sure if that meant she was agreeing to wait in the woods, but if she didn't, there wasn't time to argue about it. She crept into the clearing and over to the car.

Carla wasn't inside. Harriet circled it but couldn't see anything out of the ordinary. Lauren had waited, but when no one else appeared, she joined Harriet.

"So, where do you think Carla is?" she asked.

"I have no idea," Harriet said with a sigh. She looked around the small clearing again. "Look over there," she said, and pointed to the edge of the forest behind the car.

"Well, duh," said Lauren. "Isn't it kind of obvious the car came from the area behind it? I mean, you didn't really think whoever put it here turned it around just in case someone found it, did you?

Maybe they thought someone clever enough to find this hidey-hole wouldn't be clever enough to follow the car-sized trail back through the woods."

"Okay, you're the most brilliant. Would you just shut up so I can think a minute?"

Lauren was about to say something, but a look at Harriet's face changed her mind.

"I think we should split up," Harriet said finally. "You just said we have no cell reception, right?"

"Yeah," Lauren said carefully. "What are you planning?"

"Aiden's car must be right through there," Harriet said, and pointed. "I want to check it out and see if he or Carla is in it. If I don't find anything there, I'm going to see if I can get into that outbuilding."

"What if they *aren't* there?" Lauren asked.

Harriet looked at her. "I can't think that far ahead. You go back up to the park and call the police and tell them we found Carla's car. Bring them back here. If I haven't found Carla or Aiden by then, the police can figure out what comes next."

"I don't like the idea of leaving you here alone," Lauren said in a rare show of concern. "Someone must have overpowered Aiden, and he's a lot bigger and stronger than you are."

"If you bring the police here quick enough it won't be a problem."

Lauren sighed but didn't say anything. She turned and disappeared into the woods in the direction they'd come from.

Harriet left the clearing in the opposite direction. As Lauren had predicted, Carla's car had cut a pretty wide swath through the trees and underbrush. As she got closer to the outer edge of the woods, it became obvious some attempt had been made to conceal the car's passage.

Aiden's car was visible as she reached the edge of the trees. She paused and studied the car and then the outbuilding beyond it. Birds were singing, and a slight breeze rustled the treetops, but no other sound disturbed the quiet.

She slowly approached the Bronco, both anxious to look inside and afraid at the same time. She circled the vehicle. There was no apparent damage. She went to the driver's side door and rose onto her tiptoes to peer inside. Aiden's cell phone sat in the console under the radio. His keys were on the driver's seat. She reached for the door handle.

"Let's just stop right there," said a female voice from behind her. A hand dug into her injured shoulder and pulled her around.

"Bebe," she said. "What are you doing here?

"Well, I *was* coming to move Aiden's car, but I guess there's no point now."

"Where is Aiden? And where is Carla?"

"Oh, they're all in the garden shed getting ready for a barbecue. Here," she said, and yanked Harriet by her bad arm again. "You can go join them."

Harriet pulled her arm painfully out of Bebe's surprisingly strong grip. "I'm not going anywhere with you."

"I have nine millimeters here that say you're going anywhere I want you to." She pulled an ugly-looking black gun from behind her back. "And right now, it's saying you're joining your friends in the shed."

She pushed the gun into Harriet's side and shoved her forward.

At the door of the outbuilding, Harriet tried to break away, but Bebe was quick.

"Don't make me shoot you," she said. "I really want you all to be bullet-free. According to my calculations, there will only be ash left behind when the fire cools, but these things aren't always exact. I'd rather be safe than sorry. Now, just go in here." She pulled a key from her pocket with her free hand and quickly unlocked the door and shoved Harriet inside.

The room was dark and smelled like earth and cut grass. It took a moment, but when Harriet's eyes had adjusted to the dark she could see Aiden and Carla sitting on bags of fertilizer and Terry lying at their feet on the cement floor, apparently unconscious. She started toward them, but Bebe pulled her back.

"Not so fast, sister," she said. "I don't trust you."

"What's going on, Bebe? Why are you doing this?"

"I think it's obvious what's going on." The little girl voice that had been so annoying was gone now. "You trespassers are about to suffer a horrible accident. Maxwell should have been more careful with his rags." She referred to the long-time Foggy Point Fire Protection groundskeeper. "He used linseed oil on the wood benches in front of the building. Did you know linseed oil can spontaneously combust? It's going to be really sad. Carla followed Terry here, and Aiden followed her. No one knows why Terry is here, and now no one ever will. He'll be gone, poof, just like that." She snapped her fingers.

Harriet looked at Aiden; he was intently looking at her feet. Coils of hose were neatly stacked in a pile beside her.

"Why do you have to kill Aiden and Carla?" Harriet asked, wondering if Lauren was back to her car yet. "Carla has a baby."

"And I do feel really bad about that," Bebe said.

"Wendy," Carla whimpered. "My baby." She started quietly sobbing.

"I said I'm sorry, didn't I? I'm not a monster. I feel really bad about all this. You three have always been really nice to me. It's not my fault, though. It's his." She pointed the barrel of the gun toward the prone form of Terry. "Carlton and I are leaving this horrible place this afternoon, but Terry couldn't wait for us to be gone. He had to keep asking questions and causing trouble among our night workers. Do you realize he caused us to miss our final shipment?"

"Shipment of what?" Aiden asked, speaking for the first time.

"None of your business," Bebe snapped.

"If we're all going to die, could I at least hug Harriet one last time?" he asked. "If you feel so bad, this could make up for it."

He had a plan. Harriet couldn't see where he was going yet, though.

"Come on," he pleaded. "I promise I won't do anything."

Bebe looked uncertain. Aiden looked at the hoses again.

"Harriet and I haven't even known each other a year yet. Barely six months. Remember when we first met?" he asked her.

Harriet thought back, quickly scanning her memories. Aiden looked intently at her and then at the pile of hose again. She'd met Aiden at a Loose Threads meeting when he'd first returned from Africa. How could that help? she wondered. He'd brought his mother's quilt to her to repair after he'd wrapped an injured dog in it. She didn't see how that would help, either.

Then she knew what he wanted.

"You can leave my hands tied," he said. "Come on, we're going to be dead in a few minutes and you can go on your way. What difference will it make if Harriet and I are together when we die or not." He gave Bebe his best puppy dog look.

"Okay," she said slowly. Harriet was amazed again at how Aiden could charm the ladies—even the crazy ones, apparently. "But Carla has to move." She turned away from Harriet and grabbed for Carla. The young woman refused to move from Aiden's side.

Carla was stronger than she looked. Bebe had to turn her back to Harriet and use both hands to push Carla away from Aiden. The minute she turned, Harriet grabbed the end of the top hose stacked by her feet. The end with the industrial-size oscillating sprinkler still attached. In a blur, she swung the hose once around her head and let centrifugal force carry the heavy sprinkler into the back of Bebe's head.

Bebe crumpled to her knees, and Terry suddenly came alive, delivering a scissor kick to her body and twisting his body over hers, pinning her to the floor. Aiden kicked the gun away and added his weight to Terry's on the woman's back. Terry rolled off and turned a ghastly shade of green.

"Find something sharp to cut our ties with," Aiden said, but Harriet was already rummaging around on Max's tool bench. She found a pair of wire cutters and made quick work of the plastic straps on Aiden's and Carla's wrists. Carla then snipped Terry's.

"He's unconscious again," she said in a worried voice.

"Lauren went for help. Our phones didn't get reception, so she was going to Miller Hill and then driving toward town if needed. I told her to send the police."

"How did you know we were in here?" Aiden asked. He found some garden twine on the workbench and tied Bebe's hands behind her back.

"We didn't. Lauren has a friend who has access to real-time satellite imagery. She searched Foggy Point for Carla's missing car.

We figured if we found the car, we'd have a starting point for our search." She gently bumped her good arm into his shoulder. "We weren't even sure you were missing, actually. You said you had to work in the morning, and when you didn't show up for the funeral I thought you'd had an emergency. Until I saw your Bronco in the picture Lauren had of Carla's car."

"Well, for once I'm glad you were snoopy and took a risk. Our friend here was about to blow us up."

"So I gathered. What I don't get is why."

"I'm not too clear on that myself," Aiden said. He tied Bebe's feet together just as she roused slightly.

"I'm pretty sure it has something to do with Terry," Carla said. "He's been in and out of consciousness since I've been here. I think Bebe hit him hard on his head."

"I should have killed him when I had him down," Bebe said in a groggy voice. "His corpse would have burned just as well."

"So, why didn't you?" Harriet asked. Carla turned to her with a look of horror.

"Inquiring minds want to know," Harriet added.

"If you insist," Bebe said, and struggled to sit up. "I couldn't burn the shed until we'd shipped our last order. And I was afraid, with this weather, he'd start to smell."

"And you weren't worried someone would find his live body?" Harriet asked.

"Carlton gave the grounds crew a couple of furlough days so no one would have a reason to come into the shed. If he'd started smelling and the wind blew the wrong way, someone might have investigated."

"You really thought this out, didn't you?"

Bebe looked at Harriet for a long minute. "I had to improvise, okay? The plan was, we make our last shipment, close the operation down, and then Carlton and I leave this dump forever."

"So when Terry started snooping around and causing trouble, why didn't you cut your losses and run?"

"Does it really matter?" Bebe asked.

"I'd like to know."

"Me, too," Carla said and looked away, her face turning pink.

"They aren't the kind of customers you disappoint, okay?"

"So what is this mystery product you've been shipping?" Aiden asked.

"I think I'd like to invoke my right to remain silent."

"We aren't the police," Harriet said.

"*We* are," said Officer Nguyen as he opened the door. "Would anyone like to tell me what's going on here?"

At first, no one spoke. Then everyone spoke at once. Aunt Beth arrived with Lauren and Connie. More police arrived, and eventually Carlton came with a skinny blond officer and her chunky, red-faced partner. Harriet recognized them from the break-in that had occurred in her studio the first week she'd been back in Foggy Point, more than six months ago.

"We found him boarding a plane bound for the Caymen Islands," the blonde said.

"Detective Black asked us to find him and bring him here, since he owns the place," the chunky officer said. He looked over at Bebe. "And because he's married to her."

"You were leaving without me?" Bebe screeched, her composure slipping for just a moment. "Never mind, don't answer that. Don't say anything." She glared at him to reinforce her command.

Officer Nguyen called an ambulance for Terry, and Carla rode with him to the hospital. Aunt Beth insisted Harriet go to the hospital and get her arm checked out, and at that point her shoulder hurt enough that she agreed.

Chapter 28

Terry refused to stay in the hospital overnight, and as soon as he'd absorbed a couple of bags of IV fluids, he checked himself out. The doctors had insisted on examining Carla, too, and she was given her own fluids. Harriet went home after a sturdier brace was applied to her shoulder and Dr. Pattee had lectured her on the concept of keeping her collarbone out of harm's way until it had healed.

Aunt Beth and Connie had decided everyone should meet at Harriet's, since she had a patio large enough to accommodate the Loose Threads and friends, plus her house was still clean from the previous gathering of the Willis clan.

Harriet was once again amazed at the ability of the Loose Threads to conjure up large quantities of delicious food on short notice. There were two fruit salads, a macaroni salad with hard salami, red peppers and cubes of Swiss cheese with Italian dressing and Jenny's secret recipe baked beans. Harry Willis was at the gas grill cooking hamburgers and hot dogs. Jorge arrived just behind Terry with a large bowl of guacamole balanced on one arm and several large bags of chips in the other.

"Looks like I'm at the right place," he said, and set the bowl in the middle of the food-laden picnic table then went into the kitchen to find a platter for the chips.

Ben Willis came out carrying two armloads of folding chairs. "What did I miss?" he asked.

"Nothing yet," Harriet said. "Now that Terry's here, let's make sure no one is in the house. And see that everyone's got something to drink."

"Yes, ma'am," Ben said and saluted Harriet.

Aiden was leaning back in a padded lounge with Harriet perched upright beside his legs. The Loose Threads and the youngest Willis boys pulled their chairs into a circle. Aunt Beth insisted Terry also sit in a lounge with his feet up. Mavis pressed a tall, icy glass of water into his hand.

"Drink," she ordered.

Jorge sat at the picnic table, slightly out of the circle but close enough to not miss anything.

"So, talk," Harriet said to Terry.

"I'm sure you're all anxious to know what happened today, and what's been going on for the last two weeks—really. Before I get into that, I just want to thank everyone involved in rescuing me and apologize for any lies or deceptions I've perpetrated on you."

"I hope you're not expecting us to give you blanket forgiveness without hearing the whole story," Lauren said.

Harriet couldn't argue with her sentiment.

Terry put both hands up in front of him in a gesture of surrender. "Fair enough," he said. "As you all probably guessed already, my father did not work at Foggy Point Fire Protection nor am I doing a genealogy study of any sort."

"You got that right," DeAnn said. She must have come straight from work, as she was still wearing her green polo shirt that said *Foggy Point Video* over the left breast pocket.

"I work for a special branch of the navy," he said.

"What about the two tours in Iraq?" Harriet asked.

"All true."

"If everyone would stop interrupting the boy, we might find out what's going on," Aunt Beth said and glared at Harriet.

"As I said, I'm in a unique branch of the military. We do special investigations. Sort of like a military cold case squad." He took a long drink of water. "I came to Foggy Point to investigate a cold case that had developed into a current one."

Aunt Beth refilled his glass.

"It all started during operation Desert Shield. If you remember, that was the military action that preceded the first Gulf War."

"We remember," Mavis muttered.

"All branches of the military were hustling to arm their soldiers with state-of-the-art equipment so they'd be ready to ship out when the inevitable escalation occurred. This included body armor."

The group became quiet as the direction his explanation was going to take became clear.

"Back then, developments in ammunition and body armor were in a race against each other. Impenetrable armor would be developed and a new bullet would come along that could pierce it. Now, this is the part where I have to fill in the blanks a little, as I've yet to find a living source to confirm the Industrial Fiber Products end of things."

Jorge got up quietly with the pitchers and refilled people's glasses.

"What I know is that several lapses of judgment had to have happened. A prototype batch of body armor that was labeled Industrial Fiber Products was shipped to actual troops on their way to Iraq."

Mavis leaned back and looked at the sky. She put her age-spotted hands to her throat. Harriet was pretty sure her friend wasn't going to like what was coming next.

"The armor failed, and the entire unit wearing it was killed. According to the file of the chief warrant officer who issued the armor on the government end, Gerald Willis had erroneously certified the product as passing all the required tests."

Mavis gasped, and Ben went to her side and put his arm around her.

"What isn't in the file is any record of the government's own independent quality tests. The death of Gerald Willis is noted in the file with a recommendation to end further inquiries."

"Doesn't that seem a little odd?" Harry asked. "I mean, our dad takes the blame and then suddenly dies."

"Remember, at the time, war had just broken out. The military didn't want any more negative press, so it was all swept under the rug. And it might have remained there if body armor with the same failure problem hadn't started showing up among mercenary groups fighting in Africa. One of our former SEALs who works independently now saw the armor and remembered hearing stories from his father, who had lost some friends in the original incident. He came to us, and we checked it out."

"It only fails when it gets wet and warm," Harriet said in a flat voice.

"Exactly, like when someone in a hot climate wears it for an extended period and sweats."

"I can't believe Gerald would ship armor without thoroughly testing it," Mavis protested.

"My guess is, he didn't," Terry said. "Someone involved in the first incident decided to make some money selling the armor, which is otherwise superior, to mercenaries in Africa who weren't likely to demand a refund."

"How did you know the new armor came from Foggy Point?" Harriet asked.

"Like most criminals, this bunch made a mistake. The size tags are a folded piece of ribbon with cleaning symbols on the back… and, in very small print, the name of the company, Foggy Point Fire Protection. They apparently didn't look at the back side of their own tags."

"So, why didn't the military confront them directly?" Harriet asked.

"We couldn't. Anyone could have stolen or copied Foggy Point Fire Protection tags. I needed to catch them in the act."

"What about Gerald?" Mavis asked.

Terry rubbed his hand through the short brush of hair on the top of his head.

"This might help," said a male voice with a Dutch accent. No one had noticed Gerald's cousin Theobald join the group. He handed an envelope to Mavis. "Gerald gave me this when he first moved to the Netherlands. He said I should deliver it to you when he died—or Gerry, if you were already gone." He joined Jorge at the picnic table.

Mavis read in silence, her eyes glistening and her hand compulsively stroking her neck under her chin. When she'd finished reading the pages, she let them fall into her lap. She sat in silence.

"What did he say?" Aunt Beth asked; she picked up the pages and folded them, gently placing them in Mavis's lap.

"If Marvin Brewster weren't already dead, I'd kill him with my bare hands," Mavis said, angry now. "He knew the fabric was faulty—Gerald told him so. Marvin Brewster decided to make prototypes and send them to his contact in the army and see if they noticed. He hoped people wouldn't sweat enough to make them fail." She took the fresh glass of iced tea Jorge offered her.

"Marvin's contact was anxious to fill his order for state-of-the-art armor, so when the war broke out, he sent the prototype. Marvin assured the warrant officer in charge that the prototypes were safe. Then, when men died, he needed a scapegoat. This..." She held up the letter. "...says his first instinct was to kill Gerald and then blame him, but Gerald made him see the plan would work better if he took the blame then faked his own death before anyone could come after him. They agreed that Marvin would pay me widow's benefits and would cease production of body armor.

"Gerald had just finished testing his fabric for fireman's turnouts and told Marvin he would give him the formula if he agreed to the plan. He also told Marvin that he'd be watching."

"So that's what the whole post office box, send him a card if they used that certain chemical was all about," Gerry said. "I guess Marvin didn't tell Carlton the whole story."

"Or he chose to ignore it," Harriet said. "My guess is that Bebe was the brains of that duo, and I use the term 'brains' loosely. I'll bet she ran through Carlton's personal inheritance and then the cash reserves at the factory, and she probably told him if he wanted to keep her, he had to get more. He probably knew just enough about the armor to be dangerous."

"And my Gerald was so trusting, and he'd known Carlton since he was a baby. He probably called him and asked to get together," Mavis said.

"Someone showed up with a shotgun," Terry said. "I'm guessing that piece of plastic Harriet found in the woods was a sabot. You can put it in a shotgun shell and hold it in place with something like dental plaster, and if you shoot it at close range, you can kill a person and leave only a blunt force trauma wound. Police shoot loads of just the dental plaster to break down doors sometimes."

"Oh, my gosh," Harriet said. "Wasn't Bebe a dental assistant before she married Carlton?"

"Yes, she was," Aunt Beth confirmed. "That was pretty clever, if you think about it."

"I think you've found your killer. Bebe showed up instead of Carlton and probably shot Gerald without saying a word. And chances are good she'd sold dental plaster to the local cops and one of them told her what they were doing with it."

Aiden pulled Harriet carefully onto his lap. He hadn't let her be more than an arm's length from him since they'd gotten home.

"So, what's next for you, Terry?" he asked.

Carla got up to go check on Wendy, who was sleeping in the house.

"Wait, Carla," Terry said. "You aren't going get rid of me that quick. I have to stay around until Bebe and Carlton are indicted, and then I'll be back if they go to trial here. The JAGs on our side will figure out who gets them first."

Carla turned back toward the house.

"Wait, that's not the good part. My next assignment is at Submarine Base Bangor in Bremerton, Washington. And it's not a short-term investigation. They're relocating me there until further notice."

Her back was to the group, but Harriet was at the right angle to see the big smile on the young woman's face as she went into the house.

Robin pulled her yellow tablet from her bag, tore off the three pages of notes they'd made over the last two weeks and crumpled them up. She smoothed the freshly exposed page and wrote "*RAFFLE QUILT*" in block letters.

"Now what are we going to do about the raffle quilt?"

END

ABOUT THE AUTHOR

Attempted murder, theft, drug rings, battered women, death threats and more sordid affairs than she could count were the more exciting experiences from ARLENE SACHITANO'S nearly thirty years in the high-tech industry.

Prior to writing her first novel, *Chip and Die* (Zumaya 2003), Arlene wrote the story half of the popular Block of the Month quilting patterns "Seams Like Murder," "Seams Like Halloween" and "Nothing's What it Seams" for Storyquilts.com, Inc. *Quilt As You Go* is the third book in the Harriet Truman/Loose Threads quilting mystery series. Arlene also has written a scintillating proprietary tome on electronics assembly.

ABOUT THE ARTIST

APRIL MARTINEZ was born in the Philippines and raised in San Diego, California, daughter to a US Navy chef and a US postal worker, sibling to one younger sister. From as far back as she can remember, she has always doodled and loved art, but her parents never encouraged her to consider it as a career path, suggesting instead that she work for the county. So, she attended the University of California in San Diego, earned a cum laude bachelor's degree in literature/writing and entered the workplace as a regular office worker.

For years, she went from job to job, dissatisfied that she couldn't make use of her creative tendencies, until she started working as an imaging specialist for a big book and magazine publishing house in Irvine and began learning the trade of graphic design. From that point on, she worked as a graphic designer and webmaster at subsequent day jobs while doing freelance art and illustration at night.

In 2003, April discovered the e-publishing industry. She responded to an ad looking for e-book cover artists and was soon in the business of cover art and art direction. Since then, she has created hundreds of book covers, both electronic and print, for several publishing houses, earning awards and recognition in the process. Two years into it, she was able to give up the day job and work from home. April Martinez now lives with her cat in Orange County, California, as a full-time freelance artist/illustrator and graphic designer.

37425415R00158

Made in the USA
Middletown, DE
27 November 2016